THE GIRL FROM MENA CREEK

A NOVEL

GRACE BOGAERT

Copyright © 2015 Grace Bogaert

First Edition 2013 by M&J Dream Productions, Mena Creek, Qld., Australia
ISBN 978-0-9805367-2-0

Second Edition, Chinese Translation, 2015 by M&J Dream Productions, Mena Creek, Qld., Australia
ISBN 978-0-9805367-1-3

Canadian Cataloguing in Publication Data
PS8603.O3363G57

2015 C813'.6

c2015-902892-2

Bogaert, Grace 1959 –
    The Girl from Mena Creek/ Grace Bogaert;
    editor Glyn Davies
    Cover Design by Danny Santos
    Canadian Edition.
ISBN 978-0-9936086-0-5 (pbk.)

Photography Credits:
Back Cover, Burning of Sugar Cane Fields: Remi Jouan, Permission Creative Commons.
Back Cover Map, Geoscience Australia material, Permission Creative Commons 3.0 Australia License
Back Cover Flower: Grace Bogaert
Front Cover Top: Paronella Park, Refreshment Stand, Grace Bogaert
Front Cover Bottom: Soldiers in the Pacific, Public Domain
Author portrait: Chris Holling

Published by:
    A Scene Above Productions
    59 Neptune Drive, Unit 1
    Toronto, Ontario M6A 1X2

Printed in Canada

Dedication

To Victor Syrett of Vancouver Island and the many other soldiers of WWII who never made it back home.

Acknowledgements

I wish to thank my sons who came along for a drive through the Atherton Tablelands in 2009 and were coaxed into taking a detour to Paronella Park, the place that inspired this novel. As we arrived, Mark Evans, one of the park owners, greeted us. When he discovered I was a writer he mentioned that he wanted a novel written based on the castle's creator. Since I am mostly a screenwriter I set the idea aside at first, but before we left the park Mark handed me Jose Paronella's biography, the story of the Catalonian immigrant who built a small castle overlooking the falls at Mena Creek. Reading about Jose's struggles I thought some more about this idea of writing a novel and decided to give it a try, but I wanted to write about a young female heroine, and so Talia was born.

In the research and writing of this novel, I was blessed with help from many people. I would like to mention all those who contributed in some way.

I want to thank Antonio Acosta Castro, of Santa Clara, Cuba, for explaining the harvesting and processing of sugar cane. It was also in Cuba where I was finally able to finish the first draft of this novel.

Through the slow process of creating an outline and cobbling together the first draft and subsequent drafts, my husband, Chris Holling, provided enormous support and encouragement and for this I am extremely grateful. I am also greatly appreciative to my parents for reading the first draft and loving it even though it was far from finished.

Thank you to my friends and family who proofed and commented on later drafts: Don Angus; Dixon Trees; Robert Bogaert; Cheryl Bloxom; Gail Heaslip; Theresa Walton; Alec Walton; Sam Holling; Dorothy Bogaert who also sourced research material from a library in Perth; and Jim McElgunn, who reviewed the manuscript with great care. To Nicole Natale for regular pep talks, and to Sonja Martinez and Leticia Cervantes who corrected the Spanish phrases, and especially to Glyn Davies, my editor, who pushed for improvements and rewrites but in a very pleasant, relaxed Queenslander way.

A special thank you is due to the Evans family for preserving an important historical and cultural landmark, Paronella Park. And thanks to Bridget and Judy in particular for shepherding the novel through the publishing and printing process. Thank you to Tony Golea at Asquith, Von Espiritu, Danny Santos, and Aveek Mansur for helping in putting together the Canadian edition, as well as my lawyer, Martyn Krys.

It was a big thrill to see the Chinese edition of the novel come out in 2015, and my deepest appreciation goes out to Helen Sham at Paronella Park for overseeing this translation.

Finally I wish to express gratitude to Frances Van Ramselaar who was my first Spanish teacher, and to Susana Candelas and my other friends from Instituto Asunción, Querétaro, México.

Chapter One
Watching
Sant Feliu d'Aran, Catalonia, Spain - May 1927

The mountains above the town of Sant Feliu d'Aran had long struggled against the sun and the biting wind, and hoarded their small store of water in grey calcified fists.

A lonely shepherd picked his way over these craggy mounds like a fly moving over an old crust of bread. At last he found a path to an olive tree and settled in against the gnarled trunk.

It was as though the sun had decided his race and age, for he was as deeply hued as burnt coffee, as worn and wizened as a ninety-year-old man, but in fact this Catalan had not yet reached the fourth decade of life.

Although Arnau Queixens squinted through deeply furrowed brows, his vision was perfectly sharp and he could see with clarity into the crevices and take in the wide swath of terrain before him, knowing all the details. He read the landscape like a familiar book, keenly observing every small drama of nature as it unfolded before him: a hawk gliding low over small prey; the shadow of a hare bounding away in panic; a bird flaunting its plumage in a mating ritual.

Arnau's senses of smell and hearing were also flawless. He could pick up fragrances and sounds from far off and judge the distance to their source. Just now he heard the tolling of church bells marking eleven o'clock. The rumble of cars, the tinkle of music, and even snippets of voices, clipped by the wind currents, also reached his ears. He knew these came from the *Festa Major*, the five-day celebration honouring the town's patron saint, Feliu.

Arnau was a reclusive man and did not mind that he could only hear fragments from the revelry. He had no desire for more. The crowds and chaos he would leave to others — his sister-in-law, brother, and niece. Maybe they would eventually tell him about the festivities, or maybe not. He did not really care.

He could not tolerate the press of bodies and the inquisitive looks. The demands of conversation were not worth the effort. He found no pleasure in these human exchanges and moreover was suspicious of them.

No, he thought, best to stay away from the *Festa*.

He had learned from experience that the incidental encounters at these sorts of things only led to disruptions and complications. New people intruded into their lives and others left abruptly.

Like that woman, for example — Carmen.

Andre had given them no warning that he was going to get married and suddenly there was a stranger in the house. Of course, he could see that Andre might think Carmen was pretty, but she was far too young, Arnau thought. And what was worse, she could barely speak Catalan.

Arnau could trace the beginnings of a growing malaise in their family back to the time of Carmen's arrival.

When it was his turn to come down from the mountain and let Bart take over the flock, he noticed a disturbance in the air, picking up on it like the decaying body of a bird concealed in the rafters. Everyone was ill at ease with the newcomer: he and Bart, and their father too.

Carmen cast her nervous energy about, making many unbidden changes, altering routines, and rearranging furniture as though believing she was in her right to do so. She ruined many a meal by slipping unfamiliar ingredients into their well-loved dishes. Her mannerisms were also odd and unsettling. Moreover, she talked back to Andre. Arnau was certain that the couple's frequent quarrelling was what likely drove his brother away suddenly, leaving his new wife behind. Andre was gone even before the baby was born.

That child — she was yet another disruption of which there had been so many that Arnau now felt he had only a faint recollection of how things had been before.

And so he would never assume that the appearance of a visitor, however outwardly benign, might be harmless. Rather, like the smallest pebble skittering down a rock face, hitting other stones that in turn dislodge larger rocks until an avalanche is formed — it had the potential to bury them all.

Arnau watched the sleek black car as it wound along the sinewy road below. It advanced towards Sant Feliu from the south, moving steadily like a shiny black beetle.

He would spy the vehicle again in the coming days, making its way in and out of the town several times on forays that steered dangerously close to home.

Arnau had a feeling about that car.

* * *

It would have surprised Talia to know there might be anyone who would not want to come to the *Festa Major*, least of all a relative of hers. Her thoughts were not on Uncle Arnau at that moment, however. She would not think about him till he came off the mountain three days later and they sat together at the dinner table.

For now she was completely intent on a golden brioche, nestled in a lace-fringed basket, just beyond her reach. Caramelized pine nuts and cherries glinted like gems, making her salivate.

She begged her cousin Infanta to let her carry the basket, but the older girl refused. With a swish of her arm, Infanta pivoted it high above Talia.

"You'll drop it," Infanta declared.

At eight, Infanta was more than three years older and had the advantage of being at least a foot taller than Talia.

"I'll be careful!" Talia pleaded.

But Infanta would not be moved.

Then Talia had to give up the fight to carry the cake when her mother, suddenly noticing Talia's messy hair, pulled her aside and began to tuck in loose strands of curls.

"Such wild hair," Carmen sighed.

"Restless hair, restless girl," remarked Aunt Fina. "Just like her father." The older woman tittered, squeezing her eyes into slits and covering her mouth to hide her gold-capped teeth.

A shadow passed over Carmen's face. The subject of her husband's absence was a sore point. Five years had passed, and still Andre had made no move to send for his wife and daughter. One or two years, it was generally understood among the locals, many of whom had seen husbands or sons leave to find work abroad — two years was barely enough time for a man to get settled in the new country and learn the language, so it was not unusual to be left behind for at least that long. Three to four years, could mean he was ambitious and hardworking and was setting aside money to build a house and pay for their passage. But five years — five years and longer began to hint at something else, some hesitation on his part, doubts about their shared future, or other unhappy possibilities. A separation of five years could mean many things, but an eagerness to be reunited was not one of them.

When Talia's mother spoke again, her tone was sharper. "Talia, now listen. You stay with Jordi and Pau. I'm going to walk with the other ladies in the procession."

Jordi and Pau were Talia's cousins. The two boys could not be more different from each other. Pau was a tall and gentle youth of thirteen, while eleven-year-old Jordi was short and stocky, and angered easily.

While Talia would have preferred other arrangements, she dared not put up an argument — at least not at the moment, for when her mother had emerged after getting ready for the festival, Talia had hardly recognised her. Dressed in her best clothes Carmen was absolutely stunning — and very intimidating. Gold and garnet earrings shone through a delicate lace mantilla that fell softly at either side of her porcelain-skinned face. The sleeves of her black dress clung to her slender arms, and the cinched waistline accentuated her perfect figure. No, Talia thought, she could not complain to this beautiful woman.

Carmen walked ahead of Talia, with her aunts Fina and Matilda. These were Talia's relatives from her father's side. Andre's sister Matilda had married into a comfortable life with Gil Baltires, who now ran the family rope-making business. The Baltires factory supplied many fishing vessels and ships along the coast from Barcelona and further south. Baltires rope, twisted from the strongest strands of native *esparto* grass wound its way to wherever Spanish ships carried it, from Cape Town to Cuba.

When the three ladies entered the church, they slid onto the left side pews with all the other married women, while Talia was relegated to the back with the children.

Although the church was cool on this hot June day, Talia ached to be out in the sunshine and for the festivities to begin. The smell of incense and candle wax wafted over the parishioners. Father Jacinto's sing-song voice droned on, lulling them all to the edge of sleep. For the children it seemed forever until they were invited to come to the front of the church with pastries in hand.

The old priest bobbed his upper body and waved his black-cloaked arm over each basket, murmuring in Latin. Finally the blessings were done and the heavy church doors creaked open, letting in a stream of bright sunshine. Talia wanted to race ahead to catch up with Infanta but Jordi gripped her arm.

"You stick with us," he said.

His hold on her was firm but she wasn't going to give in that easily.

"What about the parade?"

"You won't miss a thing," he said. "C'mon." Pau gave her an encouraging smile. Reluctantly, Talia fell in behind her cousins.

While the boys raced up a narrow cobblestone street, she struggled to keep up. Her heart sank to hear the sound of the orchestra fading away, the ta-ta-tum and clanging receding beyond the maze of thick-walled buildings. It didn't seem right to be running in the opposite direction of the music.

"Jordi!" she wailed.

He turned to her in irritation. "Hurry or you'll spoil it for us."

"I'm tired!"

Not heeding Jordi's groans, Talia plopped down on the stone path and shook her head, refusing to budge.

Concerned that Jordi would just abandon her, Pau took pity and scooped Talia up, sliding her on his back. Her chubby legs gripped him as he hunched over, hobbled by the weight of her. In spite of her being well over four years old, the baby fat still clung to Talia. Pau was huffing and perspiring as they reached the top of the street.

Jordi guided them into a small passageway, between two buildings. Spindly thistles scraped Talia's legs. Pau finally dropped the little girl to the ground and pulled her along, gripping her sweaty hands.

Suddenly they were out in the open facing a blue sky and eiderdown clouds. It was a sheer drop to the cobblestone street below.

"This way," Jordi beckoned.

Talia looked in dismay as her cousin boldly clambered up a series of crumbling stones, and from there, leapt onto a balcony. With a jerk of his head, Jordi signalled for Pau to follow. Pau glanced at Talia. Not surprisingly, he saw fear in her wide unblinking eyes.

"I'll lift you up," Pau offered.

Talia's chin quivered as she tried to keep from crying, certain that this venture would lead to her death.

Pau opened his arms and coaxed her forward. He slid his hand under one of her shoulders, and then hoisted her up.

Jordi was poised to propel himself from the balcony to a nearby stone wall when there was a sudden movement. A shutter flew open, clattering against the stucco. An arm reached for Jordi.

Talia watched in horror as it fastened onto him and yanked him out of view. Pau drew back, pulling Talia with him. They listened as Jordi's cries echoed off the interior walls. His protests barely muted by the heavy stone.

Pau and Talia hopped off the ledge and scurried into the alleyway, panting and trembling.

Jordi's bawling drew the attention of a thin cat, causing it to halt its lazy amble across the street. It stood still for a moment, one paw mid-air, trying to decide whether to proceed or not. Then it caught sight of Talia and Pau and bounded away.

The pair skirted the walls for half a block, then paused to look back. Judging that no one had observed them, they retreated into a doorway and waited. Pau sighed and leaned back. He studied his young cousin. He was relieved in a way that fate had intervened to stop Jordi's stupid plan, for harm might have come to Talia.

Pau felt protective of the little girl. Seeing her after an absence of several months, he was reminded again of her intelligence and her wisdom well beyond her years.

"Pau?" She looked up at him with her large black eyes. "Shouldn't we help Jordi?"

"Nah, he got himself into this mess. He can get himself out."

"But what if —?"

She did not finish. A muffled sound drew her eyes in the direction of a shadow wobbling across the street.

Jordi appeared, sniffling and whimpering.

He shuffled forward some more and then slowed to wipe his cheeks with the back of his hand. Talia and Pau emerged from the doorway and approached him.

"Are you alright?" Pau asked.

Jordi didn't reply, but only stared sullenly ahead. Nevertheless, they could see his face was smudged from crying, and his ear was red and swollen. After a moment, the three turned and walked in silence until they reached the bottom of the narrow street. Then Jordi suddenly wheeled about.

"It's all your fault!" He said, glaring at Talia.

A burning sensation filled Talia's chest. Her eyes prickled as tears began to emerge. Was it really her fault? She had only wanted to see the procession. And now she was being blamed for something she wanted no part of and what was worse, they had still not seen any of the parade.

"The old hag was waiting for us." Jordi's eyes flashed with anger. "If I hadn't been slowed down by you I would have made it to the other side and had the best view."

"Come on," Pau said, nudging his brother along. "Maybe we can still catch the rest of the procession."

They hurried back but each time they turned a street corner, it seemed like the revellers had already come and gone.

By the time they reached the plaza, it was a confused melee. The procession had broken up and the square was crowded with people. Talia couldn't see a thing at first. Then she noticed the shiny-faced giants bobbing high over the crowd of festival-goers. Huge papier mache men and women, ominous and unsmiling, spun around.

Talia pushed her way to an opening where the giant dancers teetered. She craned her neck, blinking back at the sun as she stared up, mesmerized. The female *gegants'* skirts billowed like tents, revealing strange wooden legs beneath. Talia was fascinated by the mechanics of the limbs.

Suddenly a giant loomed over her. When it reached down and tried to touch her, a scream erupted from Talia, so violent and prolonged she did not even recognize it as her own voice.

"It's okay, it's okay, little one," a man laughed.

Suddenly, her mother was there, shaking her. "Pollita, he's not real." Carmen pressed Talia against her. "Come, come," she said, trying to calm her daughter.

At last the shrill noise from Talia stopped. She peered out from behind her mother's skirt. It was so strange. The giant was placing a hand at his neck and lifting the misshapen head, separating it from his body. Talia gaped as a normal, even pleasant-looking man appeared. The man's eyes twinkled and his mouth widened into a smile.

He crouched before Talia. He took her hand and gently guided it to the papier mache head showing her the hollow inside of the *capgrosso* skull.

"See nothing there — no teeth."

In spite of the reassurance, Talia still harboured strong misgivings and snatched her arm back, causing the man to laugh. Carmen giggled too, and it made the man look up at her and notice her for the first time. He was so taken with her that for a few seconds all he could do was stare.

"I'm sorry. I didn't mean to frighten..." his voice trailed off.

"Nonsense, she'll be fine," Carmen assured him.

"I hope she doesn't have nightmares tonight."

"Then we'll just have to stay till dawn and tire her out."

The man chuckled. "Well, I hope you do that in any case."

"Please, let me introduce myself. I'm Silvio." His head dipped in reverence to her.

"Nice to meet you, Silvio." His name slid off her tongue like satin. "Carmen."

"Your accent — you're not from around here?" he said, switching to Spanish.

"No, I'm from the south. A small place — Jerez de la Frontera."

"Ah, yes."

"You know it?"

"Well, I have never been to Jerez but I am familiar with the fine beverage made there. — It seems only sweet things come from your home town."

Talia's mother's bubbled with laughter.

"Jerez is a long way off."

"True, but everywhere is far from here," said Carmen with a hint of bitterness.

"I had quite a lot of trouble finding this town. It was like climbing into a cave."

Carmen gave a wry laugh.

As the two adults conversed, Talia noticed a change in her mother's speech. It dawned on Talia that Carmen and this man spoke the same language. After several moments of banter, Silvio bade Carmen goodbye. She flashed him a demure smile, her cheeks colouring slightly. Silvio bowed and was off, being careful to turn his mask away from Talia as he disappeared into the crowd.

*   *   *

The festivities paused in the afternoon as many retreated inside and out of the strong sun. By early evening, the band began to play again, drawing people out from their siestas.

At dinner that night, the cake blessed by the priest was cut into small pieces and Talia could finally have a taste. Inside the yellow dough was a pocket of sweetened almond paste. She licked the powdered sugar off her tiny fingertips and leaned forward, hoping for another bite. But to her disappointment, the brioche was all gone.

Her female relatives bustled about, clearing plates and serving coffee. Sounds of laughter and the clatter of dishes reverberated from the tile floors to the high ceilings.

After the meal, Talia felt her head droop. She must have been asleep for a while when what sounded like a gunshot woke her. Another loud explosion soon followed, and Talia sat up fully alert. Just at that moment, Infanta rushed into the room, skipping with excitement.

"Why are they shooting?" Talia blurted to her cousin.

"It's fireworks, silly! Come on!" said Infanta, laughing.

She drew Talia outside into the night air. The younger child looked for armed men in the streets but to her relief saw only townsfolk, cheerful and relaxed.

The smell of wood smoke wafted towards the girls. Down the block, a vendor tended over a small brazier, roasting chestnuts. When the girls neared, he held out a small paper cone towards them.

"*Castanyer! Castanyer!*" he shouted, his voice high and nasal.

A bright burst of fireworks smashed against the black sky and fizzled out. Ribbons of smoke and glitter catapulted down.

Infanta and Talia could not help but run into Jordi and Pau, Sant Feliu being such a small place, and soon they formed a little group. Talia was wary of Jordi, sensing he might still be bitter about the incident earlier that day. His sullen glances in her direction confirmed as much. He finally had his chance at a little bit of revenge. He could not resist when an opportunity arose to frighten Talia with a terror so profound it would stay with her until well into her adult years.

"There she is," cried Jordi.

"Who?" Talia craned her neck, following his pointing finger.

"The witch who tried to push me off the cliff."

Despite her fear, Talia crept forward but several bystanders blocked her view. "I can't see," she said.

Jordi shoved Talia and suddenly the dreaded woman came into view. A chill swept over Talia as she recognised the sleeve of the dress and the claw-like hand that had grabbed Jordi earlier.

"She's only got one good eye. The other's just a glass ball," Jordi whispered, his voice taunting.

"How come?" she asked, her voice faint.

"She gave an eye to the devil in exchange for special powers," Jordi said, delighting to see Talia's face go pale.

Infanta swatted Jordi. "You can't say things like that."

"You can if it's true," he hissed.

Infanta fell silent, betraying her own fear that Jordi might be right. To look at the old woman one could easily imagine a bargain with the underworld. She was small and grey, her hands rippled with bluish veins. Her steel wool hair was combed back in a severe knot, leaving nothing to soften her hideous features: a hooked nose, a sharp chin, and deep eye sockets.

"I'll give you five *céntimos* if you can guess which eye is fake," Jordi said.

It was not the money but sheer curiosity that propelled Talia to move in for a closer look. When Talia was directly in line with the woman, she paused and focused on the witch's face, trying to discern the false eye from the real eye, but the light was very dim. So Talia edged even closer, when suddenly the old woman shifted her gaze and caught the little girl in her sights.

Electric fear immobilized Talia. Yet in that instant she knew for certain which eye was dead, and which was not.

The woman cackled in amusement, unperturbed by Talia's intense stare. "One eye is looking at you and one at your mother," she uttered in a raspy voice.

"My mother!"

The hag crooked her finger and pointed. "There she is."

And indeed when Talia turned, there was her mother, dancing and laughing with Silvio, the *capgrosso* man. How odd, thought Talia, for the whole evening she had wandered about not knowing where her mother was and yet the one-eyed woman was able to locate her instantly. It made Talia wonder and worry about the force of the woman's gaze. Could the powerful eye also cast spells and curse those who crossed her? Talia was greatly relieved when a cluster of festival-goers passed in front, breaking the old woman's hold over her. Talia hastily retreated with her cousins and took refuge in other distractions, trying to put the disturbing encounter out of her mind.

* * *

Darkness was seeping from the sky and the stars were fading when they finally left for home in the early pre-dawn hours.

As he guided the horses, Talia's Uncle Bart sang a *havanera* — a mournful song about sailors lost at sea. The teetering lantern on the cart and its squeaking wheels were the perfect accompaniment to Bart's low droning voice.

Talia's feet throbbed and her body ached from exhaustion. She curled up on her mother's lap while her mother stroked her hair and loosened her plait. There was no point any more in trying to keep the mop of black curls tidy.

Talia stared up at her mother who was looking particularly beautiful and happy. Talia wanted to keep watching her mother's serene face but the weight of sleep began to roll over her. Her eyelids felt heavy, yet before they shut completely, Talia noticed something.

One of her mother's earrings was gone!

For whatever reason, Talia decided not to say anything — whether it was due to fatigue or because she knew, in spite of her young age, that it was better not to spoil her mother's rare moment of happiness. And so Talia kept quiet and drifted off to an unsettled sleep.

Chapter Two
The Wolf
Sant Feliu d'Aran, Catalonia, Spain - May 1927

When Talia came into the kitchen the next morning, she found her mother feeding her grandfather breakfast and trying to cajole him out of his sullen mood.

Grandfather Avi stared blankly at his gruel, his thumb sliding over his index finger, back and forth. He had been alone the day before and seemed to have suffered from his daughter-in-law's absence.

"How about I make you a flan, *Pare?*" she offered. Carmen hoped his favourite custard dessert would cheer him up and make him forget the day he had spent alone.

She turned to Talia and bid her to gather up some eggs. Talia's face fell. She moved out of the house reluctantly and trudged down the path to the hen house. It was already warm and large fat bees batted up against the waving stalks of lavender.

While Talia was willing to help her mother, she absolutely dreaded collecting eggs. She was wary of the chickens. She did not trust them, especially the rooster, with its fast-pivoting neck and sharp talons.

When Talia was alone in their pen, the birds approached her like feathered dragons and pecked their way around her in an ever-shrinking circle. If she faced them head on and charged them, they would scatter like dandelions in the breeze. But it seemed that it was when Talia was not paying attention — maybe staring at the hills where her uncles tended sheep, or trying to hear the sea only ten miles away — it was then that she needed to worry about them the most. They would creep up from behind her and launch a sneak-attack, pecking dangerously close to her feet.

And so with great misgiving, Talia crossed the fenced pen towards the hen house. She hesitated, finally lifting the latch and entering. Dust motes danced in slivers of sunlight. Talia glanced around the dark corners and spotted a laggard bird. It made a soft warning cluck as Talia moved past it.

Talia started at the far end of the coop, reaching into the straw hollows and feeling around for the recognizable oval shape. At last she came upon an egg, still slightly warm. She brushed off the straw and nestled it in the bottom of her apron, careful to hold up the ends to form a pocket. She continued, her spirits lifting as she found a second egg and then a third. Her mother would be pleased.

Then she heard Tortuga bark. In between his loud bursts, Talia could make out the steady rumble of a car. Tortuga's barks became louder and more urgent now, convinced there was a trespasser.

She had named her dog, Tortuga, not because he looked anything like a turtle but because she had dreamed of having a sea turtle herself. Ever since her father, whom she had never met, sent a postcard of a giant turtle on a beach, she longed to have one as a pet, or even better, to ride one across a stretch of white sand like the girl in the picture.

As far as Talia was concerned, the idea of her father in a faraway land, and the notion of someone climbing on top of an ancient tortoise belonged in the same realm as fairy tales. Her father was just as real or make-believe as Rumpelstiltskin or Pinocchio, and his fortune-seeking adventure no less magical than that of a pirate.

Talia found a hole in the wall where a knot of wood had fallen out. She peered out towards the road. She had a pretty good view of the lane and Tortuga's wide brown body, jerking back and forth alongside a sleek black car.

Her mother appeared and ran towards Tortuga, grabbing him and pulling him down off the unknown visitor.

"I'm sorry," Talia heard her apologise.

"He's a good guard dog," the visitor remarked.

That voice. It was familiar. Where had Talia heard it before? — Yes, that was it. The *capgrosso* — Silvio.

Carmen and Silvio's conversation became fainter, disappearing beneath the rumble of the motor. Talia decided to exit the hen house and get a closer look.

But by the time Talia emerged from the little shed, and tiptoed past the gauntlet of clucking hens, her mother was getting into the car. Shocked, Talia raced to the gate and flung it open.

"Mama!" she cried. "Mama!"

Her little feet flew over the rocks and past clumps of thorny shrubs. Her eyes fixed on the black car and her mother behind the glass. In her hurry, she completely forgot about the eggs in her apron. They rolled out and smashed to the ground.

As she reached the road, the car disappeared from view. Talia was left utterly winded, less by the effort of climbing the path than by the sudden disappearance of her mother.

She stood at the road for a long while, fully expecting the car to return by the same way it had left. But it did not. Her vigil ended abruptly at the sound of sharp squawking. Talia turned away from the road, her eyes disbelieving.

It was pandemonium as panicked hens fluttered about the yard, trying to evade Tortuga who snapped at their spindly legs. At each incursion, they fluttered up briefly, and then landed a few yards away, only to have Tortuga set upon them again.

"Tortuga! No!"

Talia hurried down the incline towards her dog. But she was not fast enough. He pounced on a hen and seized it by the neck. Talia tried to rescue the bird but Tortuga growled and bared his teeth as she came near.

Tortuga wrestled briefly with the struggling bird, pinning it to the ground, and summarily ending its resistance by ripping its head off.

Talia was horrified. "Tortuga!" she screamed.

The dog snatched the fowl and disappeared behind the coop,

making a beeline for the valley below.

"Bad dog!" Talia yelled. She grabbed a stone and threw it at him, but it fell far short.

After Tortuga left, Talia surveyed the disaster. Hens clustered under the fig tree and along the fence. With as much bravery as she could muster she began to guide them back to their pen. She found some corn and threw it near the open gate. Timidly, the hens began to return to the safety of the enclosure.

Talia noticed a wayward hen, pecking at the ground. When Talia came near she saw it was perched over the smashed eggs.

The bird resisted Talia's efforts to move it, so finally Talia untied her apron and threw it over the creature. Trembling more than the bird, Talia scooped up the hen and wrestled with it, pushing it over the wire fence. Once that was done, Talia bent her head in her hands and let her body give way to sobs.

A cascade of tears poured out. They collected in her dusty hands and when she rubbed her eyes, it made marks like war paint. Then when Talia could not cry anymore, she sat for a while under the fig tree, unable to get up.

The breeze rustled the cypresses. The perfume of flowering shrubs filled her nostrils. A butterfly swept by. It was hard to reconcile this peaceful scene with the horrific episode only moments before.

When Talia finally tried to get up, her legs were numb, and her feet tingled with a thousand tiny pinpricks.

She shuffled into the house, finding her grandfather with his head nodding in slumber. His bowl had been knocked to the floor and its contents spilled across the tiles. *Pare* heard her come in and stirred, clamouring for more food. She found him some bread and sausage and offered it to him, but he could not chew it and spat it out.

Pare gave her a miserable look.

"Where is my flan?" he asked.

Talia remembered the smashed eggs, and thought guiltily

that there would be no flan that day and maybe not anytime soon.

A little while later, the old man muttered: "She promised me a flan."

Talia murmured, "There were no eggs, *Pare*."

"No eggs!"

He sunk back in his chair.

"But where is she?"

Talia considered telling him the truth. She looked at her grandfather's milky eyes, his sparse white hair, and sunken cheeks with patches of stubble. She started to speak but the words stuck in her mouth like stones. She burst into tears.

Pare was baffled by this and annoyed too. He waved at her like a bothersome fly.

She ran away from him and threw herself on her cot, the coarse woollen blanket scratching her cheeks. She curled up, her sobs lulling her to sleep.

She began to dream. She dreamt of hens — not ordinary ones, but birds that could fly properly. They soared safely away from Tortuga and settled on the roof of the house. Talia was happy they were unharmed but was annoyed at the racket they made — such a lot of crashing and banging.

As the noise continued, Talia awoke and realised she had not been hearing hens but rather the clatter of pots and pans. — Her mother was back.

Talia feared her mother would ask about the missing eggs but she hardly paid attention to Talia as she bustled about the kitchen.

Talia noticed a round of cheese, butter, and a loaf of bread on the counter. She spotted another thing too. As her mother brushed her hair away from her cheek, Talia caught a glimpse of the gold and garnet earrings. *Both of them.*

Carmen hummed as she chopped parsley and rosemary. Light and happy, deliciously transformed by her spur of the moment outing, her father-in-law's sour mood did not bother her. She wiped up his spilled food and fed him bits of the soft cheese, ignoring his resentful mutterings. Her mind was elsewhere.

Talia dreaded the moment when her mother would learn of the attack on the hens, but to Talia's surprise and relief, she never did get around to asking. Her mother was absorbed in her daydreams and seemed to have forgotten her earlier request for eggs.

The hens did not lay anything for the next several days. And when the hens were counted, three were found missing.

Talia felt herself go cold when she heard Uncle Arnau cursing Tortuga. "That damned dog must have found a way into the hen house."

"It was a wolf," Talia lied.

"There are no wolves around here." Uncle Arnau stared hard at his niece. "Did you *see* a wolf?"

Talia flushed. She mumbled something about hearing a wolf howl. Arnau sniffed.

Arnau might have let it go had the remaining hens started to lay eggs again, but they were clearly still suffering the trauma of Tortuga's attack. Losing several hens and their eggs was serious.

No eggs meant no flan, no tortilla, no cakes, no pudding, and — emptier bellies. They were barely scratching out a living from the parched land as it was. Arnau could not let a dog feed freely on their scant resources. He made up his mind then and there. He decided not to tell Carmen in case she would try to talk him out of it. After all, Tortuga had done the damage while under her watch.

The next morning Talia woke up with a feeling of dread. The air was strangely quiet. The rooster's crow, the bird sounds — yes, they were the same as always, but one sound was missing — Tortuga's bark! She had not heard it that morning.

She jumped out of bed, raced past her mother busily stoking the stove, and darted out of the house.

"Tortuuuugaaa!" she cried.

She checked every corner of the garden. She called his name up and down the paths, and all the way down to the valley where the creek ran. She called his name as she crawled under the vines and between the rows of lemon and orange trees. She clapped and she whistled. Then she waited and watched, hoping for a rustle, some movement in the shadows, or the crash of his lithe body as he ran through the grass.

But he did not appear.

Uncle Arnau said he had probably wandered off, the same way he had wandered into their lives. But Talia knew her dog had not simply left. A cold fear swept through her. She knew, in her heart of hearts, he would not return and why.

Not so long ago she had seen Uncle Arnau with a litter of kittens. Watched him place the soft little babies in a sack and lower them into a barrel of water, holding them down for a long, long while so that when the wet bag was pulled up, Talia no longer heard their soft mewling. She had watched all this all from behind a tree, and kept very quiet, biting her lip as tears stung her eyes.

Arnau threw their little bodies on a trash heap and covered the mound with branches and dead leaves. She knew from the flies where they were. Was this where Tortuga now lay?

She searched through the brush pile, but saw no sign of him or the telltale flies.

It pained Talia to lose Tortuga, and all the more because she knew it had been her fault he died. It was she who had left the gate open. It was she who had led Tortuga to the temptation that would be his undoing.

Carmen did not pay much attention to Talia's distress and only offered a few distracted words of reassurance. Her mind was on other things.

The morning after her mysterious trip in the car, Carmen began to watch the road. The day after that, she was there again. This continued for several mornings in a row. Carmen would linger by the side garden and occasionally walk up to the road and peer down it, searching the horizon. She would come back to the house, her face even more closed off, and her eyes filled with a troubled faraway look.

As the weeks went by, Carmen stopped going to the road altogether. The black car was like a ghost that failed to reappear, and that she had perhaps only imagined in the first place.

Yet, the car was real enough. It had taken all of Talia's mother but had only returned a part of her.

Chapter Three
The Letter from Afar
Sant Feliu d'Aran, Catalonia, Spain - November 1927

Nadal, or Christmas, was approaching but unlike other years Talia's mother made no preparations for the holiday. It could have been because she was sick.

It was an illness that crept up slowly. Talia would often find her mother lying down in the middle of the day or staring out at the valley, lost in thought.

She moved through her tasks slowly and heavily, rarely smiling. The gold and garnet earrings were returned to a velvet pouch at the bottom of her dresser.

Sometime in late November, a letter had come from Talia's father and Carmen stole away to read it. Talia asked her if he had seen any more turtles but her mother was distracted and did not answer right away.

"I want to see a turtle," Talia said. At last her mother heard her. Slowly, she turned to face her daughter.

"Well, maybe you will."

"What?"

"We're going to Australia."

Talia was shocked. She hesitated to press her mother with more questions. A fear lingered beneath her reluctance.

"Me too?" she finally asked.

"Yes," her mother laughed.

"What about *Pare*?"

A shadow passed over Carmen's face. "He'll stay with Bart and Arnau."

When Arnau first learned of Carmen's plan, he was surprised and suspicious. "Australia! Why now?"

Carmen did not reply, but Arnau persisted.

"Does he have a home for you?"

"It's time to join him. It's been too long," said Talia's mother keeping her eyes averted.

"Wait till Bart hears about this."

At the time Bart was on the mountainside with the herd.

"It's not his decision."

Arnau stared at her. He doubted his brother was sending for Carmen. He felt he had let Andre down by not looking after his brother's wife and daughter better.

Whatever Arnau's misgivings, Carmen was not to be dissuaded. She let her two brothers-in-law know it was her plan to leave in December, just before Christmas.

Talia knew the time of their departure was getting closer when her mother pulled out an old trunk and began to fill it.

In spite of her ill health, her mother found a reserve of energy and burst into a fit of cleaning, as though expecting the results of her work to last for as long as she was gone.

She took down the curtains and washed them in the stream. She placed them with the rest of the weekly laundry over the bushes to dry. In the morning she stoked the stove and placed a flat iron on it for warming, and spent the day pressing linens. When Carmen hung the curtains up again, Talia could not really see much of a difference as the flowered print was still faded, but now there was a faint fragrance of lemon.

Carmen next tackled the kitchen furniture, polishing the table with beeswax until it gleamed and repairing the grass seats of the chairs. She boiled water and took a brush to the stone floor, scrubbing until the rinse water came up clear.

She scrutinized the family's few bits of clothes and took care of the holes and worn elbows and cuffs. From these she selected a few items of Talia's and hers to pack in the trunk. The chest was slowly being filled.

The day before they were to leave, Talia picked some flowers and gathered some of her favourite things — the turtle postcard, a tuft of Tortuga's hair found in a thorny bush, an abalone button, a speckled egg shell, and a gnarled root shaped like a dwarf. She bundled everything in an old kerchief and asked her mother to place it in the trunk.

Her mother opened the bundle and held up the root, a small smile forming on her lips, but then she let the bundle drop on the bed.

"We can't bring all that. There's no room."

Talia's face reddened and tears threatened to fall. Talia's mother stroked her daughter's hair. She sighed, turned back to the trunk and pressed down on the contents, making room for Talia's bundle.

"There, Pollita, you will have your souvenirs."

Talia smiled, relieved.

The next day, her mother woke her before the sun was up. "We have to go," Carmen whispered.

Although Talia was too tired to be hungry, Carmen encouraged her to have some warm milk and bread with fig jam.

Arnau was in the mountains but they had already exchanged goodbyes with him. Talia hugged and kissed her grandfather who seemed bewildered by the goings on.

"When will you get back?" the old man asked.

"We're going to join Andre in Australia, *Pare*." Carmen had already told him this several times in the preceding weeks. She tried to remain patient but her voice became louder as she repeated her plans. "Remember, we're leaving for Aus-tra-li-a."

He looked at her blankly and then said, "Bring me back some good coffee," wagging his finger so she would not forget.

Carmen nodded, realizing sadly he did not understand, and probably never would, even after they were long gone.

Bart coughed. "We have to hurry to get you to the train."

Carmen and Talia climbed onto the cart next to Bart, and pulled a travel rug over their legs as it was very cold. The grass and shrubs were coated in silvery frost.

They rode in silence until their little stone house was gone behind the curve in the rocks. They reached a fork in the road and turned right, travelling past the town of Sant Feliu. Faint light revealed the church tower. Talia's mother glanced at it and then looked away.

"Isn't that where the cousins live? Auntie Fina and Auntie Matilda?"

Carmen didn't answer.

"Can't we say goodbye to my cousins, Mama?"

Bart gave Talia a sympathetic look.

"We have to hurry to get the train," he said. "Besides they're all still sleeping."

Talia watched as the church tower shrank in the distance. It seemed to her that it had been a very long time since they had been to town to see her relatives.

As they rode towards Girona, morning light began to brighten the sky. Talia watched as they passed stone houses with smoke curling from the chimneys. Dogs ran alongside the cart before dropping away, unable to keep up. A shepherd warmed himself by a fire, clasping a heavy blanket around himself. Next to him sat a little boy holding a woolly lamb around his neck, with another at his feet.

Soon they were in Girona and the cart pulled onto a cobbled street near the train station. The smell of burning coal tainted the air.

Bart loaded the trunk onto the train and then gripped his sister-in-law's hand. "Give Andre my greetings. Tell him, maybe I too will come in a few years."

"Why don't you come now?" Talia asked.

Bart pulled out the insides of his pockets and showed Talia that they were empty.

Carmen spoke up quickly, "As soon as we can, we'll send you the money."

Bart shrugged. The sharp train whistle startled Talia. Bart made a move to go. His face twisted as though he might cry. He patted Talia's head.

"Take care of your mother," he said. He nodded to Carmen and then left.

Talia watched her uncle from the window as the train set off. She watched until he disappeared, eclipsed by buildings and trees as the train picked up speed.

Talia rested on her knees, with her face pressed against the glass, staring out as the countryside whipped by. Rolling hills, green pastures, peasants stopping to watch the train. Faces there for a second, gone the next — she saw it all through a sooty film.

Finally, with her knees aching she leaned back and slid down into her seat. The rattling of the train on the tracks, the regular clickety-clack, lulled her to sleep. She awoke some time later to a rumbling noise. A man now sat across from her. His bulbous nose whistled as he snored. When he opened his eyes, he was disconcerted to find Talia watching him intently. He pulled a watch from his pocket and glanced at it. He wound it and returned it to his waistcoat. When he looked up again, Talia's gaze was still fixed on him. Carmen nudged her daughter, turning Talia's head to the side so her staring eyes would shift away from the man.

"Are we almost there?" Talia asked.

"Ah, Pollita. It's going to be a long, long trip."

Her mother unfolded a bundle of food and passed Talia a piece of cheese and bread. Carmen drew out a bottle of wine and offered some to the man across from them. He shook his head.

"*Non, merci,*" he replied.

In the afternoon, Talia stared out the window, catching glimpses of a beautiful blue sea with colourful fishing boats and nets strung out to dry. Then she fell asleep again.

Talia awoke later feeling disoriented. The air in the train had chilled with the setting of the sun and her legs were cold where the shawl had fallen off. Her mother tapped her gently. Carmen hurried to gather their things, and hustled her daughter out the door and down the narrow train steps.

After the closed and stuffy air of the train, Talia was struck by a new smell — raw and weedy. Then she saw the source of it. Between gaps in the crowds, there was the sea.

"Is this Australia?" she asked her mother.

"No, Pollita." Carmen laughed. "This is Genoa, Italy. We'll be on the boat for six weeks, and then, only then, will we be in Australia." Her mother pointed to an immense vessel, looming up from the dock. This was the ship that would carry them away.

They followed the crowd and were swept up in a thick column moving up a gangplank, struggling with babies and parcels. Talia held tight to her mother's hand, afraid of falling into the water. Finally at the top, the space opened up. Talia looked back towards the dock, marvelling at the distance they had covered.

The dock swarmed with workers busy with their duties; curious folk, interested in the comings and goings of the large ships; and the families and friends of travellers, cheering, waving goodbye, and tossing paper streamers. Talia searched the faces, as though expecting to see someone familiar among them.

It seemed a long while before the trail of passengers from the gangplank finally ceased. They jammed the deck, clinging to the railings, and shouting their goodbyes. The boat's sudden horn blast sent Talia's fingers flying to her ears. In short order, it began to rumble and shake, vibrating throughout as though coming alive. Chains rattled and the gangplank groaned as it was lifted away.

The boat began to pull away from the shore, and the city that had once seemed so large and sprawling slowly shrank until it finally disappeared altogether. They passed a few fishing boats and soon these too became small specks on the glittering sea, and at last Talia and her fellow travellers were alone on the water.

Chapter Four
A Wave of Friends
Departing Genoa, Italy - December 1927

The metal railing felt cold and wet to Talia's small fingers and when she pulled them away she saw that they were blue and stiff. She tucked her hands under her arms for warmth as she waited for her mother to tire of staring out at the grey shifting sea.

Water the colour of lead formed in troughs, rolled up, and crested. Rolled and folded — over and over again. In spite of the boat's size, it lurched with the sea's movements. A small city of people staggered and pitched, held ransom to the water's uncertain moods.

Wind whistled as it whipped across the deck cutting into thin overcoats and piercing woollen shawls. The flags overhead were pulled taut by the strong air currents.

A creeping sense of desolation overtook Talia. There they were in the middle of the sea, surrounded by strangers, and her mother, the only person in her life now, seemed so ill.

Carmen leaned over the railing and gave a heave, her face ashen, spittle hanging from her lips. Her half-lidded eyes barely took in the surroundings.

A column of rain that had long been angling towards the boat was now suddenly upon them. Talia's mother cowered under the cold driving spikes. Her sticky hand reached for Talia as the rain sent them below deck. The stairs to the steerage were narrow and wet. As they descended, the closed air hit them, sour with seasickness and sweat, old wet clothing and damp leather.

As they entered their cabin, they were met by curious looks from an old woman, dressed in black, and another younger female. They exchanged greetings. Italians, Carmen guessed.

Carmen shook the rain from her shawl and hung it on the end of the berth. She helped Talia out of her wet coat and removed the girl's shoes. She poured herself a cup of water and drank it thirstily. Then she washed her face and patted it dry.

Carmen drew back the sheets and slid in. She beckoned for Talia to follow and draped her arms around her, pulling the little girl close. They cuddled there, still shivering, and eventually they fell asleep.

Talia woke before the dinner bell to the sounds of voices, thumping of heavy doors, and the low rumble of the motor. Finally her mother stirred and got up. By then the two Italian women were already gone.

Carmen pulled open the trunk and retrieved a white cotton dress for Talia. She combed and plaited her daughter's hair, weaving in a red ribbon.

Talia fingered the satin ribbon as though pondering the reason for such an adornment.

"It's Christmas Eve, Pollita," Carmen explained.

"Oh!"

"And Jesus' birthday is tomorrow. You remember what else is special about tomorrow?"

Talia thought for a second. Her eyes widened in delight. "Is it my birthday too?"

"Yes."

"But will Saint Nicholas find us, Mama?"

"Of course. He always knows where the children are."

"Even on the water?"

"Even here."

Carmen studied Talia's face and smiled at her unbridled excitement. She envied her daughter's apparent freedom from worries and sadness. It was a blessing the little girl was too young to fully understand the circumstances, Carmen thought.

Her mind went over all they had lost: the little farm, their relatives in Sant Feliu and her own family back in Jerez. When would she see them again? She felt her chest tighten and got up quickly in an effort to hide her pain from Talia.

Carmen felt badly about their abrupt departure. But things would get sorted out in Australia, she thought to herself. Their new life there would make up for all the sacrifices.

Carmen briefly forgot her worries as they entered the dining room. They were greeted by off-tune voices belting out 'O *Sole Mio'*. Red-cheeked guests sang and swayed around a trio of musicians.

The nervous steward beckoned for those still standing to be seated. "*Signore y Signori, la cena è servita.*"

The guests finally responded to his appeals and began to fill up the chairs.

He saw Carmen and Talia standing by themselves, looking a little lost. He glanced behind them as though half-expecting someone else as well — a husband, a father. Realising that they were on their own, he found two empty seats and led them there.

In spite of her queasiness, Carmen was still tempted by the menu: a pumpkin soup, potato gnocchi and roast pork with apples. Talia and her mother ate greedily, undeterred by the boisterousness of their fellow passengers. Wine was passed up and down the table and when the main course was done, cream-filled cannoli flew off the dessert plates like feathers in the wind.

Suddenly her chair scraped back and Carmen hurried away, her hand to her mouth. Talia wheeled around just in time to see her mother hurtling out the door. There were a few giggles and sideways looks and then people returned to their conversations.

The meal had been too much for Carmen. The bulk of it disappeared again down the toilet, some of it missing its mark and landing on the floor and down her dress — her only good dress.

She rushed back to their cabin and changed into other clothes, rinsing out the fouled dress first before rejoining Talia upstairs.

The little girl was almost exactly where her mother had left her, although the tables and chairs had been moved to the side. Talia stood in wonder as dancers swirled in pairs, boots and shoes turning quickly, almost flying above the floor. The thunderous force of the thumping feet fascinated her.

The raucousness of the crowd and the bluish smoke-filled air forced Carmen to retreat again but this time with Talia in tow. They returned to their berth and were getting ready for bed when a knock sounded on the door of the cabin. It opened and a cheerful face with luminous black eyes peeked in.

"*Buenas noches.*"

A woman entered, apologising for disturbing them. She introduced herself as Maribel and explained that she worked every day with the Candelas, a well-to-do family in first class, helping the mother who was travelling alone with her daughters. Maribel was from Alicante and had started with the Candela family when their eldest daughter was a baby and continued as the family grew, adding three more girls.

"Another one on the way. They say this one is going to be a boy, but my guess is it will probably be another girl. — Which would make five girls altogether! Can you imagine!" Maribel opened her hand wide to show Talia all five fingers.

"That's how old I am — tomorrow!" Talia said.

"Aaaah! Aren't you special! A Christmas baby!" Maribel smiled at Talia and patted her head. Her fingers playfully scooped up a few of Talia's curls.

"And your hair — isn't it wonderful!"

Talia blushed. She glanced at her mother, expecting her to disagree with Maribel's assessment and throw in a complaint about Talia's hair, but Carmen said nothing. It struck Talia how unfriendly and aloof her mother seemed at this moment.

Perhaps Maribel had the same perception too for she was suddenly apologising again.

"There, you're very tired. I'm sorry for keeping you up. I'll try to be quiet from now on when I come in."

Talia stood still, awestruck by Maribel and her vivacity. Finally, her mother's voice broke the spell.

"Come to bed, Pollita."

Early the next morning, Maribel descended from the upper berth and dressed in the darkness. Before she slipped out of the room, Talia heard her whisper.

"Feliz Cumpleaños!"

"Gracias," Talia replied, feeling a rush of warmth from this kind stranger.

After morning mass, the children were invited out to the deck for a surprise. Talia hurried there joining a crowd around San Nicolo, a bearded man in a red, fur-trimmed coat. He gesticulated with his staff, questioning the eager boys and girls.

"Have you been good this year?"

They replied quite loudly, *"Sì, sì"* as though the louder they were, the more true it would be. Based on the level of their voices alone, they were certainly very deserving.

San Nicolo teased them a little by dragging out their wait with an elaborate examination of his scroll of names.

"Let me check my list."

At last he began to read out the names, prompting a child to rush forward, claiming a small present. Tops, rubber balls, a skipping rope. Not homemade toys, but real store-bought gifts.

Talia was sure she had been forgotten as name after name was called, but never hers. Didn't they know it was her birthday too?

And then.... "Natalia Qw-Qw--Qway—sens." The Italian Santa struggled with the pronunciation so Talia wasn't sure if that was her. Yet no one else came forward.

"I hope she didn't fall off the boat," San Nicolo joked.

Children laughed.

"I'll take it," someone suggested.

"Na-ta-lia Qway–sens," Santa repeated.

Finally, Talia's mother whispered in her ear.

"Go, Talia, I think it's you."

Talia gathered her courage and pushed her way through the crush of children. She reached the bottom hem of San Nicolo's coat, but he pretended not to see her to humorous effect. She tugged on the felt garment and at last he peered down at her.

"Ah! There you are."

He handed her a small parcel. She took it and pressed it to her chest as she skipped back towards her mother. Talia peeled off the wrapping and found a tiny tea set decorated with small pink roses. It was so delicate she hesitated to pick it up at first.

After they returned to their cabin, Talia laid out the dishes on the trunk and offered her mother some tea. Maribel returned in the middle of their tea party.

"Look what Santa brought!" Talia exclaimed.

"Oh, my," said Maribel. "Isn't that fancy!"

"You want some tea?"

"Please. I am so thirsty."

The governess sipped her imaginary drink with gusto and then produced a bundle of sweets wrapped in a napkin, contributing them to the party.

Maribel glanced at Carmen, who was resting on the berth. She gave her a comforting smile. "You'll get used to it in a few days. It doesn't bother me so much. I'm from a family of fisherman so I have the sea in my bones."

But Carmen never did get used to the boat, nor did the colour return to her cheeks for the duration of the trip. She continued to suffer from a stomach ailment attributed to seasickness and spent many hours below deck.

On another one of those days when Carmen lay in bed, Maribel came into the cabin and saw Talia playing alone again. She took pity on the little girl and invited her to keep Maribel company at work. When Carmen expressed concern that Talia would be a nuisance, Maribel dismissed the idea outright.

"With so many little girls underfoot, one more won't make a difference," Maribel said reassuringly.

And so it came to be that Talia accompanied Maribel as she escorted her charges, the four Candela sisters: Aracely, seven; Ofelia, five; and the three-year old twins, Lucia, and Maria

Eugenia. They seemed more than happy to have Talia tag along.

Besides, Talia offered something very special, and that was her hair. Since the little Candela girls themselves had short bobbed hair, Talia's long curly locks entranced them. And even better was that Talia patiently endured their amateur attempts at hairstyling. Talia for her part was thrilled to suddenly have so many friends after a relatively lonely childhood.

With the Candela girls, Talia explored the decks of the boat, listening to Maribel's lively stories. They were elaborations of books she had read or true-life experiences that showed worldliness beyond her twenty-three years.

When the sea became rough and the upper deck too rainy or windy to be out, they spent their time in the Candelas' cabin, which seemed quite luxurious especially compared to the third class accommodations. Talia marvelled at the Candela girls' collection of dolls. Each girl had at least two, so their quarters were awash in tiny garments, from lace-trimmed petticoats and fur-fringed shawls to velvet dresses decorated with gold embroidery and beads.

"My father is building a castle for us, and mama didn't want to be around the mess. But then she found out she was going to have another baby so that's why we're travelling now."

Talia was amazed. A castle, she thought. So that meant Aracely, Ofelia, Lucia and Maria Eugenia were princesses.

"So is their father the king of Australia?" she asked Maribel one day.

Maribel sputtered with laughter. It was a while before she could stop her giggling. She wiped away tears and bit her lip. "No, Pollita. In Australia, anyone who wants can build a castle."

This was an astonishing revelation. Perhaps her own father had been building a castle for them, Talia wondered. Surely this would explain why he had not sent for them until now.

The enchantment of this notion, and the lifting of the clouds, began to push Talia's mood to a new level of excitement. They were about to leave the Mediterranean and the weather was moving from cool and overcast to hot and sunny.

As the boat entered Port Said at the tip of Egypt, the statue of Ferdinand de Lesseps towered over them, pointing steadfastly towards the next stage of their journey. They did not heed him right away but remained overnight in the port while supplies were loaded on board. All around them small boats flocked to their ship. Men in caftans hawked their wares, sending the goods up to the ship via rope and pulley.

Their journey down the Suez Canal began the next morning. The days passed with only a bland shoreline in view and the occasional glimpse of a camel caravan or herd of goats, but Maribel's stories enlivened the dull sand and flat landscape for the girls.

She claimed that on a clear day one could see the faint outline of the great pyramids along the Nile, including the Sphinx, which had the head of a woman and the body of a lion. The Sphinx, Maribel explained, could answer the most puzzling questions. Talia tried hard but could not see beyond the haze and the vibrations caused by the intense heat.

Maribel's tales became even more fabulous as she recounted the astounding life of Empress Cleopatra, the most beautiful and powerful woman in the world. "She decided when she would die, because she knew she could come back at anytime, in any form — even as a cat! So she took the deadly asp and made it bite her."

Just as Talia was wondering whether one of the kittens Arnau had drowned could have been Cleopatra, Señora Candela, the mother of her friends, interrupted in a stern voice that seemed to come out of nowhere.

"Of course, Maribel knows, as all good Catholics do, that only Jesus can choose to come back from the dead, and that Cleopatra is rotting away in her tomb and will remain there, sinner that she was."

Maribel turned to see Señora Candela settle back down into a wicker lounger. She pulled out an embroidery hoop and began to jab the taut linen fabric with her needle. From under the brim of her hat, she met Maribel's eyes briefly.

"Yes, your mother is right," Maribel conceded reluctantly. "Cleopatra was a sinner and will not live again." And then as though not wanting to dwell on this sad possibility she moved on to a new topic of interest.

"Ah, you see those camels. They're probably carrying salt all the way from Timbuktu. Salt is like gold in this part of the world."

They passed through the Red Sea, leaving behind the leaning dhows, the minarets and the distant sounds of chanting. From there on, the horizon opened up again as the ship entered the Indian Ocean. And still the heat grew.

Several days later, they stopped in Colombo, Ceylon, a city of white buildings and red tile roofs, beyond which lay hills of leafy green. Its harbour was cluttered with fishing boats. After a short sojourn, they were back at sea, with more days of azure skies, and the occasional warm rain. They had many lazy, carefree hours.

One morning on the deck, Maribel lifted Talia to show her something that at first Talia mistook for a large dragonfly.

"You see it? It's a flying fish!" said Maribel excitedly.

The strange creature skipped above the surface of the water, zigzagging from side to side, and then suddenly folding its wings, it plunged underwater. But soon it emerged again and took up the same odd meandering, lifting off hesitantly just above the peaks of the waves as though undecided about where it really belonged, in the sea or the sky.

The days passed and blue sky after blue sky allowed the sun to turn Talia as brown as tobacco. The Candela girls all wore wide brimmed hats and their skin retained a powdered paleness in spite of the hours spent outside.

The Candela girls and Talia played tea and jacks, hopscotch and cards, and dressed up the dollies and took them for walks in the tiny wicker pram. They made fun of the steward, sang songs, and played hairdresser. Meanwhile Señora Candela did needlework, or read from novels, but more often than not she fell asleep in the rattan lounge chairs. She became more rounded as the weeks went by and her walk took on a funny side-to-side tilt.

"Maribel says the baby could come any day now. It might just be a child of the sea, not born to any one country," remarked Aracely.

Talia thought about that — a sea child. A baby raised by mermaids or dolphins and carried on the wings of flying fish until it learned to swim. It would be a special child indeed.

As the weeks went by, boredom had forced even the shiest of the passengers to open up. Stories and cigarettes had been shared. Friendships had formed. They had been travelling for nearly a month and now in the middle of the Indian Ocean, they were just hours away from crossing the equator. The already convivial mood became positively festive as they reached this important marker.

Maribel held up a rubber ball for the girls to see and pointed to a stripe that went all the way around. "We're on the north half now and tonight we move to the south."

The first class dining room, where Talia was a frequent visitor — thanks to Maribel's ability to charm the steward into turning a blind eye to an additional guest — was decorated for this important occasion. As dinner ended, a fellow passenger dressed in a white robe and crown, and bearing a trident, sang as the revellers toasted with champagne to King Neptune.

Fireworks fired from a small companion boat marked the actual crossing. That moment, the moment when they passed over the line dividing the earth into north and south, caused many of the passengers to pause and think about the eventual end of the journey. What grand plans and ambitions did they nurture that would either come to fruition or fall far short of their expectations? For a little while longer at least, these hopes and dreams were left untarnished by reality, deferred for the few remaining carefree days of travel.

Not long after, the boat finally arrived in Fremantle, Australia, and several groups of passengers went ashore, including the two Italian women who had shared the cabin with Maribel, Carmen and Talia. They had indeed reached Australia but this was not the right port, Maribel explained to Talia.

It was after the first group disembarked that Talia's mother made one of her rare appearances on deck. She was pale like a seedling that had sprouted under a rock. She stood out not just for her wan complexion, but also for the strangeness she exuded, having hidden away from the company of others for most of the journey.

Señora Candela's eyes seemed to latch onto her immediately. Looking down at her from the first class deck, she took note of Carmen's condition, her loosely draped clothing, and the heaviness with which she moved. Señora Candela leaned towards Maribel and whispered something. Maribel nodded gravely.

Spying her mother from afar, Talia felt a pang of guilt at how little time she had spent with her and how much more she preferred to be with Maribel and the Candelas, whiling away the hours while her mother remained below deck, all alone. Now that the two Italian ladies had left the boat, the cabin was even more solitary.

Talia felt a distance from her mother, as though she had changed families and her mother was slipping away from her, much like a lighthouse along the shore, disappearing further and further, until almost out of sight.

Even though they had landed in Australia once, they were still far from their destination. An air of restlessness grew among the passengers. Now that they had seen it, they were eager to be there. Like candy behind the glass at a confectionery shop, the country remained a tantalizing distance away. From what Talia could see of it, Australia was a cold grey line on the horizon, hardly welcoming.

It was on the thirty-fifth day that the air changed abruptly.

The wind picked up and smoke-coloured clouds billowed up and curled into ominous and ever-changing shapes — devils and winged horses — scurrying across the ship's path until they clustered, the whole gang of them, looming, as if to block its way. After the warm Indian Ocean, this air was almost frigid. Maribel led the girls from their play outdoors as droplets began to pelt their lovely sunhats. They returned to the shelter of their quarters.

Talia was now used to making her own way to the cabin below. But that particular day, just before she turned the handle she had a sense of foreboding. Opening the door, she found her mother doubled over on the floor, gasping, baring her teeth like a rabid animal. Her eyes bulged, her lips thin as her face stretched in agony. What frightened Talia most was her mother's unearthly moaning. She was convinced her mother was about to die.

Time sped up while also seeming to slow down as Talia raced to alert Maribel. She found her and the Candela girls dawdling at the entrance of their cabin. Talia burst upon them, hiccupping words between tears. Maribel understood something to the effect that Carmen was dying. Señora Candela came to the door and asked what the fuss was about. Maribel directed the girls inside then whispered something to Señora Candela. There was a quick exchange of words, then Maribel was dispatched to see to Carmen. Talia wanted to come along but was ordered to stay behind.

The rain lashed steadily against the windows through the late afternoon and evening as the girls huddled indoors. The mood was tense, and Talia and her friends argued over silly things, boredom getting the better of them.

That night, Talia slept next to Ofelia. She kept her eyes fixed on the door, waiting for Maribel's return and news of her mother. She couldn't remember falling asleep but she must have, for the next thing she knew she heard the ship's horn, and the ring of the bell announcing the first seating for breakfast. Maribel had not returned that night, and Señora Candela remained tight-lipped about Carmen's condition.

Chapter Five
Sea Child
Crossing the Bight, near Australia – February 1928

Over his thirty-odd year career as a ship's doctor, Dr. Gennesario had delivered many babies and he was expecting to deliver yet another quite soon — that of Señora Beatrice Candela, the Spanish lady with the four daughters. She had already come to see him a number of times with various complaints — swollen ankles and other discomforts. In spite of these minor matters, her pregnancy was progressing well and the baby's heartbeat was steady. He had even felt a kick or two while examining her. Things seemed to bode well for a healthy, vigorous child. The only thing he had to caution Señora Candela about was to walk regularly and take the air so as to improve circulation and not to allow herself to grow too plump.

The doctor would tease her by saying that he would have to declare the child Italian because it was going to be born on an Italian boat, but Señora Candela insisted that her baby would not be born until they were in Australia. Her previous four children had all arrived late and so would this one. But Gennesario was sure she would be proved wrong and the Señora's new baby would make his or her appearance at any moment.

And so some time later when he was interrupted at lunch with an urgent message from Nurse Farinelli that a patient was in labour, he rushed down fully preparing to see Señora Candela. He was taken aback to find someone else instead, a woman with whom he had not yet had contact and for whom he had received no prior warning that she might be with child. It was even more confusing as Maribel, the Candelas' governess, was with this stranger.

He had little time to sort this all out as the pregnant woman was in extreme distress. She writhed in agony, barely coherent.

The contractions were only a few minutes apart. It would have been difficult to get names and details at this moment so he focussed instead on the more pressing problem of ensuring the wellbeing of mother and child.

Dr. Gennesario administered a dose of ether and immediately the woman's moans were quieted. He turned his attention to the baby that had started to make its way down the birth canal but for whatever reason had stopped progressing. Nurse Farinelli handed the doctor a pair of forceps and he began to work them around the infant's head.

He had an odd feeling that while the baby wanted to be born, this woman had been trying to keep him inside, keeping him from showing his face. But she no longer had a say in the matter. At this moment she was deathly still.

* * *

Maribel stood waiting outside the infirmary. The rare noises that penetrated the walls were unnerving and she fretted for Carmen's sake. Regret plagued her as she brooded over what she could have done to help Carmen and her unborn child.

While Maribel paced, the baby finally made his appearance. He was by all accounts a healthy child even though he did not begin breathing right away. Gennesario thumped him on the back and the infant took in his first inhalation. The doctor and Nurse Farinelli were even more reassured when the baby uttered a small cry.

His blue-tinged skin turned a mottled pink and his body vibrated as his lungs filled, and then he expelled an even heartier cry. This next bout was so loud and feisty that even Maribel could hear him through the door, and she hurried away with the news.

When Maribel arrived at the Candelas' cabin she found Beatrice moving restlessly. Despite her fatigue she had not been able to sit still. She quickly crossed the room to meet Maribel.

"Well?" she asked.

Maribel was about to answer but just then spotted Talia lifting her head off the pillow. The girl had woken up almost immediately, even though Maribel and Señora Candela had tried to be quiet. She jumped out of bed and ran towards Maribel.

"Is my mama going to die?" she asked tearfully.

Maribel felt a swell of pity for the little girl and picked her up, folding her into a hug. The question was also in Señora Candela's eyes, but Maribel's expression was unreadable.

To Talia she tried to be reassuring. "No, no, Pollita. She's getting better. She'll be fine," and Maribel hoped in her heart that this would not turn out to be a lie. In fact, she had no idea how Carmen was managing.

"I want to see her," Talia pleaded as she clung to Maribel.

"The doctor is taking care of her now," Maribel replied calmly.

Maribel carried the girl to her bed and murmured some more reassurances. When Maribel returned, the two women slipped into the adjoining room. They were careful to speak in hushed voices, knowing that Carmen's daughter was still awake and probably straining to hear every word.

"Maribel, I cannot bear it — tell me what's happened!" urged Señora Candela.

Maribel gave her a weak smile. "It seems that she has given birth to a baby. I don't know if it's a boy or a girl. I only heard it crying."

"And the mother?"

"I have no idea, but when I was sent out earlier she was in a lot of pain," replied Maribel.

"But that's every woman's lot at childbirth."

"Perhaps, but she seemed particularly ill."

Señora Candela frowned.

"Maribel, this is how I will appear to you in a few weeks when my labour begins." Señora Candela rubbed her abdomen almost as though making a plea to her baby to be gentle and merciful.

"And what about the baby? — You did not see it?"

"No, no. I wasn't allowed in. I only heard it. And my, this baby has got a strong set of lungs!"

Señora Candela smiled.

"What do you think she is planning to do?"

Maribel shook her head. "I mean, *what is there* for her to do?"

Señora Candela nodded. She had been pondering the situation. The circumstances were delicate and at sea there were limited ways of dealing with the problem. But being at sea might also be an advantage. Señora Candela's mind raced as she contemplated Carmen's dilemma.

Talia was still awake when Señora Candela and Maribel returned to the room. She kept her eyes closed but heard the outer door shut. Sometime later she noticed that Señora Candela was gone and Maribel was slumped over, fast asleep.

* * *

Once the little baby boy was in the clear, Dr. Gennesario had Nurse Farinelli remove the child to the adjoining room and then they returned to the baby's mother who seemed to be doing poorly. The new mother was very weak and running a fever. She had lost a lot of blood, and her skin was damp and grey.

The air was raw in the little boy's lungs. More than likely, it felt uncomfortable. He was also very tired, but mostly he was angry. Furious actually, that he had waited nine months for his first proper meal and it was not ready when he needed it.

When she left her cabin, Señora Candela moved with a sense of urgency, even before she first heard those cries. She hurried towards the infirmary, like a hunting dog tracing a scent. She found him, the squalling babe, famished and red-faced.

"You poor thing. There, there."

There was no hesitation in Señora Candela as she picked the

newborn up, uttering soft, cooing words. She was a mother above all else and knew instinctively what to do. All she wanted to do was comfort him.

She brought his little face to her bosom. Through her confident purposeful movements, she briefly assuaged him, changing the frantic wails to whimpers of hope, letting him believe that someone near understood his needs. He sensed maternal help was at hand and was appeased for a few seconds. He opened his mouth wide like a little bird, expecting nourishment to be dropped in. But he had little patience, and when he was still not fed his cries rose up again, sharp and angry.

Without much thought, Señora Candela's fingers flew to her buttons, unfastening them quickly. She loosened her clothing and retrieved a breast, placing it against the baby's cheek. The nipple tapped his upper lip, guiding him. He turned his head and opened his mouth wider, whereupon she pressed the breast into his mouth, cutting off his next cry. It was a little uncomfortable fitting him above her rounded belly, but he made do in the awkward space like a puppy in a crowded litter. Once he was latched on he held on tight. After the first few tugs, she felt a tingling in her breast as he suckled. Her milk had come in. Her body was remembering from the many times before.

And as if her own unborn child were sensing competition, it gave a jealous little kick — a sort of caution to its mother not to forget her priorities and obligations to its own offspring above all.

While her thoughts these days had been mostly on her soon-to-be born baby, Señora Candela could not help it now but look upon Carmen's little boy with adoration. How easily he had moved from frantic starvation to sweet satiation, from crimson angry cheeks to plump sleepy peacefulness. His chest lifted and sank softly with each breath. His downy black hair rested lightly against her skin.

His fingers curled tightly around her index finger like the tendrils of a vine. It was a wonderful feeling, this fervent, blind attachment. How helpless he was, and how much he needed her.

She was basking in a feeling of emerging love for this baby when suddenly her body was wracked by a powerful and painful thrust.

She could barely stand up and staggered to the bassinette with the boy, scarcely having enough time to deposit him safely before another violent spasm seized her.

It was like a rogue wave, sneaking up on her and hitting her with a mighty force, almost as though the creature inside her was retaliating for her disloyalty.

Señora Candela was stunned. She had been so certain of the timing, but her predictions for this birth were turning out all wrong. Her baby was coming very soon, and very fast. She wondered if by nursing the other child, she had inadvertently triggered something, disturbing the natural order of things.

*   *   *

Dr. Gennesario would remember this night for years to come. Everything seemed to happen at once. There was only a small sick bay on this ship. The workload had always been quite manageable up until this point, but in the space of a few hours the number of patients had doubled, tripled, and would soon quadruple.

Dr. Gennesario was still in the midst of trying to bring down Carmen's fever when he was called away to see to Señora Candela. Just as he suspected, her baby would not wait for their arrival in Australia.

He and Nurse Farinelli left Carmen to rest and recover, not realizing that more dangerous than her fever was the first stage of delirium that had begun to worm its way into her mind.

Dr. Gennesario was feeling weary from the long day but tried to offer Señora Candela a bright smile when he saw her. She was doubled over and moaning when he came in, but he soon determined he would at least have just enough time to boil water and properly clean instruments from the earlier delivery.

*   *   *

Waves of intense heat rose up through Carmen like a pot boiling over. Her whole body was like dry tinder and just as flammable. Water brought to her lips evaporated like water thrown on an inferno. Her eyes were sore and dry, and her lids moved as though over sand, unable to glide shut. She was forced to stare upward to the heavens to suffer what she imagined were accusing looks and stares. She saw the stern, disappointed faces of her mother and father, her brothers-in-law, and even her husband who had somehow reached the boat. There was nowhere to hide from her shame.

It consumed her. It was as if the devil himself tended to her like a log on his hearth, giving her over to the flames of hell. She thought about making a full confession if only they would bring a priest to her bedside, but no one came. She was plagued with the worry of what would become of her child if she were to die. There was no way to make amends. No way to make anything right of what she had ruined.

In a corner of her feverish mind, an idea formed — a way to take care of the baby, a way for him to have a chance at salvation. Visions of baby Moses adrift between the reeds came to her. The images bubbled and boiled in her brain, making her dizzy. She thought about how Moses was saved by being placed in a basket on the water. He was found and given a new home. Carmen would do the same for her son.

She grappled with how to carry this out. She glanced about the room looking for a hamper or other vessel of some sort. She slid off her cot. Sweat dripped from her as she groped around. Finally her hand came upon a small blanket — something to swaddle him. She wrapped it around him twice hoping it would keep him warm. She spied a metal basin and dragged it near. She removed her gold chain with the tiny cross and placed it on him. Her head was throbbing and salty beads of sweat stung her eyes. She paused to rest, feeling the room tilt around her. She got up and braced herself. Pulses of pain crippled her, yet she managed to lift the swaddled infant and stagger outside the room and towards the railing.

Using all the strength she could muster, she lifted her bundle over the railing, and released him. She thought she could hear the basin splash and she prayed that it had not tipped in its descent towards the water.

She peered over the edge but saw only inky black, and heard the restless waves against the hull of the boat.

The cool night air hit her strong and full. It struck her then in a small window of lucidity, the appalling madness of her deed — the sickening realization that she had thrown her baby to his death.

She let out a piercing scream and immediately tried to climb the railing. She was too weak to do even that and her body dropped in exhaustion. She felt the deck beneath her, wet and slippery from the sea spray. She shook with sobs, crumpled by the weight of her guilt and her grief. She had no idea how much time had passed when a firm hand shook her on the shoulder.

She glanced up to see Maribel, looking puzzled and worried.

"What are you doing here?" Maribel asked.

Carmen could not speak at first. Then the words came out dry and harsh. "I put him on the river."

"Beg your pardon?"

"I set him down — on the water!"

"Who?"

"My son. I let him — drown." Her voice was strangled, barely audible.

Maribel's face clouded over as she struggled to understand Carmen's statements. Maribel shook her head softly, offering a look of pity. "Your son is inside, Señora."

Carmen gave her a look of disbelief. And as if offering proof, at that very moment they heard him cry. Maribel helped Carmen back inside the infirmary with the aid of a ship-hand. They eased her through the doorway, her feet dragging. Then hoisted her onto the bed.

When the baby cried again, Carmen made a movement to go for him but the ship-hand and Maribel stopped her and insisted she lie down. They let her see her son but then carried him out of her reach and she did not protest.

The fact that he was alive surprisingly did not give Carmen any relief at all but rather sent her into a fit of self-flagellation. She tore at her hair and clawed her skin, her body shaking as she raged. Even though all her anger was directed inward, it terrified the ship-hand, a Greek boy, who was on his first sea voyage. He was greatly relieved to be sent away to get Dr. Gennesario. The physician appeared moments later with a sedative, and for the second time in two days Carmen was knocked out cold.

Whatever the distraught woman had thrown overboard, or thought she had, it had fortunately not included her infant son. But they were not taking any more chances with her and determined to keep her well away from the child as well as from the other newborn.

The other baby was Señora Candela's child. Her predictions had been wrong, and her baby, yet another girl, was born at sea, less than twenty-four hours after the birth of Carmen's son.

With the need to keep the baby boy safe from Carmen, he was removed from the infirmary and placed under the care of Señora Candela and Maribel. As though it was meant to be, Señora Candela tucked a baby under each arm and nursed them together. She had already chosen a name for both a girl and a boy so she simply gave the infants those names — Gloria and Roberto.

The two infants brushed against each other, meeting for the first time in their lives. They might not have even been aware of each other as they began to nurse, and though they had not had the benefit of cohabiting a tiny watery womb for months on end, the two babes nestled side-by-side and bonded as though they had always belonged together. Even people who met the family for the first time would say Roberto and Gloria looked alike — they shared dark eyes and dark hair, and within months babbled a common language.

The bonding at the breast was soon matched by paperwork written up by Dr. Gennesario, recognizing Roberto as the natural offspring of Señora Candela. Carmen gave them no argument, and if she had, there might have been a veiled threat to bring her to face justice for attempted infanticide. It was surely divine intervention that Carmen had only managed to throw an old blanket and a basin overboard and not her own child.

The secret adoption of Roberto solved Señora Candela's longstanding desire to provide her husband with a son, and having given birth to twins once before it was not unreasonable to believe it might have happened again. Señora Candela insisted that Carmen keep the adoption a secret and extracted from her a promise not to try to find the Candela family again. Carmen sombrely agreed.

When all was said and done, there was no one more tired than Maribel. She withdrew to the Candela cabin, and after giving the girls a brief explanation, fell asleep.

The next day, Maribel asked Talia to rejoin her mother. Because Señora Candela had given birth to twins, she explained, they needed peace and quiet. This threw Talia into emotional turmoil — she had been so excited about seeing the baby twins but now she was being asked to leave. Maribel saw the hurt in Talia's eyes but emphasized that her mother now really needed her.

When Talia finally returned to Carmen, she was sleeping, still looking very pale and sick. Talia awoke in the night to hear her mother crying.

Talia's mother remained in bed for the rest of the journey, with Maribel coming in to bring her food.

In spite of these kind gestures, Carmen could not look

Maribel in the eye. And Talia could not understand her mother's coldness towards Maribel. Talia incorrectly blamed herself for this without really knowing what she might have done to cause the ill will.

The confusion of this behaviour was nothing compared to the deep pain Talia felt when Maribel told her she could not come back to play with the Candela children at all. She could not fathom what she had done to have herself completely barred from her circle of friends. Maribel explained to Talia that she needed to stay with her mother for the few days that remained of their journey.

"Your company will help your mother get better, Pollita."

But her mother hardly paid any attention to Talia. Carmen was lost in a world of melancholy and her state of health did not seem to improve for the remainder of the trip. Talia felt miserable and lonely.

One morning when her mother was asleep, Talia sensed a change in the boat. There were more noises than usual: thumping, clanging, and shouts. She went up on deck to see what all the excitement was about. A crush of people was leaning against the railing, shouting and gesturing. Talia tried to squeeze in between the bodies but the wall of humans was impenetrable.

Suddenly, a familiar voice shouted to her.

"Pollita, we've arrived!" It was Maribel.

Talia was ecstatic to see her.

"Where?" Talia asked.

"Sydney, Australia."

"Where the turtles are."

"Well, maybe."

"Oh, yes. Giant turtles." She pulled out her worn postcard and showed it to Maribel.

"I guess you're right," Maribel murmured.

Maribel turned the card over and scanned it. She eyed the date — January 1926 — more than two years earlier. She gave it back to Talia with a sad smile.

Maribel lifted Talia up so she could see the stretch of land before them. On either side of the boat were sandstone cliffs veiled in a gauzy mist. As they approached, the rock face became more defined.

Slowly the ship glided through the wide gap and entered a bay. Beyond, a city with tall buildings sprawled before them. Small green and yellow ferry boats criss-crossed the harbour. Talia closed her eyes and opened them a few seconds later to find the buildings taller and the shoreline closer.

Maribel released Talia, letting her glide down. She kept a hand on Talia's head.

"Pollita, I've got to go run and finish packing. I hope to see you again, but you know it's a big place. — Thank you for all the lovely tea parties. You're a dear brave girl."

Talia felt a vast emptiness as Maribel disappeared. Overwhelmed, she could not make a move right away but remained where she was, letting the activity swirl around her. Ship-hands scurried by and porters heaved the trunks and bags in piles. Then there was a lurch and a thunderous splash as the anchor was lowered. The rumbling of the motor died away. They had docked. The sea journey was over.

People jammed the deck in organized chaos. The exodus began with first class passengers streaming down the gangplank while third class steerage watched, impatient to set foot in the new land.

Talia craned her neck, looking for the Candela family. She managed to climb onto a heap of luggage, and from her perch, scanned the line of passengers. At last she caught sight of them — the Candela girls in neat coats and hats. A red-faced porter struggled with their trunks and bags. Behind them was Maribel, walking with Señora Candela, each carrying a bundle. Surely these were the twins.

Talia blinked. Her eyes strained as they fixed on the swaddled infants, carried with such delicate care. She was excited when a tiny doll-like hand popped into view.

Talia teetered as she leaned further over the railing, trying to get another look at the babies before they were gone altogether.

Suddenly, a rough hand grabbed her arm and yanked her back. Talia gulped.

"Get down from there, little miss!"

The reprimand came from a stranger, an older man in a suit and hat.

"You wanna get yourself killed?"

Talia blinked. She did not understand the question, but sensed the man's anger.

"Where's your mother?"

She spotted her mother just then, staring fixedly. Her starkly tragic expression was in sharp contrast to the excited happy looks all around her.

When Talia arrived by her side, Carmen did not even notice her daughter, so intently was she staring at the spot where the Candela family had passed by only seconds earlier.

Chapter Six
A Father, a Stranger
Ingham, North Queensland - February 1928

The long train trip to North Queensland was made more dreary and lonely by Carmen's silent, brooding state. It did not help that the strangers around them spoke languages they could not understand.

In addition to the monotony, Talia struggled to find a comfortable position on the hard seats. For endless hours she stared out at the slow-changing scenery, coloured in the same sandy brown, and only occasionally broken by a small settlement — a post office, a hotel, a bank, and a general merchandise store. On the edge of these villages, they might see a few wood and corrugated iron shacks, the harshness of their exteriors softened by clusters of wispy trees with grey bark.

The first night was quite cold and they bundled themselves in their shawls and travelling blanket, shivering against each other, but as the sun rose in the sky towards the middle of the day, it became very hot. And then when they opened the window a little, they were blasted with sticky, sooty air, and in no time their clothes were grey and filmy.

Apart from the stops in small towns to pick up or drop off passengers, the train would often come to rest in the middle of nowhere, and they would wait puzzling at the cause of the delay, only to lean out of the window and find a large herd of sheep ambling in confused fashion across the tracks. The animals moved like low tan clouds, their soft backs of fleece undulating, kicking up dust as they bumped against each other.

The shepherds made Talia think of her Uncle Arnau and Uncle Bart. She wondered how they were managing without her mother. She felt a pang to think of her grandfather and his lonely days in the old house.

As time wore on, Talia fell into the rhythm of the terrain. It was no longer the vast emptiness she had originally perceived. She began to notice and watch for subtle changes in the landscape. But nothing brought more excitement than the appearance of the agile and energetic kangaroos.

In their own odd way, they were quite majestic. Their small heads and kindly, docile expressions seemed at odds with their large muscular limbs that pulsed forward in powerful leaping movements. They startled Talia by bursting onto the empty landscape with breathtaking speed.

"Mama, look!"

Carmen opened her eyes and nodded. "Ka-ga-roo," she explained to her daughter.

"*Kan*-garoo," someone corrected.

Carmen turned to look at a sandy-haired man with a battered hat. He continued speaking, adding some other things which neither Talia nor her mother could understand. Carmen nodded politely.

"What did he say, Mama?" Talia whispered in her mother's ear.

"I have no idea."

Whatever the beasts were called, Talia kept a look-out for them whenever her eyes were open.

After the second night on hard seats, morning came and houses and other buildings began to appear closer and closer together. Then the train slowed and squealed to a stop at the South Brisbane Railway station.

Carmen became flustered looking for the connecting train to North Queensland. She approached another family and with gestures and simple words they finally understood each other.

"Roma Street?"

The father nodded and beckoned for Carmen and Talia to follow.

From there, they piled into a large cab, their luggage strapped to the running board and roof, and crossed the river to the Roma Street Station. There they boarded another train heading north.

This train was a little different but the seats were just as hard and uncomfortable. Talia was so weary even her bones hurt. She slouched against her mother whose hands felt hot on her skin.

It was some days before they were finally rewarded with a glimpse of the sea. Talia ached to go to the beach for a swim and perhaps find the fabled turtles at last, but refreshment breaks were only long enough to buy a sandwich or a cup of tea. As they travelled north, the dry lands and flat grassy expanses eventually changed to a greener, lusher landscape.

Many travellers got off at the next stop, a town called Rockhampton, and Talia wondered why they were not disembarking too. Carmen assured her that they were getting much closer.

It would be just one more day until their arrival in Ingham where Talia's father was to meet them. Carmen became tenser at that point, and fussed with Talia's appearance, trying to tidy her hair.

The temperature increased as they travelled north. The air closed in on them like hot breath. Talia begged her mother to allow her to remove some of her several layers of clothes, pointing out that all of the other passengers wore short pants or sleeveless shirts. To Carmen this attire seemed quite indecent and she resisted at first. But finally, weary of Talia's complaining, she relented. She held up a shawl over Talia and helped her remove her camisole.

Late that afternoon the sky began to darken. Tentative rumbles sounded in the distance. Palm trees and shrubs began to bend in the wind. And then it came — a few tentative drops at first, and then all of a sudden — a deluge. The rain battered the train in a deafening rhythm. The windows were still open and in seconds the floor was drenched. They were hurriedly closed except for a small gap, but even so the rain managed to get in.

Lightning flared, followed in quick succession by the crash of thunder that felt so close they were convinced it was right above them. Talia gripped her mother at each new burst of noise.

Through the night the rain continued. It seemed as though the ocean itself had been whipped up and thrown against them. There was so much water, and it showed no sign of letting up.

In the middle of the night the train chugged to a stop, sighing as though weary of the storm's antics. The great iron horse creaked and moaned until soon the only sounds left were the coughs and shuffling of restless passengers, and the occasional drip of water. The inky black offered no real clue as to why they had come to rest there. Only with the morning light would they know the reason.

As soon as day broke, curious heads leaned out of the windows and gaped at the sight. The train had come to rest at the edge of what seemed to be a lake. Only the top of the rails crested above the water's surface.

The train's conductor and fireman waded into the water to inspect the line. Talia watched as they became smaller and smaller. They eventually returned, gesturing and shouting.

There they waited for several hours, and at last the water seemed to subside enough to allow the train through. The train came to life again with a lurch, shifting forward and easing into a gentle chug-chug.

Talia had the strange sensation of being back on the boat, with the splashing of water on all sides. Everyone held their breath as they crossed the 'lake'. As the last of the water disappeared behind them, there was a burst of animated talk and cheering.

But their relief was short-lived. It was not long afterwards that more water was sighted. It seemed the whole landscape was sodden and any hollow or depression was filled to the brim. But this time, the train did not stop. It continued on at a slow, steady pace, slow enough that one could look out the window and catch the perfume of flowers and pungent smell of mangrove and bark.

Talia marvelled at the glossy sheen of the plants, the colourful birds and butterflies.

Several hours later the train pulled into a small town. By then Carmen had braided and rebraided Talia's hair several times. Her nervous hands flitted over Talia, making a futile effort to tidy her daughter's sooty, sweat-stained dress.

"*Ya llegamos, Pollita.*"

Talia was surprised. After all that time, they were finally there. It seemed incredible.

"Is this Australia?"

Carmen sighed. "We've been in Australia since we got off the boat. This is Ingham where your father is coming to meet us."

Talia pressed her face against the grimy window. "Is he there?"

Carmen stared out the window but saw no one she recognised. "Come, let's get off."

Talia and her mother hobbled down the stairs, their limbs aching and vibrating from the impact of the constant rocking of the train. It was as if they had to remember how to walk again.

Carmen and Talia settled on their trunk at the entrance to the station and waited. They studied faces as people came and went. Eventually the crowd thinned and Carmen began to look worried.

"I'm hungry," Talia complained.

Carmen dabbed her face and neck with a handkerchief.

"We'll eat as soon as we arrive at your father's house."

"But I'm so hungry, Mama."

Carmen sighed.

A cab driver offered to take them to their destination but Carmen shook her head.

They listened to church bells. Two o'clock. Still Talia's father had not arrived.

"You stay here with the bags. I'll be right back," Carmen told Talia.

Talia squinted in the sunshine, watching her mother cross the street. Carmen was careful to tiptoe around the mud and the wide puddles. Horse-drawn buggies rambled by. Talia was fascinated by a couple of Chinese women in pigtails and black silk jackets. They walked arm-in-arm, holding up a blue umbrella.

Her mother soon returned with some fried fish and potatoes wrapped in newspaper. She also brought a papaya, a fleshy orange-coloured fruit. After the fish and chips, Talia was still hungry and ate the fruit so quickly she had no time to decide whether she really liked it or not.

It did not matter as it filled her belly and allowed her to drift off to sleep, leaning against her mother. It did not seem that she had been asleep very long when she heard her mother gasp.

"Andre!"

Talia's eyes flew open as her mother rose abruptly.

There he stood, outlined against the sun — her father. At long last.

He was sinewy and muscular, with coffee-coloured skin. He wore the customary short pants and sleeveless undershirt.

He gripped Carmen tightly, kissing her on the face. Carmen unleashed a sob, and then another.

"Why are you crying?" he asked.

"It was so long!" she blubbered.

"I am sorry, I'm late — I was here earlier today ..."

"No, no. So long since I've seen you!"

"Ah, yes. But you're here now."

It was then he noticed Talia, and his look seemed to reveal he had nearly forgotten he had a daughter. Talia had been keeping still, watching timidly.

"Who is this? Is this my little girl?"

He scooped her up off the trunk and lifted her so she was eye level with him. He studied her face, his eyes crinkling. She in turn scrutinized him. He had an unusual smell of sweat, and fruit, and tobacco.

"She certainly looks like you, doesn't she?" Carmen said.

He laughed at Talia's expression. Talia had not yet said a word to him. She was tongue-tied with shyness. Even though he was supposed to be her father, he was still a stranger to her.

Finally he let her go, plopping her on the front seat of the buggy while he went to gather up the trunk. Then he helped Carmen climb aboard.

Andre jumped in beside his wife, took up the reins and with a clicking sound, set the horse and cart in motion. After a mile, they turned off the main street and down a rutted road, soft from the heavy rains. They lurched from side to side as the wheels dug into the mud.

"How was the trip?"

"Tiring. Very tiring."

"Of course. But you'll be able to rest here. Life is easy in these parts." He laughed as though it were a private joke.

They came upon a car stuck in the middle of the street. The owner, a lady in a wide-brimmed hat gestured while two men attempted to pull her out using their cart. The car tires spun and spattered mud in a wide semi-circle. Carmen lifted her arms up defensively against the spray. Andre chuckled as he wiped away spots from his face. Finally the car lurched forward and rolled clear of the large puddle. The woman's rescuers cheered.

After the car drove on, Andre skirted the soupy mess and continued on the roadway, but soon there were other soggy spots.

Talia listened as Andre spoke animatedly to her mother. Every once in a while he used words Talia could not understand.

"You've arrived in the middle of the 'Big Wet'" he said. "We get more rain here in one year than Sant Feliu gets in ten."

As the sun baked the moist earth, steam rose up from the ground. Talia caught a whiff of something strong as they crossed a bridge. On either side was a dank swamp.

"Mangroves," her father explained. "And that, over there, that's a banana palm. And that's a coconut palm."

And just then as he was pointing them out, the trees began to dip and sway. He frowned as he glanced up at the sky and noticed it turning a smoky blue. There was a faint rumbling noise in the distance.

He made a clicking sound and urged the horses on, and they struggled all the harder. They were given a brief reprieve from the mud when they reached a section of the road lined with logs placed lengthwise from side to side. There the hooves clumped noisily and the cartwheels rattled over the corduroy path.

The volume of the threatening rumbles increased along with the wind. It tossed everything about from the glossy leaves to Talia's hair. She brushed a loose strand out of her face. A few seconds later she felt a splash on her arm and then another on her leg. The three of them looked up almost in unison to see the sky, now the colour of ash. Without further warning, it opened up and the rain fell in a sudden burst.

There was no point in pushing the horses harder for they already had difficulty making headway with the soft earth. Red soil, picked up by the rushing water, ran like a coppery soup.

Andre pulled a tarp over the trunk and handed Carmen an old raincoat. She held it over Talia and herself but the raincoat did little good. By the time they pulled in between the gateposts that marked their homestead, they were completely soaked.

Andre leapt out of his seat and grabbed Talia. He helped Carmen down and they ran through the streaming rain towards a small building on stilts. Besides the fact that rain was streaming down, Carmen and Talia had no time to give their new home more than a passing glance.

They clattered up the wooden steps, onto a verandah, and burst inside. The hammering of the rain on the tin roof echoed Carmen's unsettled thoughts. Was this really where they were expected to live? Could it be just a misunderstanding? Perhaps this was a temporary layover until the storm was done. But no, she was soon forced to give up any illusions she might have had of a wonderful new home.

When Andre returned from putting the horses away, he smiled to Carmen and said, "Lemme show you around."

There were just two rooms to the small shack. A roughly woven curtain served as a door between them. Rough split timber boards formed the floors. Fraying jute bags were tacked haphazardly across the walls. And like so many of the little houses they had seen from the train, the building was clad in corrugated tin.

Andre launched into an explanation of the features of the house as though he were describing the luxuries of some grand palace. He pointed out the water pump that sat atop a sink made of an old kerosene can. All of the furniture had been fashioned by him from old packing cases and fruit boxes. In some cases the labels were still affixed.

When Andre asked Carmen what she thought, she struggled to hide her disappointment.

"You don't like it?"

"I'm just really tired, Andre."

Talia whispered to her mother, asking for a toilet. Carmen in turn asked Andre.

"Ah," he said. "Come this way."

He grabbed some scraps of newspaper and handed them to Carmen. He lit a kerosene lamp and carried it out, leading Carmen and Talia down a plank gangway from the back of the house, towards a small shed.

Even from a distance of fifteen feet, the strong odour hit them. This was the 'dunny', the most foul-smelling of places. As Talia approached, she heard rustling sounds and worried about the strange creatures that might lay in wait there. She hurried to get it over with, holding her breath for as long as she could.

At bedtime, Carmen removed Talia's soiled clothes and washed her, dressing her in a thin slip. In spite of the cooling effect of the rain, the air was still very warm and humid. Talia crawled into a small bed, recently built for her from three wooden crates. She drew up a rough cotton sheet and lay down, watching as Andre closed the white gauzy net around her bed. He bade her goodnight and carried the kerosene lamp away to the other room, taking the light with him. Talia was left alone in the dark.

Although fearful of being by herself in this strange place with its unusual night sounds and buzzing of insects eager to have a nip at her, her exhaustion soon took over and she fell asleep.

Chapter Seven
Shades of Green and Grey
Ingham, North Queensland - February 1928

Talia slept soundly until the following afternoon when rain beating on the roof broke the quiet. After dinner she dozed off again and dreamt she was on the train once more, jostled about in the rattling carriage with endless miles of scenery flying by.

At the end of the second night, she arose feeling that she could not sleep anymore even though her brain felt as if it were full of cotton wool. Her legs were spongy as she stood on them for the first time in days.

There was a break in the showers, and a stunning span of cloudless blue beckoned through the open doorway. The garden was lush with smells and sounds. The greenery glistened in the sun, waxy leaves polished and beaded with droplets of rain.

Talia was drawn towards a well-worn path, chiselled away in the dense vegetation to a clearing where various crops were organized in rows. She found her father there, tending to a giant plant, drooping under the weight of several huge orangey-red tomatoes.

He was not at work at the moment as the sugar cane harvest was finished for the year. Like many other cane cutters, he whiled away the months waiting for the harvest to begin again. He filled his time with fishing, hunting for rabbits or possum, or snaring the wallabies that fed off the cane. But his great passion was gardening. It was an enjoyable pastime, but more importantly, it was a vital source of food during the lean months.

"There she is — sleepy head." He smiled at her. "You come to help?"

She looked at him shyly, unsure of what to say.

He laughed. "How about I make you into a gardener?"

"This piece here can be Talia's selection." He brought his hoe down and loosened the dark soil. He hacked away until a sizeable rectangle was formed. As he worked, thin lines of sweat snaked down his neck.

He paused and leaned on his hoe.

"What is your mother doing?" There was a distance in those words as though Carmen belonged to Talia more than to him.

"I don't know," Talia replied. In fact, she had not seen her mother that morning.

"She was very sick on the boat?"

"Yes."

"And what made her sick?"

"The waves. Lots of people were sick of the waves."

Andre grunted. "But you didn't get sick?"

"No, never. I liked the boat."

He grunted again. The conversation was put on hold when he spotted a weed. He pulled it up, shook off the soil, and then tossed it to the side. Then he pinched off a leaf riddled with lacy holes and crushed it in his calloused hands. He found another weed and removed that as well. Meanwhile Talia waited for him to begin his questioning again.

"So why did you like the boat so much?"

While he attacked the pests and invaders in his garden, Talia began to talk about the trip. She prattled on about flying fish, and Maribel, and playing with dolls. Andre grunted an acknowledgement every few words but it didn't seem like he was really listening. In fact, he was thinking about Carmen and her illness. How worn out and different she looked from the woman he had left behind in Spain five and a half years earlier.

She seemed moody and evasive, and her eyes wore a veiled look. He wondered how different things might have been had he brought her to Australia right away, or — if they had never married at all.

Talia could sense he wasn't listening anymore and stopped talking. Andre noticed her silence and turned to stare at her. It occurred to him that she might be getting bored. He got an idea and told her to wait while he left, returning a short while later with a cotton sack from which he took out a handful of seeds.

"Now, you watch what I do."

He created a furrow in the tilled soil and dropped seeds in the ground every few inches. While he crouched over the ground, he turned his head and spoke.

"How are Arnau and Bart?"

"Fine."

"And my father?"

She cocked her head as though not understanding. He clarified, "Your *pare*?"

"Oh, … he's old."

"Yes, he's old. But how is he?"

Talia shrugged. " I dunno."

"What does he do all day?"

"He watches the yard."

"Just watches, doesn't go out and work in it?"

"No."

"No, what?"

"He just sits, no work."

"Hmmm," Andre sighed.

"He can't."

Andre gave her a quizzical look.

"He's old. His hands are — er — I dunno."

She curled and folded her hands to demonstrate her grandfather's infirmity. "And he can't walk."

Andre made a sucking noise and shook his head.

He paused and stood up, looking across the stalks and plants, as though he might find there an explanation for all that had gone wrong. He gave up and turned to Talia.

"So my daughter — are you my daughter?" he said, scrutinizing her.

She became very still. It was an odd question and she did not understand what he was driving at, only that it made her uneasy. Then as if finally locating some paternal resemblance in her features, he released her from his probing stare.

"Would you like to grow some pumpkin?"

She blinked.

He chuckled. "You don't know what pumpkins are?"

She dropped her head rather than admit to this further bit of ignorance.

"Well, you'll find out once these come up."

He uncurled her fist and dropped in a handful of thin pale seeds.

"Every one of these little fellows can make five or six pumpkins. Bright as the sun inside."

Talia looked at the seeds with greater interest now, seeing them as somewhat magical. He poked the soil with his finger and gestured for her to throw in a seed, which she did.

"That's right. Keep going."

She deposited the whole handful one by one until an entire row was planted and her hands were empty. Andre mounded earth around the seeds and marked the row with a wooden stake.

"There. Now we wait for nature — and here we have all the sun and rain you want. Good soil too." He waved at the vegetable patch. "Here you can grow anything."

Andre was very proud of his garden and enthusiastic about cultivating new varieties of plants. He explained about pests, how certain plants grew from seeds, others from rhizomes, others from spores. He sliced open giant seedpods and gathered feathery strands from dying blooms. He nursed cuttings in rows of cans and pots. These were the beginnings of other plants. The supplies for new crops seemed endless. He saw the region as bountiful with potential as rich as the soil and verdant landscape. The land would provide them with everything they needed.

After Carmen and Talia arrived, the garden became a sort of refuge for Andre. It gave him an excuse to escape from Carmen's moody spells. He made no demands on her as she often seemed tired and lethargic. He wondered if she was still recovering from the long journey, or suffering from a lingering illness, or if she simply could not accept that this place was her new home. In fact, it was all of these things, but mostly the latter.

Carmen was very discouraged by the primitive living conditions: the destructiveness of the constant dampness; the ferocity of the insects — the meat ants, the mosquitoes, and the marsh flies to name a few. She would stare in surprise each time a new red welt appeared on her arms or legs.

Unlike Andre who saw the land as close to paradise on earth, Carmen saw it as hostile and dangerous. Andre's warnings about certain spiders, snakes and toxic plants did nothing to convince her otherwise. Andre told her and Talia that the red-backed spider hid in dark corners, and the deadly King Brown was powerful and fast. Andre also cautioned Talia and Carmen about several troublesome plants: the thorny Lawyer Cane or 'wait-a-while', whose razor sharp vines caught on clothing and skin; and the stinging tree that was to be avoided at all costs. Its large heart-shaped leaves had fine prickly hairs that became embedded in the skin and caused horrible pain that lasted weeks, even months.

The frequent rain showers seemed to feed a ravenous green beast that was the jungle. Greedy for water. Greedy for sun. Andre would hack away at the scrub and within a short while, green tentacles sprang back, risking being lopped a second, third and fourth time. Day or night, nature never seemed at rest. It was hungry and restless, as though following some instinctual plan to take back the land from humans.

After one rainfall came another. The steamy sauna-like air made it almost impossible to dry the laundry so the smell of mildew was everywhere.

The mud that was all around them invariably found its way to every bit of fabric where it became firmly embedded. Even boiling the clothes in the big copper could not rid them of the grey hue. So dry or not, the laundry never seemed clean anyway.

Moreover, Carmen was aghast to discover how quickly mould bloomed on their shoes and on the clothes and things left in closed spaces. The damp ate away at their skin too. Cracks opened between their toes and festered, never really healing.

Carmen made the mistake of not unpacking everything from the trunk after they first arrived. One day when Carmen had already been in Ingham for a few weeks, she opened the trunk and gasped. With trembling hands she pulled out her linen tablecloth fringed in lace. The once-white fabric was now blemished with grey and black stains. She dug further into the trunk, and became still more heartsick at what she found.

That same afternoon, Talia was working in the garden helping to harvest a crop of potatoes. She scooped the potatoes from the dirt as Andre turned over the soil. He piled them into a kerosene can and placed it before her.

"Can you carry that?"

Talia nodded, although she was not sure she could.

"Take them to your mother."

It turned out to be far too heavy for her but she did not want to complain. The can bumped against her legs and the wire handle dug into her palms. She carried the potatoes back to the shack, stopping every few feet to rest and rub her sore hands.

When she got to the foot of the stairs, she paused setting the bucket down. She heard an awful sound — a strange keening.

She crept up the stairs and found Carmen's face buried in an antique christening gown. Her hands wrung the little garment that was dark and stained. She mourned for the ruined gown as she might have cried over a dead child.

No matter what she did to get it clean, soaking it in vinegar, lemon juice, or setting it out in the sun to bleach, the precious heirloom was ruined.

Chapter Eight
The Swaggie
Ingham, North Queensland – May 1928

Late one afternoon when her mother was skinning a rabbit that her father had trapped, a thin weary man came trudging into their yard. His red-rimmed eyes peered from under the brim of a tattered hat, small corks hanging from the edge like brown cocoons. A fraying cloth bag weighted with his worldly possessions dug into his shoulder, causing him to lean to one side and making it seem as though he might topple over at any moment.

Talia understood by his hand gestures that he was hungry or thirsty and she ran to get her father.

Andre invited the stranger to eat with them. While waiting for the rabbit stew to cook, the man, whose name they would later learn was Cliff Berklin, happily accepted chunks of papaya and mango from Andre's garden. Cliff was a sheep shearer who had come up from the south.

That night at supper, he ate ravenously, barely stopping to take a breath. Then when he had eaten his fill, he began to reveal more about himself. Slowly his life story came out and while he recounted his difficult tale, Andre translated for Carmen and Talia.

Cliff had been on the road a long time, travelling from the parched outback, going from station to station looking for work but everywhere he went, things were desperate. He talked at length about how the drought had savaged the sheep herds. Thousands of sheep were dying for lack of water and food. The sun had scorched the vegetation and all that was left was red sand and thousands of bleached skeletons. The remaining sheep were so weakened that at times the only thing that kept them from keeling over was the lack of a breeze. Only the crows that pecked at the carcasses thrived.

"At least up here you're not going to starve — you got lots of rain. Everything grows like crazy."

"Yes," Andre agreed. "It's paradise here."

Carmen cast her eyes downward, unable to share in her husband's enthusiasm. She had still not overcome her initial disappointment.

Cliff stayed for nearly two weeks, helping Andre to fix some fencing and lay down new boards on the bridge over the creek. Over the course of those days he seemed to flourish; his posture straightened, the colour returned to his skin, and his eyes became brighter.

At night Talia listened to the drifting strands from Cliff's harmonica and caught the scent of tobacco. The visitor and her father sat up late talking. Their conversation was like a strange melodious concert, light-hearted and companionable.

Andre was happy for the distraction that Cliff had given him; otherwise evenings were usually passed in relative silence and gloom. In spite of their language and cultural differences, Andre chatted more easily and laughed more often with Cliff than with Carmen.

The visitor, accustomed to roughing it, was happy to bunk down on the verandah. He was always up before Talia, and on the last day she nearly missed him altogether, as he was packing up to go when she came out of bed.

The swaggie thanked the Queixens profusely for their hospitality. Loaded up with sandwiches and fruit, he went on his way again down the road, heading towards a banana plantation where he hoped there might be work.

Andre shook his head after their visitor had gone, remarking that work was hard to come by this time of year. Many big projects, railway repair, construction, and farming were usually put off until after the 'Big Wet'. But this year the slack period was even longer as the four-year-old drought in the south had begun to affect the economy up north as well.

Like her father and the swaggie, Talia appreciated the lush

natural bounty around them. She delighted in the many strange and wonderful discoveries she made every day. A dewy spider's web scintillating in the morning sun. A nest of six dingo pups, tawny-coloured, eyes still closed to the world. The strange spindly-legged brolgas dancing as part of their mating ritual.

She even befriended a kookaburra, taming it — or so she thought — with presents of food. Nico was an intelligent bird and learned to respond to Talia's rewards by chattering on demand or approaching when directed to do so.

Just like at their old home in Sant Feliu, they kept a pen full of chickens, or 'chooks' as they were called here. While Talia was still intimidated by chickens, her attitude would change following a strange and frightening incident involving Nico.

One evening as dusk was creeping up, and the yard seemed peaceful, Talia stood watching the hens softly clucking, when suddenly, Nico swooped down on one of them, grabbing it by its neck.

Amidst frightful squawking from all of the hens, the kookaburra swung its victim against a tree trunk, knocking the poor bird around again and again until the feathers were loosened from it. Then the kookaburra set upon the hen with its sharp talons and beak, ripping it apart and devouring it.

Talia was shocked at the power of the kookaburra and even more so at the fact that this sociable creature would attack a fellow bird in such a cruel and violent way.

When she told her father about the incident, he did not believe her at first, but then when he saw the mess of feathers on the grass and the blood on the tree trunk, he came to realise Talia was telling the truth. He found a length of wire mesh and covered the top of the chicken pen.

The chickens slowly drifted towards Talia where she stood against the fence, clucking softly as though in their own way offering thanks for her part in removing the threat of the predator.

Chapter Nine
The Cane Gang
Ingham, North Queensland – June 1928

As soon as the 'Big Wet' ended, the roads became more passable, and the Queixens were able to leave their home without fear of getting bogged down in the mud. Andre had many acquaintances and friends among the other Spaniards in the area and he was eager to bring his wife and daughter around to meet them.

He also secretly hoped a little socialising would draw Carmen out of her depression and show her that one could lead a happy and satisfying life here in spite of the hardships.

And so they set out for the Roncesvalles property, taking with them a basket of produce and cakes. They were joined by the Llorencs, the Collioures, and the Murgias, who were also cane cutters in the district.

As Talia stepped off the cart with her parents, she was immediately surrounded by several children who peered at her with friendly curiosity. Talia's arrival was opportune, for another player was needed just then to even out the teams for a game of rounders.

Talia's lack of English in this company did not seem to be a problem. Whenever she spoke in Spanish or Catalan she seemed to be understood, although the response she would get was more often than not in English.

When the game failed to develop into anything more than a match between two boys because the majority of the players simply did not know the rules or were too young to properly participate, Hector Roncesvalles, a boy of about eleven, decided to lead the bunch to view something he claimed was a true marvel. The children followed, traipsing through a paddock, carefully stepping around cow patties until they came to the back of a precariously leaning barn, with boards so withered and riddled with termites they looked like the ribs of a skeleton. There, clinging to a hollow under the eaves was something akin to a greyish boil — a swollen beehive.

Hector had brought along a pea rifle, the perfect instrument for wreaking havoc on the little yellow-jackets. As the other children watched in awe, he took aim, and with a burst of pellets perforated the shell of the hive. Initially there was little reaction from the bees, but not satisfied to leave well enough alone, Hector proceeded to hurl stones, and then a heavy branch of wood, until finally the hive crashed to the ground, scattering stunned bees. When they recovered, the bees bounced up and sought the children out, buzzing with rage.

"Run!" Hector cried, taking off with scant regard for the littlest ones, who lagged behind, screaming and yelping as they raced away from the barn. Whether the bees caught up with them they were not sure, but they were still trembling in terror as they sought refuge under the trees where their parents were gathered. The children, sweaty and flushed, and some even crying, still worried that the bees had followed them. Julio Roncesvalles, Hector's father, listened to the panicked stories and then he spotted his son hanging back with a few of the older boys, and he frowned at him, the corners of his mouth turned down in displeasure.

Hector was not ready to put away his pea rifle just yet. He and his posse crept into another corner of the paddock where some horses were enjoying the shade under a gum tree. As the others watched in a mix of horror and fascination, Hector directed his gun towards the rump of one of the horses. The first shot missed but the horse must have sensed something for it jumped and whinnied, pulling hard on its rope. The children laughed and gasped as Hector took aim again, this time targeting the entire cluster of animals. But before he could fire, a large hand clamped down on the gun and snatched it away. Hector looked up just in time to see his father swing at him, but not soon enough to duck the blow.

"Where's your sense, boy!"

"Aw, I wasn't going to hit 'em."

"I've been watching you. You've been up to no good the whole day."

The elder Roncesvalles told his son he was not done with him yet and Hector could expect more punishment later. The other children gave Hector looks of pity but he took the threat in his stride. Even the loss of his weapon proved to be of little consequence for he quickly devised other forms of mischief using a slingshot and a supply of candlenuts.

Meanwhile the wonderful smell of roast meat wafted through the yard. The source was a large pig suspended over a fire. It was strange to see the pig's expression frozen in a contented grin as though quite happy to be impaled from one end to the other and suspended over searing heat. Throughout the day it was the object of much admiration and interest as it slowly broiled, attaining a glistening caramel brown. The noisy spatter and sizzle of grease on the coals from time to time seemed to applaud its increasing appeal.

When the pig's skin was crisp and its flesh cooked to tender perfection, the families squeezed around two long tables improvised from wide boards. The pig was carved up and heaped onto plates with rice and beans. The meal was devoured, mingling with homemade wine before settling in the picnickers' blissful bellies. And even though they ought to have been satisfied with that, they still made room for cakes and the better part of a giant watermelon until they were full to bursting.

Talia enjoyed several pieces of the fruit, wiping off juice as it ran down her chin. But she was disconcerted to see Sonia Roncesvalles staring at her.

"You mustn't swallow the pips," Sonia said. "If you eat them, a plant will grow in your tummy and come out your ears." Her hands traced an imaginary vine trailing from Talia's stomach to the side of her head.

Alarmed, Talia watched as Sonia displayed a black seed on her tongue and then spat it out. From then on, Talia followed Sonia's advice by ejecting the pips before she could swallow them but quietly worried about those she had already eaten.

As the day waned and the friends were still digesting their heavy meal, Hector's father pulled out a mandolin from a tattered case and began to pluck at it. One by one, the guests turned to listen. They did not mind the half-started songs, abandoned and then resumed as Julio tuned his instrument or tried to remember notes. The same large hands that had smacked his son earlier, were now delicately coaxing the mandolin strings. Julio played several old-country songs that prompted a sing-along. After each piece ended, Carmen applauded enthusiastically and Andre was pleased to see her smile and laugh, something she had done only rarely since her arrival.

Andre was further encouraged when they rode home together later that night and Carmen recalled some amusing stories and bits of gossip. The Señoras Murgia and Llorenc had been generous with their advice and encouragement. Sympathetic to Carmen's disappointments, they shared tales of their own struggles after first arriving in Australia.

As the buggy twisted and careened with the deep ruts in the road, a full moon cast a silvery light on the wet ditches and glinted off the stalks of cane. Andre pointed to the fields with enthusiasm. There was excitement in his voice as he spoke about returning to the gruelling work of cutting cane.

"It's the best kind of tired — the first day after the lay-off."

"I can't imagine."

"You'll see. You'll like the fellas."

It was there on the ride home, as the cart was lurching into a deep dip in the road, that Carmen learned for the first time that she was to prepare the food for her husband's gang of cane cutters.

"And they're going to love your cooking."

Carmen looked at her husband sharply.

"Why would they care about my cooking?"

"Because, Carmen," Andre faltered, "I thought you could feed them. It'd be so nice for the men to get some decent meals for a change."

At that moment the moon went behind a cloud, and all was dark and the road ahead unclear. Talia heard her mother's silence louder than the resonant croaking of the frogs or the singing of the cicadas.

"Andre, you never mentioned this before!" she replied. "How do you expect me to manage?"

Andre reasoned with Carmen that it would not be much more work to cook for another eight people than for their own family. Besides they could use the money to pay for new clothes for Talia and herself. And so, Carmen was convinced — or resigned — to do Andre's bidding.

As the cane-cutting season was set to begin, the old gang reunited. The barracks behind the Queixens' shack filled with eight men — two Italians, a couple of Maltese and four other Spaniards.

The men laid out their cane knives and sharpened them, refastening the blades with new handles where needed. They talked and joked till late, getting caught up on each other's activities over the last few months. A few of the men had been at a mine in Cloncurry while others had been fishing or logging wood. Three-finger Joe had been in Townsville staying with his sister and her husband.

Joe still managed to cut as much cane as everyone else in spite of losing two fingers in an accident several years before. Talia's father told her that a cane knife had slipped and cut off part of his left hand, but Joe liked to entertain Talia with farfetched stories about his fingers being bitten by a crocodile or alternatively a shark, forgetting that he had already told her a different version of the story. Since Talia liked Joe's tall tales she never let on that she knew the real reason for his mangled hand.

The first morning of the season, the men were up before dawn, clad in long trousers, long-sleeved shirts, wide-brimmed hats, and kerchiefs tied around the neck to catch the sweat. They ate a hearty breakfast and then traipsed off to the fields talking boisterously, their jovial voices trailing behind them.

Talia and her mother began to keep the same schedule as the cutters, rising before dawn and going to bed not long after supper.

Carmen familiarized herself with some of the local foods — foods they had never eaten before much less used in cooking — yabbie, and kangaroo were among them. She also drew on familiar staples from the old country — dry cured sausage, beans, and rice. She purchased olives, almonds and pickled capers from a hawker who came by with his cart, adding these ingredients on occasion in an effort to recreate some of the dishes the men were accustomed to in their home countries.

At first she relied on a Calgoorlie safe to keep perishables cool. It was raised above the floor and sat in pans of water to keep the ants from climbing in, but it was still difficult to keep meat fresh in the heat. On one occasion after finding meat overrun with maggots, Carmen decided from then on to only order a two-day supply from Sullivan's butcher.

The cart from Sullivan's came from Ingham every other day. Butter, milk and cheese were also distributed this way, following a set route. The deliveryman for the Greek baker came by on horseback with a big bag of fresh rolls and loaves of crusty bread. Watchful birds followed him closely, scavenging for crumbs or spilled merchandise.

Carmen was not prepared for the voracious appetite of the cane workers. The men came to the house twice a day for a warm meal, arriving with an enormous hunger. Talia's mother realised after the first day that she would need to increase the portions of food as the men devoured everything on their plates and still demanded more.

The main kitchen was built in a lean-to away from the house

because the heat from the wood stove was so intense. The sides of the back kitchen were open to ventilate the hot air. The only problem with that was that many creatures interested in the food sometimes ventured too close for their own good. They ranged from the meat ants to all sorts of flies and mosquitoes, birds, bush turkeys, snakes, gliders, geckos, and even large lizards like the goannas.

Talia watched with amazement one day as a gecko ran along the wooden railing propelled towards the pot by the smell, and with a splash, plunged headlong into the steaming vat. She was speechless and did not move, fearful that the beast would emerge a few seconds later, angry and dangerous.

She was still expecting and hoping it would leap back out, when her mother returned just then with a tin of salt. Talia tried to get up the nerve to tell her of the disaster but instead watched mutely as her mother added the salt, stirred it in, and tasted the stew, apparently pleased with the result.

"Mama, I don't think it's good to eat that."

"Nonsense, Pollita, it's delicious."

After a long silence, Talia started to explain.

"But Mama..." she faltered.

Once her courage returned, it was too late as just at that moment the hungry workers came in from the fields and sat themselves around the long table. Carmen passed them enamel bowls overflowing with the piping hot stew.

Talia was overwhelmed with a sense of impending doom as she stared at the workers, waiting for them to discover a claw or a tail.

"What ya lookin at, chook?" Pietro asked when he noticed her gazing intently.

Talia remained silent as Pietro lifted the spoon to his mouth. Talia winced as the man chewed and smacked his lips. But it was strange. It was as though all trace of the beast had mysteriously vanished into the pot. The workers complimented Carmen on the delicious meal and even asked for second and third helpings.

Thereafter Talia was more cautious about what she ate, studying the contents carefully to ensure it contained no accidental ingredients, especially of the reptile sort.

*   *   *

After witnessing so much excitement about the cane fields, and watching her father and his fellow cutters disappear onto the block for hours on end each day, Talia was curious to know more about it.

She had only glimpsed the fields from a distance — the thick green stalks waving and beckoning — and she imagined a wonderful area beyond the wall of tightly spaced green, a place that was the source of all things sweet and delicious.

She had her heart set on visiting this mysterious realm and found her opportunity one day when she learned her mother had forgotten to pack the cakes for the crew's morning tea. Talia used the excuse to take the basket to the field in time for their break.

She relished being in the company of the cutters. She enjoyed their ready laughter and easy camaraderie. There was something comforting about the smell of the rolled cigarettes, and the musk of their sweating bodies, mixed with the scent of the freshly cut cane.

She was also drawn to them because they were very kind to her. Joe told funny stories and Salvatore went out of his way to teach her new words in English every day — from the scant few he knew himself. She would eventually discover, when she began school, that much of what he had taught her was not grammatically correct. But it did not matter, as hanging around Sal, Joe, and the rest of the cane cutters made her feel special.

And so that morning, she was determined to sneak away from her mother and find her father and his friends.

Clutching the basket, Talia ventured out, and following a

well-trod path, eventually arrived at the edge of the selection. Staring at the wall of green she began to have some misgivings about her plan but she pressed ahead, entering the field. As she penetrated the maze of cane, she began to feel more and more uneasy. The tall stalks loomed up, and everywhere she looked seemed the same.

Just then she thought she heard their voices and changed direction, and then did so again, until she was no longer sure where they might be or how she might find her way back.

Shortly afterwards she heard a rustling sound and a crackle. And seconds later, she smelled the first odd scent, like burnt treacle. Suddenly the ground began to boil with movement, spewing creatures up from the earth. Dust flew up as a multitude of brown rats raced towards her, and long dark snakes slithered by.

Talia shrieked and began to run, heading directly into a curtain of smoke that only got thicker as she scurried here and there in panic.

Then before her, out of nowhere, a wall of orange flames leapt up, spreading from stalk to stalk, running vertically up the length of the plant and then moving on.

Talia was sure she had stumbled into hell. Trapped in between the fire and the scrambling vermin, and unable to see her way out, all she could do was scream.

But just as she thought her life was over, she was grabbed about the waist and scooped up. Rough hands held her so tight she could no longer scream or even cough. She was swept away through the walls of cane. The stalks beat against her legs as she and her rescuer smashed through layer after layer. As the grey haze thickened it seemed as though they were travelling blind until at last they cleared the border of the field and passed out of the bank of billowing smoke.

Talia was placed on the ground, where she tried to catch her breath between her hacking coughs. Through her stinging eyes, she could see the men gather round to look at her.

Only then did she realise her rescuer was three-finger Joe. It was he who had found her and carried her out although all of the men had plunged into the smoky field to look for her.

They regarded her with sober, serious eyes. Tears drew white lines down Talia's sooty cheeks. No one dared scold her.

What hurt the most were not the scratches from the stubbly ground where she was plopped down, or the bruises that appeared later, but her father's silent look, brimming with fury.

Finally he spoke, trying to contain his deep anger.

"What were you doing there?"

"I was bringing cakes..." her voice trailed off, suddenly noticing she no longer had the basket with her.

"Any one of us could have been killed looking for you! What a stupid thing to do! Now, go home! I don't want to see you anymore today!"

She slunk away, crushed by her father's rebuke and embarrassed by the fright she had given them all.

Chapter Ten
First Australian Christmas
Ingham, North Queensland - December 1928

The months during the cane harvest flew by and it seemed like no time had passed before the shops in Ingham began to display signs announcing Christmas specials. There were holiday socials and stories in the *Northern Gleaner* to warn children of the need to be especially good during this time of the year. Talia hoped that Santa would have forgotten about her foolish escapade to the cane field a few months earlier.

This would be Talia's first *Nadal* in her new homeland. She found it odd to think Christmas was approaching while the weather only got hotter and the days longer. For her Christmas usually brought to mind cold, a layer of ice on the water basin, frost on the trees and grass, and mornings where she hated to leave the warmth of her bed. But like almost everything else about this place, holidays here would be very different too.

Even with the preparation of *turrón*, the dessert made from sugar, almonds and eggs, there were adaptations. Since almonds were more difficult to come by, they used macadamias. Talia helped her mother crack open the nuts and retrieve the pale nut meat. They ground the pieces into a fine powder and stirred it into a mixture of beaten eggs and sugar.

Then they pressed the mixture into a flat square box lined with waxed paper. They dusted the top with powdered sugar and covered it with more paper, and then weighed it down with a heavy piece of wood. It was left on a shelf to dry out over a few days. Every now and then Talia would tiptoe to the tray, lift the wood to peek at the dessert, and brush away any trespassing ants. When the *turrón* was firm, they cut it and dusted it with a little more powdered sugar.

There was a rare moment of harmony around this time, for

they all worked together as a family to recreate the nativity scene. Andre built a small manger and Carmen wove a roof from palm leaves. They decorated it with greenery, twigs and bark.

The small ceramic figurines Carmen had packed away in the trunk and brought from Spain were unwrapped and arranged in and around the small wooden barn. Mary, Joseph, and the baby Jesus had survived the journey more or less intact, but the two shepherds now held crooked staffs and one of the angels had lost a wing. Andre chuckled as he discovered the *caganer* figurine, a strange little man in a red cap and white dressing gown, squatting to do his business. Andre placed him at the back of the manger, partly hidden behind a tuft of grey moss.

Although she doubted he could possibly be cold with the weather so hot, Talia covered the blessed baby in a scrap of faded calico cloth and placed fresh bedding underneath him.

On Christmas Eve, the Queixens family got up early and dressed in their finest clothes. It was strange to see Andre, who only ever seemed to wear a singlet and shorts, now looking smart in a suit and fedora.

Talia had grown so much that Carmen had to sew a crocheted fringe to Talia's best dress to make it longer, but there was nothing she could do about the girl's shoes, which were suddenly too small.

Andre proposed a solution, and ignoring Carmen's objections, whipped out a knife and cut rough holes in the shoes turning them into sandals.

"Andre! Now one is different from the other!" Carmen moaned.

"Nah, they're good. Is it better Talia? You can walk in them?"

Talia nodded and walked a few paces in the sandal-shoes, pretending that they were fine when in fact they were still painful. She decided not to complain for fear of escalating her parents' disagreement.

Pinched feet aside, Talia was very excited as they drove to town. When they passed cars and trucks, they exchanged shouts of "Happy Christmas" and friendly taps on the horn.

The rains had returned and the roads were rough, so the buggy veered around puddles and deep ruts. As they neared Ingham, the landscape cleared, and buildings and wide streets lined with poles and wires came into view.

Turning off the main street and heading north, they entered the Ingham Showgrounds where a large crowd had already assembled. As soon as the buggy came to rest, Talia rushed to get down but her mother swiftly grabbed her hand and held her back.

"Stay with me, Pollita," she urged, looking askance at some vagrants camped out under a tree. Even at that early hour they were stumbling about, flaunting beer bottles.

Carmen pulled Talia away from them and steered her towards a cluster of children watching a puppet show. Two brightly dressed characters with large hooked noses and pointed hats shouted and punched each other, provoking laughter from the children.

"Remind you of anyone?" Andre teased as he and Carmen stood watching the puppets battle. Carmen smiled in spite of herself.

When the curtains came down on the puppets, the throng of children moved to other sources of fun. A clown amused a small crowd with his clumsy antics and silly tricks. A juggler tossed rings into the air and kept them spinning above him as he kept another ring twirling around an ankle.

A group of young girls took to the stage and danced, each with one hand held high and another positioned at the waist. Their pleated skirts swayed and their feet drummed lightly on the timber boards to music provided by a fiddler.

Not long after, a trumpet sounded. Talia broke free from her mother's grasp and joined the crush of children running in the direction of the fanfare.

Behind a group of musicians, a large crepe paper emu rose up, its skinny neck and head towering above the crowd. Talia's father scooped her up so she could see Father Christmas himself in a red and green chariot pulled by six horsemen.

Children hurried along with the parade as it rolled towards the stage. Father Christmas dipped his hands into a sack and cast handfuls of candies towards the children. They went wild searching the grass for them, and when a new handful was thrown in the other direction, they scrambled to keep up, like a flock of hungry gulls.

Talia wriggled out of her father's arms and dropped to the ground to join in the hunt for sweets. She soon found two pieces of toffee that she gobbled up all at once, her mouth bulging.

Her fingers were still sticky when she was given a slip of paper and hustled into a line-up with the other children. The queue led to the front of the stage, where they waited to greet Father Christmas. Talia watched anxiously as child after child went up to receive a gift. She secretly prayed the sack would not be empty before her turn came. And suddenly she was first in line, but instead of stepping forward she froze, her knees locking. Andre nudged her and she stumbled towards the old bearded man.

He bent down and spoke to her, mopping his shiny forehead with a handkerchief.

"Have you been a good girl?" he asked in English. Talia felt bewildered. She turned towards her father in wordless panic.

"Yes," her father answered. "She is good girl."

And so, with this recommendation, Talia was handed a brightly coloured kaleidoscope. On one end was an opening, and when she looked inside, tiny bright pieces shifted forming beautiful patterns. She twisted the cylinder to the sound of soft tinkling and yet another colourful picture appeared at the end of the tube.

Talia was giddy with delight at all the treats and the novelty of this Australian Christmas. And as if that wonderful day was not enough, the next day was also very special, but in a different way.

In the morning, Talia found a little parcel sticking out of a sock at the foot of her bed. She unwrapped it with great excitement as her parents looked on.

"Happy Birthday, *hijita*," Carmen smiled.

Inside the package was a cloth doll with long floppy limbs. Her hair was made of yellow yarn and she had dark button eyes. She wore a gingham dress and white cotton bloomers. But best of all was her coat — a luxurious garment of glossy rabbit fur.

Talia exclaimed her profuse thanks to her parents. She immediately named her dolly, Maribel, after the kind lady who had stayed with them on the boat.

After breakfast, the family dressed up again and climbed into the buggy. They returned to the Roncesvalles property, where once again the Llorenc, Murgia, and Collioures families were gathered. Even though Talia had met the children on a visit before the cane harvest began, she was still a little shy at first, but that soon wore off. She began to join in the games with the other children — the usual hide and seek, tag, and a Christmas tradition she remembered from Sant Feliu.

A wooden log was wrapped in an old red blanket, and the children beat it with sticks, while they sang:

> *Caga tió, caga torró,*
> *avellanes i mató, si no cagues bé*
> *et daré un cop de bastó, caga tió!*

> Poop log, poop turrón,
> hazelnuts and cottage cheese,
> if you don't poop well, I'll hit you with a stick!

As they hit the hollow log, treats rolled out — *turrón*, peanut brittle, candied pineapple, apricot and mango *dulce*. Finally when the log was almost empty, a clove of garlic appeared, signalling the end of the log's munificence.

They sang songs until late in the day and finally the log was added to the fire.

It had been a lovely party and Talia was blissfully happy, at least until the subject of school came up. She learned then for the first time that she was to begin Grade One right after the holidays.

The news caught her off guard and anxiety swept over her. How could she possibly manage at school if she did not even know how to speak English?

Chapter Eleven
Shoeless to School
Near Ingham, North Queensland - January 1929

While Talia worried about learning English, Carmen had other concerns. The lack of proper footwear was uppermost in her mind when she pleaded with Andre to let her buy Talia a new pair of shoes. Talia's improvised sandals, even with the extra holes, were simply too small for her. But Andre refused to budge on the matter.

"She doesn't need them. Kids here don't wear shoes much."

"It's not proper," argued Carmen.

"Proper or not, I am not spending money on shoes when she doesn't need them."

"Andre, you're so tight with the money."

"You think so? Someday we want to buy our own farm, own a piece of land. And we can't do it if you're throwing away money left and right."

Carmen was silent. She too wanted to buy a property but it was difficult to set aside any money. Difficult because Andre was unemployed and would be until the cane-cutting season began again. No money would be coming in unless he found other work. And so with no money to spare, there would be no new shoes.

Talia, her hair neatly braided, her cotton dress carefully pressed but her feet bare, joined up with a group of other kids, most also shoeless, and headed on foot to the school several miles away. As they followed the winding track, other children joined them, some also on foot, others on bicycles.

Before long they arrived at the school, a neat timber building on high posts. Its wide verandah and canvas awnings kept the sun at bay, and when it rained, the showers too. The school was only two years old, replacing the previous one that had been destroyed by white ants.

At the back of the building was a paddock where a few horses grazed. They belonged to students who lived too far away to walk.

Headmaster Stephens appeared at the top of the school stairs, and stared out at the students. He recognized most from before the summer break, but spotted several new faces as well. He secretly hoped they would not be troublemakers. He sighed as he lifted the hand bell, thinking how the holidays had gone by far too quickly. Many of the students probably had the same thought as they heard the harsh clang interrupt their last moments of freedom.

Talia followed the other children as they lined up. Mr. Stephens addressed the assembled group and reminded them of the importance of punctuality and respect for their school and community. He nodded to one of the older boys and the flag was raised. Everyone broke into "God Save the King", standing with straight backs and solemn expressions. Talia made an o-shape with her mouth and pretended to sing along, hoping no one would notice she did not know the words.

After this, Talia was relieved to see they were to go inside and out of the sun. Her classmates raced ahead to get a drink before school started and jostled to hang up their satchels and hats on the rack outside the classroom. Talia tried to do the same but she could not reach the already full hooks. She tucked her lunch bag against the wall, praying it would not be trampled.

As children filled up the seats, Talia hovered at the back of the classroom unsure of where to go or what to do. She wanted to sink in between the floorboards and disappear.

She felt a pair of eyes drill into her. They came from a large forbidding woman at the front of the class. This was Miss Constance Purcivell, a spinster and teacher for the last eight years at No. 14 State School.

"Come forward," she commanded, her hand jutting out like a spear towards Talia. "Sit here," she said.

Talia hurried to obey, still uncertain of what was expected of her. She slipped into the empty seat, not daring to look at Miss

Purcivell, much less breathe while the teacher was still near.

When the woman finally left, Talia risked a glance sideways and saw, next to her, a pretty little girl with bright brown eyes. This was Lucy Danetti. Talia did not know it at the time but she and Lucy would soon become good friends, and Lucy would be a great comfort to Talia, especially during the first few months at school.

The fact that both their fathers were cane cutters was something they had in common. But there were even greater differences. Unlike Talia, Lucy had the advantage of speaking and understanding English, and she had an older brother, Manuel, who had already filled her in on how to survive school: how not to upset Miss Purcivell; and which kids were to be avoided in the playground. Moreover, Lucy was wore nice clothes and shoes, and had smooth, tidy hair.

Another thing she already knew, but that Talia did not, was that writing with your left hand was forbidden. And so when Talia set about copying the alphabet onto her slate, quite pleased that the results were looking much like what was printed on the board, she had no idea she was in for big trouble. Her only warning was the appearance of a shadow over her shoulder. Suddenly she felt a sting on her left hand.

"You are to use your right hand."

The smack on the fingers from Miss Purcivell would be one of those things that Talia would remember for a long time. There was nothing worse than the humiliation of being the first child to be chastised on the very first day of school. It was all Talia could do to keep from blubbering on the spot. Lucy gave her a sympathetic look and Talia felt grateful to her.

In her sharp voice, Miss Purcivell made the class repeat tables and spelling again and again till Talia's head throbbed from the effort. As the day wore on, the children began to slouch from the heat and boredom. Miss Purcivell noticed the change in attitude and snapped at the students.

"Sit up straight. Hands on your desk, and face forward!"

The children eagerly awaited the final bell and as soon as it rang, they all stood up at once, nearly trampling each other to get outside.

Over the coming weeks, Talia continued to struggle with English. Many times she felt bewildered and frightened but soon learned to guess the meaning of Miss Purcivell's sharply delivered instructions by watching others and cautiously following along.

The consequences for any sort of intransigence were severe. They ranged from standing in the corner and facing the wall, being banished outside the room, or even worse, being caned.

Talia was shocked the first time she witnessed a caning. Fabrice, a rowdy boy with black hair, stood yelping as Miss Purcivell struck his palms ten times. The delivery of the blows was so fierce Talia could hear the air whistle as the cane came down. Later in the school yard Fabrice showed the other kids his wounds — several deep red welts branded into his fleshy palms. He seemed almost proud of them.

"Dinna hurt," Fabrice claimed.

"Cors it did. I saw ya was cryin," taunted Ambrose, a red-haired boy with crooked teeth.

Looking at the marks on Fabrice's hands Talia could almost feel stinging on her own palms. It was a fresh reminder to keep her pencil firmly in her right hand, although writing would have been so much easier with her left. Sometimes when she caught herself slipping the pencil into the wrong hand, she quickly switched sides and sat on her left hand just to reduce the temptation to use it.

In spite of her struggles, Talia soon began to learn the alphabet and do some simple sums, practising these on her slate. By winter she could manage reasonably well in her new language. She started reading words wherever they appeared: labels on crates, jars, and tins — *Rinso, Bovril, Eades Gout Pills*, and *Clement's Tonic*. Sometimes she translated for her mother. Together they read the *Wee Gumnuts* and *Ginger Meggs* comics from the newspaper, sharing a rare moment of levity.

At school, Talia was introduced to all sorts of new games — Red Rover, hopscotch, jacks, and a horse and buggy game in which the girls were yoked together as a horse team to be galloped around the playground.

A visit to Lucy's house was a special treat for Talia. Though similar in construction to the Queixens' household, and filled with the same style of crate and kerosene can furnishings, the Danetti house had a completely different look and atmosphere.

It was because Lucy's mother was an accomplished seamstress and had a flair for decorating. She dressed up everything in bright fabric and ruffles. Crocheted fringes embellished the curtains and towels. The scent of lavender trailed behind Mrs. Danetti as she bustled about cheerfully, humming arias from her homeland. There was none of the gloom that Talia felt when she was with her own mother. For this reason, she eagerly accepted any opportunity to spend time with Lucy and her family.

Not too long into the school year, the headmaster announced that there would be a picnic excursion to the seaside. Talia and Lucy, like the other children, looked forward to the special occasion.

The morning of the excursion, rather than meet at the school, the children waited under the awning of the train depot for the seaside special to arrive. As soon as the conductor opened the gates and the teachers boarded, the children rushed in, shoving and pushing for the window seats.

Talia was struck with the memory of her previous train ride. It was less than a year earlier, yet it seemed so long ago. She recalled the smell of soot, and the ache from sitting so long on hard seats.

The trip to the seaside was relatively short. They disembarked at the siding near the jetty where steamers loaded and unloaded cargo. Huts dotted the land near the shore.

The children ran across the white sand, swinging their

hampers. They plopped them down under a tent set up to provide shade and areas screened off as change rooms.

Before exploring the beach and shore, the children were severely cautioned by Miss Purcivell. She warned them to watch out for stinging jellyfish, to take care when picking up certain seashells that might still be inhabited, and most of all not to swim out too far.

The sea was calm and the breakers rolled in rhythmically, providing a source of fun for those who wished to glide in on the surge.

The children broke at mid-day for a picnic lunch under the canvas awning. A man pulling an ice cream cart along the jetty drew a rush of children who came away with dripping cones.

After lunch, Talia and Lucy wandered the beach and discovered a unique ribbed imprint in the sand. The tracks led to a nest of eggs that Mr. Stephens identified as belonging to a tortoise. Talia was thrilled to get just that much closer to her dream of seeing a giant turtle, but whatever had deposited the eggs was now gone.

"The mother turtle has done her job and is now back in the water."

Mr. Stephens saw to it that the overly curious explorers did not disturb the eggs. "Please don't touch — that's right. We don't want them destroyed. They make a fine soup," he added, shooing the children away.

His last remark disturbed Talia and she was secretly glad the mother turtle was safely out at sea.

From there, the girls moved to the tidal pools among the low rocks. The waters revealed anemones of all colours and sea urchins like vibrant pincushions. Colourful fish swam around rocks shaped like Chinese temples, and narrow bands of seaweed danced and swayed.

Talia's hands soon filled with beautiful shells and polished stones. She returned to the tent and deposited them near her bag and went back out again looking for more.

As the day wore on, the breakers became more powerful, rolling in with pounding fury, churning up the sand. The children were thrilled but Miss Purcivell looked on anxiously. Her face puckered with worry. At last it was time to pack up, and she seemed to be relieved each time a child returned to the tent, heeding her whistle call.

But it was hard to hear anything above the roar and crash of the waves hitting the beach, and two boys, Cameron and Ambrose, continued to play on the broken hull of a boat in the deeper water.

Afterwards, it was unclear whether the shark's fin was spotted from the shore or whether Cameron or Ambrose saw a shadow in the water. At some point the shark butted against the rotting vessel and startled the two boys onboard.

There was a great wrenching scream and then panic ensued. Children still making their way out of the water made a mad dash for the shore. Feet sped like whirligigs, kicking up spray. Screams and shrieks scared off the gulls. Miss Purcivell blew into her whistle and gestured frantically. Cameron and Ambrose flew off the broken hull and tumbled into the water. Cameron swam away quickly, while the other boy, Ambrose, was caught somehow.

His arms beat the water, and he staggered and tripped. Blood streaked the surface behind him. He screamed and floundered. Two sixth grade boys, Donald and Lawrence, ran into the surf and grabbed him. Thankfully the wrecked hull had bumped the shark and forced it to back off, otherwise these boys might have been struck as well.

The older boys rushed to the tent carrying their wounded classmate. The fact that Ambrose was able to scream was a good sign. When they got him under the awning, they wrapped cloth around his leg and lifted it up to help curb the flow of blood.

The first thing he said was, "Don't tell my mum!"

The Headmaster pulled away the cloth and patted down the wound, determining it to be a bad scrape and nothing more. There was great relief all around.

Miss Purcivell scooped up Ambrose into a teary embrace. "Thank heavens," she cried.

It was hard to tell in the chaos whether others had been hurt, or were simply sobbing in reaction to the fright.

An initial headcount was done to make sure there were no other victims. Then, for good measure, Mr. Stephens directed Lawrence to do a second head count. Miss Purcivell was too distraught to be of any help. She clung to Ambrose, uncharacteristically emotional and protective of a boy she had only ever treated with great harshness. It was perplexing to him.

She began to blubber, blurting out a story in between sobs.

"It was just about this time of day too, when the waters are murkiest and he was thinking of coming in. And if only he had. If only." She paused and sniffled. "First the beast took his left arm but he managed to get away. Then the monster followed him into shallow water and got another piece of him."

"Constance, please."

Headmaster Stephens tried to cut her off, but she continued, as though in a trance.

"They brought him by train to hospital, but by then he had lost too much blood. Within hours he was gone," she added, her voice catching. "Oh, the cruelty of it."

Ambrose's eyes were wide and he held his breath as he listened.

"Yes, but Ambrose is fine. He's quite alright." Stephens spoke with authority.

The children were quiet and did not move. They were still reeling from the scare but perhaps even more from the strangeness of Miss Purcivell clutching Ambrose.

Finally, Headmaster Stephens corralled the dumbstruck children away from Miss Purcivell and sent them on towards the train. They gathered their things and traipsed through the hot sand, the mood so different from when they had arrived.

The Headmaster was overheard speaking sternly to his colleague. "Really, Constance, was it necessary to alarm them like that?"

It was as though she did not hear him.

"He had only just come back from the Great War where he'd eluded bullets and bombs for two years, only to be felled by a beast hiding in the sea."

Miss Purcivell stared across the horizon as though visualizing the shark victim floating above the water like an angel.

"I'll see that the boy gets home," said Mr. Stephens with a hint of impatience. "Can you manage on the train with the others?"

"Yes," she said softly, her eyes glassy. And finally she turned away from the water.

Chapter Twelve
Pestilence and Plague
Near Ingham, North Queensland – December 1930

The cane-cutting season had begun again in June. Talia's father had taken up with his gang after a hiatus of several lean months. But the harvest had not started well — not just on the block Danetti's men were cutting, but also on several other properties in the Ingham district. Large patches of faded yellow stalks were discovered as well as huge sections of dead cane, leaning or toppled over, eaten from the roots up by grubs.

The men muttered about the poor yields, the soil crawling with the grubs — white shiny creatures with black eyes and small dark hairs along their stomachs. So small and helpless they seemed, yet so destructive. These were the larvae of the grey-backed cane beetle.

The voraciousness of the insects was staggering. Even for those growers who had misted their fields with carbon bisulphide or drilled between the rows of cane with white arsenic and other poisons, the devastation persisted.

Heeding the appeals of desperate growers, the local cane-pest board stepped in and announced a campaign to collect beetles during their two-week mating period in early December when the insects emerged from the ground and settled in the trees. All hands were called upon to help collect the insects, and children too were recruited to help with the 'beetling'.

To Talia, Lucy and their schoolmates, the beetling expedition seemed like a wonderful adventure and a welcome opportunity to make a little pocket money that was otherwise hard to come by. The cane pest board was offering tuppence for every can of beetles collected. The supply of the pests seemed limitless and so too seemed the things the children might buy for themselves. Talia ran through the wish list in her head — sweets, ribbon, drawing paper and paints, even cloth for a new dress.

She was eager to participate and convinced her parents to let her stay with the Danettis for a week of 'beetling'.

The evening before beetling was to start, Andre took Talia to the Danetti home. En route they could see farmers already busy trying to stem the invasion of the beetles. Small fires had been lit along the cane fields, and lanterns were suspended over tubs of water topped with kerosene. Beetles, attracted by the light, would bump against the glass and then fall into the kerosene, dying almost instantly.

For Talia the glow of the lanterns and the bonfires gave the fields a festive atmosphere, but for Andre it was like a military camp with troops preparing for battle.

Beyond the sound of voices and crackling fires, Talia detected other strange noises — the eerie humming of the beetles; the soft plunk of the insects hitting the glass; and the rustle of leaves from the hordes in the trees.

That evening, Mrs. Danetti sent the children to bed early in the sleep-out, instructing them to get plenty of rest, but the girls found it hard to settle down. Lucy and Talia giggled nervously as they talked about the prospect of scooping up beetles with their bare hands. Mrs. Danetti had to scold them several times to be quiet because Mr. Danetti was suffering from a severe headache.

Although they were outside on the verandah, their voices still disturbed him. It was strange — even Jet's barking put the usually jovial Danetti on edge.

"Ida, those kids won't stop jabbering."

Mrs. Danetti rapped on the wall next to the sleep-out. "Girls, quiet now," she ordered. "I don't want to have to tell you again!"

Lucy and Talia dropped their voices to a whisper, and at last Lucy fell asleep. But, for Talia sleep was elusive. She was restless, perhaps because the bed was unfamiliar.

After what seemed like hours, she drifted into a fitful slumber, unable to completely block out the cacophony of the cicadas and other night creatures, and the shaking trees that she imagined being devoured leaf by leaf, sharp mandibles passing through the greenery like scissors through paper. So at four a.m., when Mrs. Danetti roused the girls from bed, it seemed to Talia like she had not slept at all.

Tired as she was, she found energy nevertheless in the exciting prospect of the beetle hunt. She, Manuel, Lucy, and Mrs. Danetti hurried with lanterns, sheets, and empty syrup tins to the foot of a large Moreton Bay Fig. Sheets were spread out beneath it to deter the beetles from escaping and burrowing back into the ground where they could lay eggs.

Manuel clambered up into the tree and began to shake the branches. As he did so, the little beasts began to rain on the girls below. They screamed in horror as the insects landed in their hair or slipped through gaps in their clothes. At first Lucy and Talia refused to touch the beetles, but at Mrs. Danetti's urging, they came around and began to snatch them and thrust them into their tin buckets, keeping the insects in their hands for as short a time as possible.

It became a bit of a game with bursts of laughter and shrieking, as beetles pelted them in unpredictable waves. Manny took delight in shaking the branches just as the girls passed below.

Ida Danetti worked steadily, her fingers darting towards every dark wriggling spot. She did not share in the children's excitement, and she saw nothing humorous at all in the situation. She was intent only on removing the destructive insects, for uppermost in her mind was their ability to chew their way through the Danettis' livelihood. She was also preoccupied by her husband's sudden moodiness and uncharacteristic impatience, snapping at the children for no apparent reason at all.

Ida vowed to single-handedly pluck every beetle from the trees, if only to ease her husband's worries and restore harmony at home. But when they returned with many buckets full, Mrs. Danetti was disheartened that Frank said nothing at all about them.

Talia and Lucy were oblivious to this lack of enthusiasm. They were over the moon with excitement as they counted their syrup tins and tallied up their earnings in their heads.

After a week of beetling, the first payments were made. Talia and Lucy spread out their newly earned pocket money on the kitchen table while Mr. Danetti looked on, his brow furrowing and his eyes red, almost glowering. Lucy noticed him staring.

"What's the matter, Papa?" she asked.

"Go on outside!" he growled.

It was just because he was usually so good-natured that Lucy dared to persist with her questions.

"But why?"

"I said get out! Now go on! Out with youse!" he blasted, and the girls jumped from their chairs and dashed out the front door.

Talia was perplexed by the behaviour of Lucy's father, and she tried to comfort Lucy as tears tumbled down her friend's cheeks.

"I thought he would be happy," Lucy wailed.

"Never mind, never mind," reassured Talia. "He's just tired from all the noise at night."

"No, he's cross about something. I just don't know what."

The next day, Mr. Danetti came home early from the cane fields and retired to bed, shivering in spite of the heat.

Mrs. Danetti covered him in blankets and spoon-fed him soup to counter his chills. His teeth chattered and he complained of aching joints. He vomited up the small meal she fed him, and he refused any more food. The next morning, Ida did not go out beetling. She sent the girls out with Manuel.

Within the week, Mr. Danetti's flu seemed to have passed, and he returned to work with his fellow cane cutters, but his friends could see his stamina was not the same. He was still quite weak and often needed to sit down and rest. Midway through the second week, his skin became the colour of onion peel and the whites of his eyes turned a sickly yellow.

"Ya sure, Frank, ya alright?"

"Bit tired, I s'pose."

Joe insisted that something was wrong. "Ya look terrible. God's truth."

"Well, you don't look so good yourself."

Joe shrugged. At least Frank was still fit enough to make a joke. But that would be his last bright moment.

That afternoon, Frank moved as though he were drunk. His feet shuffled clumsily and every step was slower than the one before. A small clump of cane stubbles rose up before him like a fence in an obstacle course and tripped him. He fell hard, landing face down.

He remained there quite still, and his friends rushed to his aid. Pietro and Joe, who lifted him, were struck by how light he had become. His sallow skin hung from his bones. His recent illness had slashed pounds off his already lean frame.

Ida wanted to take her husband to the hospital right away but he refused saying he only needed to rest. Andre also tried to convince Frank to seek medical help, but he would have none of it, mumbling something about hospital fees. The mysterious illness, while running Frank down in every other aspect, had done nothing to diminish his stubborn will.

Talia's father and the other cutters took turns at dropping in to check on Frank but there was little encouraging news over the following days. His condition worsened and his energy began to ebb away. At the end of two days he could no longer speak coherently and it was then Mrs. Danetti took matters into her own hands.

She insisted on driving Frank to Ingham in their old Model T, but it seemed as if even the car had caught some of her husband's obstinacy, because its wheels dug into the mud, becoming bogged down. Now thoroughly panicked, Ida sent Manny to find Andre and have him bring his wagon.

At the sound of wagon, Mrs. Danetti sprang up. Andre had

come with Pietro, and with Manuel's help, they lifted the ailing man into the cart. Mrs. Danetti climbed in and cradled her husband on her lap, trying to cushion him during the bumpy ride. She stroked his forehead, pushing away his matted hair.

During the rough journey, he drifted in and out of consciousness, babbling in Italian and English. Every jolt of the cart was torture for him, and he grimaced and moaned as the wagon wheels creaked over the bumps and ruts.

Coming up to the outskirts of town, they encountered a group of men blocking the road with a truck and an over-turned cart. Andre guessed they were strikers. There had been trouble at the mill in town.

Andre stopped the wagon, watching apprehensively as the mob came up and peered at them with hard eyes. They encircled the cart, and scrutinized the travellers. Suspicious of scab workers, they started to question Andre and Pietro about the purpose of their trip, but when they saw Frank lying across the wagon, ashen-faced and trembling, their anger and hostility dissolved. The strikers hastened to remove the barriers and waved the party through.

Andre tried to make up for lost time by flogging the horse, but as they approached the main road through Ingham, they were delayed again. The town's thoroughfares were congested. The park was jammed with tents and lean-tos, providing shelter for the swaggies who continued to flood in, driven out by the drought in the south. Soot-stained and dirty from jumping the train, hungry and desperate, they roved about, relying on handouts and a few days of relief work here and there. They had reached the end of the line, expecting to find steady work in the cane fields or the mills or the Far North, but had only found more disappointment. Their numbers crowded Ingham, a town already thick with disillusion.

With nothing to lose, the destitute men joined impromptu brawls and swelled the strikers' numbers, lending their own anger and frustration to those of the local men, tipping cane bins, barring scab workers, and blocking the route to the mill. If they could not work, then no one would.

They fought against deprivation and hopelessness, and now with the spread of cane fever, they also fought death by disease. The enemy now had several shapes: the mill owners who paid too little for the raw cane; the growers who refused to burn the cane fields to rid them of the rat-borne plague; and of course the rats themselves.

The cart with the sick man waded through this sea of discontent. Time was running out for Danetti. He had stopped his babbling, and became quiet. Foam appeared around the corners of his mouth. Then his body slackened, and his eyes stared rigidly skyward, as though already fixing on a star on which to end his journey.

A wail pierced through the mob's disgruntled muttering and querulous voices. It stopped the men cold. It was Ida as she cried for her dying husband. Andre lashed the horse, urging it on. Anyone in the way of the travelling cart, who saw him whip the animal, knew they had better jump out of its path or risk being run down.

Finally the wagon arrived at the hospital, and the nursing sisters hurried Frank in. They glided alongside him like angels in starched white, but it was too late. Frank was already dead, and nothing they could do would revive him.

The attending doctor guessed from Danetti's occupation and his jaundiced appearance that the cane cutter had died of the leptospirosis bacterium. The Ingham hospital had already received eighty cases in August, and the number of new cases was still growing. Danetti had probably been infected through one of the many small cuts or sores on his hands coming into contact with water tainted by rat urine.

Mrs. Danetti secretly cursed her husband's stoicism, his reluctance to be brought to the hospital sooner. He might have been saved had he come in right away.

Meanwhile, Carmen sat up with the girls and Manuel, and then finally urged them to go to bed. But no one slept that night, as they were still wondering how Mr. Danetti was faring.

They rose before dawn to continue with collecting beetles. It was a welcome distraction to their worries, and they had the sense that they were doing some good, however insignificant their efforts. They pawed at the ground, moving their hands back and forth — beetle to bucket, beetle to bucket — like soldiers on a grim but doomed mission.

After their beetling was done, they went back to the house to rest. Midmorning, they were napping on the lounge and inside the sleep-out, when Andre and Mrs. Danetti returned. Mrs. Danetti descended from the wagon, doubled over with grief. She staggered towards her children and folded them around her. They did not need to ask; for they knew from the way she held them that their father was dead.

Talia was thrown into a state of disbelief. It was incomprehensible that Lucy's father could not be there any longer. Surely a mistake had been made, and they ought to check again at the hospital.

The other cane cutters and the church folk took up a collection for the Danettis. Even Talia handed in her earnings from the beetling, but all in all the donations would not last long.

Mrs. Danetti began to take in laundry and sewing, but this was barely enough to keep the household afloat.

Talia learned that Manuel would not return to school and that he would take his father's place on the cane gang. He was no more than a boy, and he struggled to keep up.

When Talia returned to visit Lucy following her father's death she noticed the dramatic change in the Danetti home. The odour of illness lingered. The normally bright curtains seemed dull and limp. The kitchen, previously so spotless and orderly, was now untidy, with piles of clothes in heaps, waiting for their turn in the copper.

The once bright and fashionable Ida Danetti was unkempt and haggard. She no longer had the time or energy to smile or sing, or even hum. And this was what saddened Talia the most.

Mr. Danetti's favourite chair, a carved rocker, sat empty. No one was allowed to use it. Jet would come in and lie down in front of it at the end of the day, still waiting for his master to return.

Frank Danetti's death and those of other cutters touched off a firestorm of anger among the cane cutters, and soon the cutters' union declared an all-out strike. After a rally, workers gathered in the pub on Main Street. Bundy rum and spirits helped stoke their anger and bitterness to new levels. A group stumbled out of the pub at closing time and wandered the streets, gathering in number until a large mob had amassed in front of the mill gates.

They surrounded a truck laden with cane and prevented it from entering the mill. The driver was pulled out of the cab and roughed up and the truck was overturned, its load of cut cane spilling into the street. When the mill owners tried to bring in scab workers by train, the mob of striking cutters climbed aboard the train and scuffled with the replacement workers, frightening them into turning back.

Andre and the fellow cutters joined some of the protests. Carmen sympathized with them but worried that they would not have enough to eat. While the cane rotted in the fields, mill buildings and cane trucks were vandalized.

The strikers continued to push for the cane to be burned to make conditions safer for workers. Finally, the mill owners and growers came to an agreement with the cutters, and the strike ended after nine long weeks.

It was a hard-won victory. The strike had cost the workers many weeks of wages, and the plague had killed dozens of cutters and sickened many others. The happiness of the Danetti family was destroyed and Frank's horrible and painful death cast a pall over the whole community, knowing they were all vulnerable to the same pestilence.

But as a result of the strikers' struggle, the law was changed, and from then on it required cane fields to be burned before the start of the season in order to get rid of the rats.

For many years afterwards, every time Talia passed the drifting smoke from burning cane, her throat catching and her eyes smarting, it always reminded her of the season of the strike and the tragic toll suffered by the Danettis.

Chapter Thirteen
The Big Blow
Near Ingham, North Queensland – March 1932

When they looked back they would remember that there had been many hot days that summer. This one in particular began as just another scorcher in the long heat wave they had endured for several weeks now.

Talia lounged on the verandah, too worn down by the heat to do much of anything. She lay on the bench and kept still, the weight of the humidity keeping her there. She watched with heavy eyelids as a skink popped out of the shadows and scampered up the verandah post. She turned her lazy eyes to a giant spider, a wiry black cluster that had been absolutely motionless all morning long.

The skink scrambled back down and pranced on the railing before slipping below the house by way of a slat. It seemed scattered and confused — uncertain about where to settle.

When Talia glanced back, the spider was gone. Strange, she thought. What had possessed it to move after spending all morning in the same spot? Had it found something to feed on? And where was it now?

Birds zipped by overhead. Possums, normally only active much later in the day, scurried through the scrub. So many creatures were on the move.

An ominous rumbling first alerted her to a change. A swift cooling breeze rustled the leaves, lifting them over and exposing their dull undersides. Fat cumulonimbus clouds clustered like sheep. Rain was now certain and Talia was glad. It would mean a break in the cloying humidity, at least for a day or two.

But this would be no ordinary rainstorm, as Talia and her family would soon discover.

The first fat drop of rain was soon joined by another, and then another, striking hard surfaces in an increasingly frenetic beat. The drops quickly pooled between the tall grasses, stirring up the soil.

Carmen hurried from inside the house to fetch the laundry from the line and beckoned for Talia to help. They tossed the clothes in the basket and raced inside. Carmen decided against stoking a fire to heat the iron. She would wait till after the storm to do the week's pressing. Instead she smoothed the white shirts and pillowcases and set them aside.

She watched from the front door as the storm gathered momentum. The rain was coming down now in sheets. It battered the cane fields, the palms and gum trees, and hammered the roof of the house.

It rained steadily for hours. And just when one thought the heavens must have been wrung dry, the rain only picked up in intensity, and with it the wind too. Thunder continued in the distance, punctuated by silvery streaks of lightning.

From their house Talia and Carmen could see the nearby creek become swollen and the water turn yellow in colour. They looked on with worry as the water rose and increased speed. Andre arrived home just as the creek began to crest at the bridge. His expression was grim as he watched the wind whip the palms until they were nearly sideways.

There seemed no way to keep the water out of the house. It drove through the cracks in the walls. There were not enough pans and tins to catch it all. Tacking tarps to the ceiling also proved futile, as the water collected and pushed the tarps back down.

They noted with increasing alarm the low-lying swampy areas growing in breadth, widening until they joined with the creek to form a large lake.

As the light drained from the sky so did their hopes that the storm would simply blow over. For several hours, they cowered inside the house feeling it shake and shudder under the force of the wind. The crate furniture blew off the porch and an empty kerosene can spun across the meadow like a runaway tire. Talia jumped and gasped as something large smashed against the house. Finally, Andre yelled something to them, but he could not be heard above the din.

"What?" Carmen shouted.

"Let's get out!" said Andre, gesturing towards the door.

"Where to?"

Andre pointed downwards.

Carmen shook her head. He grabbed her shoulder and gestured frantically. "The whole top is going to rip away!"

Carmen was doubtful. Surely it was safer inside their house than anywhere else.

"Come on!" Andre insisted.

Carmen gave in to Andre's urging. They lashed themselves together with a rope and moved in chain formation down the stairs, braving the wind as they exited the shack. Clinging to each other, they crawled underneath their home to take refuge.

Andre hung up the hurricane lamp but it was not long before the light was extinguished. Thereafter they could only guess at how bad things were by the roar of the wind and the glimpses offered by occasional flashes of lightning.

It was as though they were shipwrecked and clinging to wood salvaged from their sunken vessel. For twelve hours, they held onto the stumps, shivering in the ever-rising water. Andre and Carmen had to bend their head and shoulders to fit under the floor, and Talia took shelter between them. Her own small body shook from the fear and the cold.

All night long they listened to the wind shriek and howl about them, throttling the ramshackle house and threatening to wrench it off its footings. It creaked and groaned against the powerful force, swaying with the whims of the storm as though at any moment the temperamental giant would finally succeed in pulling it off its stumps.

With its roof torn off and the linoleum stripped away, the house offered no real protection from the rain. The water drove through the cracks in the floorboards, soaking them as they huddled below.

As every hour passed, Talia clung to her mother and father. Still the water rose, and they waited in awe and fear of the tempest's fury. Talia had never experienced such terror, yet a small part of her was fascinated to witness the sheer power of it. They waited out the long hours, not certain how they would meet their end — buffeted on the one hand by increasingly high surges of water, and on the other by the relentless wind that tossed timber and tree limbs about like toothpicks. Just when it seemed they could not hold out any longer, as the water was creeping ever higher, fingers of light began to peel away the darkness. And then, the roar began to subside.

When the wind had died down at last, Andre guided them out from underneath the house. They stayed close, Carmen hugging Talia to her chest as the water was still high. The little girl shivered from the cold and wet, and lingering fear.

They emerged to find the world as they had known it only twelve hours earlier, completely devastated. Pummelled and flattened. The cane fields were gone, palms and other trees were uprooted, outbuildings were torn apart, and pieces of corrugated iron lay twisted and scattered about.

The roof of their shack had been sheared off and lay some distance away in several pieces. However humble their house had been, it was still a great disappointment to see it destroyed. To be without any shelter was beyond comprehension for Talia. Even though they were out of immediate danger, she began to cry.

The landscape was now a sea, broken only by clusters of trees and islands where the ground level was higher. Water surrounded them everywhere and there was nothing they could do but wait until it receded a little.

They climbed into what remained of their old house and slept as the sun beat down on them. Talia was hungry and thirsty. Although she could easily reach out and scoop gallons of water from her front steps, none of it was safe to drink.

Currents of water, dull and cloudy with silt, flowed past in the middle of the creek, bringing with them all manner of things from elsewhere — small animals, broken furniture, logs and wheels. Some of this flotsam got caught in the shrubs and trees on the edges of the creek and became trapped. Andre and Carmen eyed these things — things that could be useful for rebuilding their devastated house if only they were within reach. At the moment the water was too strong and it was not yet safe to venture out.

Carmen encouraged Talia to take a nap. The only place was the bare floor. Talia slept fitfully, dreaming that their house was floating along a river. She woke some time later to her mother's sharp voice.

"Please, Andre! Stop! I beg you! You'll drown trying to save that mutt!"

Talia went to the front of the verandah to see what was upsetting her mother. She saw that her father was out on the water. He had lashed together pieces of tin and scavenged timber to create a makeshift raft. He teetered on this rickety vessel, making his way towards an island on which a black dog was stranded, whimpering, and begging, in his own way, for help.

"Jet!"

Talia recognised the dog — it was Lucy's pet. The dog's cries became even more frantic at hearing his name being called.

Talia watched with her heart in her throat as Andre moved towards the animal. After the death of Lucy's father, the loss of the dog as well would be too much for her friend, but Talia also feared for her father, who had trouble keeping the tin raft afloat.

The dog whined as Andre pushed the raft forward unsteadily, but without having any real control over it, he overshot the island. As the raft drifted close, Andre tried to coax the dog towards him, but the animal would not budge. Andre reached for the dog and the raft tipped precariously.

Andre grabbed the dog, just as the raft flipped over and sank.

"Oh, my God!" Carmen gasped, waving her arms.

Andre and Jet floundered. Andre tried to swim while still holding onto the thrashing dog. They splashed around, gulping water as they slipped below the surface.

Carmen dropped to the floor. "Andre!" She covered her head, unable to continue watching.

A few seconds later, Talia shook her mother, "Mama, look!"

Carmen glanced up to see that her husband and the dog had managed to swim to a fence post and were now clinging to it — or, rather, Andre was holding on to the post with one arm, with the other around the dog.

"It's okay, Carmen," reassured Andre. The dog yelped, seemingly in disagreement.

"Now what?" Carmen said in despair. "All for a dog. *Dios mio!*"

A regular splashing sound caused her to turn. The source of the sound was a small boat with two men paddling towards their property. She yelled at them, gesturing in her husband's direction to signal his predicament. Andre also saw the men.

"Hulloooo!" he shouted.

The visitors spotted Andre and began to paddle towards him.

"Crikey, got yourself in a spot over a blunny dog!" one of them snorted.

There was a brief discussion about whether there was room for the dog on the punt, but soon enough Jet, whimpering and yelping, was hoisted on board with Andre. The men moved the tippy boat towards the shallowest part of the water whereupon Andre and the dog leapt off.

Andre thanked his two rescuers profusely.

"God bless."

The men warned Jet, "And you rascal, stay out of trouble."

Carmen exhaled in relief. "May God protect you," she called after the men in the departing boat.

After pushing away from shore, the men skirted a clump of

bushes and grabbed something from the branches. It was a hoe. They tossed it onto their laden boat along with their many other finds and continued on their journey up the swollen creek.

Andre's eyes crinkled in a rueful smile as he saw the men grab their reward from among his scattered possessions.

Carmen sighed. "All for a stupid dog! You could have drowned!"

Andre shrugged, "Yes, well, I didn't."

Jet seemed oblivious to the turmoil he had caused. He recognised Talia immediately and showed his delight by leaping onto her and pushing her down. Talia laughed at the enthusiastic greeting. She threw her arms around him, hugging him tightly. He was damp and scrawny, his fur matted with mud and debris, but he was probably the happiest dog for miles around.

Days later, once the water had receded a little, Talia and her father left on foot for the Danetti home with Jet in tow. Carmen was strongly against the idea of setting out so soon after the storm, but Talia knew her friend would be frantic at the disappearance of her dog.

As they travelled, they came across many signs of the storm's wrath. Debris was strewn everywhere. The bloated body of a horse lay across a small bridge. The stench of it reached Talia and her father long before they came upon it. Blowflies clustered at the horse's mouth and eyes. Talia ran by, disgusted and horrified, but Jet brimmed with curiosity. His nose dove towards the rotting animal, scattering the flies briefly. They buzzed and hovered at a safe distance, eager to return to their feast of dead flesh. Finally, Jet had to be wrenched away from the carcass.

They walked slowly for several miles, plodding along the mucky road and climbing over uprooted trees. Jet seemed to know that they were close because the dog gave several excited yelps and then took off, bounding into the tangled brush and heading for home. The joy on Lucy's face when Jet returned was one of the few wonderful moments during that black period following the storm. Talia and her father took note of the sorry state of the Danetti property. The cyclone had not made any exceptions for this place where tragedy had already struck only a few months before.

Andre set about helping Manny drag timber and farm implements from the scrub. Together they rolled the old truck out of the mud and up to a drier piece of land. Andre scavenged plant seeds and cuttings and planted these in an effort to restore the garden. By the time they had worked a few hours, it was too late for Talia and her father to return home, so they bedded down for the night. Andre slept in the front of the old Model T while Talia lay down alongside Lucy on a mat of palm leaves. She was happy to be able to spend a little time with her friend. In whispers, they talked about the night of the storm and Jet's dramatic rescue. The dog's antics and adventures were a welcome distraction for the girls amid the gloom of recent death and devastation.

"It was so foul, the way he put his nose right up to it," Talia squealed, relaying Jet's encounter with the dead horse. Lucy gasped, in disgust.

"You mustn't let him kiss you!" Talia advised.

Lucy groaned. "I think he already did!"

Talia broke into giggles, but then became serious again. "You ought to wipe down your mouth with iodine."

"Iodine? Where am I going to get that?"

Talia sighed, remembering the current bareness of their homes. She sat up, thinking. "Lemon juice might do."

"I think our lemon tree was stripped bare."

They lay in silence, thinking about this. Finally, Lucy added, "if Jet survives, then I should be alright too."

They peered over at Jet, who was curled up nearby, snuffling peacefully. Lucy smiled.

"Yes, Jet seems quite fine."

They finally settled down to sleep, soothed and comforted by their friendship and shared experiences.

Around the middle of the next day, Talia and her father headed back home. Carmen was waiting for them, anxious and puffy-eyed. She hugged Andre tightly.

"I couldn't sleep last night. I heard the wind pick up again."

As the water settled still further, Talia and her family combed the scrub for their belongings, but they recovered few of their original possessions. The wind had scattered everything far and wide. But it was not only their things that had been blown away but those of their neighbours as well.

Over the coming days, they salvaged objects that the creek had given up and left on its banks — enamel plates, a sodden boot, kerosene cans, rugs, a door, a chair, and an umbrella. The recovered items now became part of the Queixens' household. It was a haphazard form of redistribution.

For Talia's family, the loss from the cyclone was enormous. Not only were most of their household possessions gone, but also their livelihood was in shambles. The garden was washed away. Cane fields and crops everywhere were damaged. They and many of their neighbours were left destitute.

Combined with the disappointing harvest of the previous season, this new loss was too much to bear. With hungry stomachs and weary hearts, Andre and Carmen argued over how best to sort out this problem. The solution they agreed on was for Andre to search for work in another area.

He took only enough time to locate and salvage the metal pieces to restore some semblance of a roof to the shack. He replanted the garden and restocked the pantry. While the land was still damp from the floods, he left to find work further north, in an area the cyclone had left untouched.

And so it came to be that Carmen and Talia were left on their own, once again. Talia felt a numb panic as she and her mother faced these new desperate circumstances. They could only hope that Andre would soon send for them.

Chapter Fourteen
Promise of Paradise
On to Innisfail, North Queensland – September 1932

It was weeks after the cyclone and long after the main floodwaters had receded that Talia caught sight of something on the ground as she was exploring. A smooth white patch just at the surface. She clawed with her fingers at the mud until it revealed — a small teacup!

It was part of the set she had received at Christmas more than four years before, at her fifth birthday. She was now almost ten years old.

She rinsed the tiny cup off, exposing the pink roses. She cleaned and dried it. At first she was very pleased with the find, but in the end it only served to remind her of what else was missing. No matter how hard she looked she could not find any more of her tea set.

It was like her own family and their lives. There were pieces missing, their existence incomplete. Blown away in the wind and buried somewhere in the mud.

Within two weeks of the storm, Talia and the other children were back at school but nothing was the same again. The reappearance of her dog, Jet, had only cheered Lucy for a brief while. She was distracted and melancholy when she did attend. But often she was absent in order to stay home and help her mother.

Talia looked back fondly on the days when they had been carefree and happy. How short that period was and how long ago it seemed. Now a sense of loneliness overwhelmed her.

Talia and her mother lived for several months in a strange uncertainty. The household was just a shell of what it once had been and Carmen made little effort to restore it, knowing that they would soon be on the move again. But weeks went by as they waited for word from Andre about their new home.

It could not come soon enough. However, it was not until February of 1933 that a message was sent through a neighbour that he had secured a place for his family. Shortly thereafter a letter came with travel instructions.

Carmen and Talia packed what little they still had and took a cane tram to the Herbert River. From there they travelled on a launch towards Lucinda, and then by steamer up the Hinchinbrook Channel to Innisfail. Andre met them as they disembarked and took them for the last leg of the journey by horse and cart.

Her father's buoyant mood and healthy appearance raised their spirits somewhat and Talia began to allow herself to feel a little bit optimistic. As they travelled, he raved about his new place of employment, the domain of a fellow Spaniard. Incredibly he had secured a job in a castle, where his family could also stay.

A castle? Talia had trouble believing this. She studied her father, looking for signs of tropical fever, wondering if his story might be some frothy invention brought on by illness.

But closer to their destination, Talia began to see evidence that he might be telling the truth. There had just been another rain shower, and with the sun beating down, the moisture rose up in a steamy haze. It was through this mist that Talia first caught sight of an outline of turrets. And then when they rounded a corner, there were more enchanting glimpses.

Talia's heart beat harder as they approached. Now she could see the fabled castle in its entirety, standing majestically. It was such a magical vista.

Little did she know this place would be her home for many years to come. It would be the place where her life dreams would be born. A place of great happiness as well as heartbreak.

High above the wrought iron gate a sign announced Castillo Candela.

Not only was it a visual feast, but a delight for all the other senses too. As they drew nearer, the sound of waterfalls reached them, as well as the perfume from many flowering vines.

Bright splashes of colour contrasted with the shade and deep greens of the garden. Purple bougainvillea clung to the whitewashed walls, and huge flowerpots with clusters of orange lantana and crimson geraniums decorated the many patios and balconies.

To the left of the castle was an English-style cottage on a hill. As they pulled up, the sound of a barking dog grew louder. Three girls skipped out of the cottage, turning with inquisitive looks towards the oncoming buggy. Seconds later a man with dark olive skin and dark hair also emerged. He nodded and shouted a greeting to Andre. Moving with brisk strides, the man approached Talia's family.

As the dog's barking grew more agitated, still more curious faces appeared. Then a regal-looking woman, dressed in a light summer dress, exited the cottage. Talia gasped. It was Señora Candela!

Talia realised that this was the castle the Candela girls had bragged about years before on the journey to Australia.

Talia leapt off the cart and raced towards her old friends. There followed many hugs and exclamations and Talia finally got to meet the twins, Roberto and Gloria, now four years old.

Talia's mother seemed strangely drawn to the little boy to the exclusion of everyone else. She clasped the child's chubby cheeks and exclaimed, over and over, "Oh, my!"

Señora Candela made a clucking sound and it was then Carmen noticed Señora Candela's warning look. Carmen collected herself and made an effort to acknowledge the other children.

"Everyone's been well, I hope?" Carmen asked as her eyes again drifted in Roberto's direction.

"Yes, with good food and a healthy environment, they have all thrived," added Señora Candela. "I am thankful my husband has been able to provide well for them."

"So you know each other?" Señor Candela looked quizzically

between his wife and Carmen.

"Yes," said Señora Candela stiffly. "We crossed from Genoa on the same ship."

"*¡Qué milagro*! It's a miracle that you have met up again. What are the chances of that!"

Talia was baffled at Señora Candela's cool demeanour towards her and her mother. She had remembered her as such a kind person from the boat trip, but their arrival at the castle seemed to have caught her completely off guard.

The Candela girls, on the other hand, were just as cheery and as much fun as before. They grabbed Talia by the hand and whisked her off for a tour of their castle, the family home, and the vast grounds.

As she entered the luxurious home, Talia suddenly felt ashamed of her shabby clothes. Against the backdrop of the beautiful house with its fine furniture and drapery, she felt her poverty more than ever.

Ofelia beckoned her to follow. On one side of the wide centre hallway was a parlour outfitted with overstuffed velour furniture. A polished mahogany piano stood in one corner.

"Is that a real piano?" asked Talia.

"Of course," Aracely answered. Her tone suggested she thought the question almost ridiculous. Talia flushed in embarrassment.

Aracely sat down and began to play. Almost immediately, Gloria and Roberto crowded around their older sister and began to plunk down on the keys with their chubby hands, playing to a separate beat. Aracely stopped and groaned.

"Oh, bother! They're so trying. Honestly, Talia, you don't know how lucky you are not to have younger brothers and sisters."

In fact, Talia felt quite deprived to be an only child, but she said nothing. She often felt very lonely. What she would give to have a younger brother and sister like Roberto and Gloria! The twins were lovely little children, so funny and so adorable.

In a fit of annoyance, Aracely pushed Roberto and Gloria's fingers off the keys and started playing again. But soon the little hands came back and once more trampled on Aracely's lovely notes.

While the concert played on, Talia gazed around at the rest of the room, admiring the plump upholstered chairs and matching sofa. Between them was a crystal wireless set built in a dark wood case. A giant potted palm filled another corner of the room. An oil painting of a landscape with a shepherd and a flock of tan coloured sheep hung above the settee.

"What did you think?" asked Aracely when she had finished playing.

"It was beautiful," answered Talia honestly.

"My piano teacher says I have the hands of an artist." Aracely lifted her fine, thin-boned fingers for Talia to admire.

"Papa says the piano teacher just wants to teach more lessons," huffed Ofelia.

Talia turned to the younger sister. "Do you play piano too?"

"I do Irish dancing," Ofelia replied. "I danced at the Innisfail Show last fall with my troupe."

"Someone told her that Dagos shouldn't be allowed." Lucy revealed. Ofelia shrugged. "It only happened once. Most people think I'm Irish if I stay out of the sun."

Talia wasn't sure what a Dago was but was too shy to ask. It was obviously something undesirable.

After her performance, Aracely led Talia into the dining room. Above the table hung a crystal chandelier. Light travelled from a side window and reflected through the glass pendants, casting gold and yellow dots throughout the room. Talia watched in awe as Aracely pushed a button on the wall and suddenly the room was filled with brilliant light from the chandelier. How easy it was to get rid of the darkness. There was no fussing with matches or the wick of a kerosene lantern. Light came instantly with a small push from Aracely's artistic fingers.

Presently, they moved on towards the back of the house, following a long hall of polished tile to a series of bedrooms, two for the girls and one for the parents and another for Roberto. He had a plump bed and a shelf full of toys. Talia marvelled at the sheer number: a teddy bear, a miniature sailboat, alphabet and picture blocks, a train on a string, and several tiny metal cars.

But Talia's astonishment was unsurpassed when she was shown the bathroom with its indoor plumbing. Water flowed from the tap with a simple turn of a handle. She had never witnessed such a thing before. Talia peered up the tiled stall towards a metal disc that protruded from above, wondering what it was.

Maria Eugenia noticed Talia's curiosity and bragged, "We can have hot showers any time we want."

Talia was astounded. The closest thing she had ever come to a hot shower was a sudden downpour of rain. This was truly luxurious. The Candela girls indeed lived like princesses.

But there was still more. Aracely was bursting to show Talia the electric stove and led the group towards the kitchen. Just as they were about to enter, Talia could hear the discordant voices of Señora Candela and her mother.

"We had an agreement —"

"I swear I knew nothing about this. That is the honest truth." Carmen pleaded. "Please let us stay. There will be no trouble from us."

Aracely seemed not to notice and pushed through the swinging doors. The two women suddenly became quiet. Talia was struck by her mother's distraught look and Señora Candela's drawn face.

Señora Candela spoke sharply to her eldest daughter. "Don't go dragging the whole crew through the kitchen just as I am showing Señora Queixens around."

The girls, taken aback by the severity of their mother's tone, quietly withdrew. Aracely was puzzled.

"Why was Mama so mad?" Lucia asked.

"I suppose it's because there's going to be a big party on Saturday — a wedding with three hundred guests and the cook just quit," Aracely informed them.

"She's probably very happy your mum has come to help as she has had no luck with other helpers," added Ofelia.

Talia was not so sure Señora Candela was happy but kept her troubled thoughts to herself as the tour continued. The next stage was a visit to the castle itself. Any worries Talia may have had were soon eclipsed by the stunning beauty and grandeur of the castle.

The entrance to the castle was flanked with wide columns painted to look like marble. Beautiful mosaic patterns were set in the floor.

After the foyer, they passed through heavy doors and into the grand ballroom. Adorning the wall was a giant mural of a seaside fishing village. It seemed vaguely familiar to Talia. It was not unlike one of the last images she retained of her homeland.

In the cavernous hall, Señor Candela and Talia's father were busy setting up the room for the wedding. Andre unfolded chairs and arranged them around the long tables.

Suddenly there was a soft swishing sound and the flash of something small and light. A current of air blew by them at shoulder length. Talia's skin prickled with a sense of danger.

Maria Eugenia shrieked, "What was that?"

"A spider!"

The girls scattered, looking back from a safe distance to see what type of spider had attacked.

They heard sniggering and they all looked up at once.

Talia saw a gangly boy with dark skin perched on a crossbeam. His white teeth glistened as he peered down at them, laughing. Aracely huffed.

"Alwyn, you're terrible!"

"What was that you threw at us?" Lucia asked accusingly.

"Weren't no spider," he answered with a chuckle.

Alwyn showed them a roll of crepe paper streamers. He dangled it from above, letting the end of it unfurl just enough to graze their shoulders. He went from one to the other, delighting the twins who tried to grab the streamer. When he arrived at Talia he stopped.

"Crikey, I thought there were just five sisters! Where'd she come from?"

"This is Talia. She and her mother have come to stay and work. That's her father." Aracely pointed towards Andre.

"Aha! Thank the stars she's not another Spanish princess." Alwyn grinned.

Aracely made a face. She explained to Talia, "Alwyn says we're spoiled but we really do work hard. — As a matter of fact, I spent all of yesterday helping to unpack and wash the new china. It arrived this week from England. Four hundred place settings. It's really beautiful. Come on, I'll show you."

Before Aracely led her away, Talia glanced back up at Alwyn, who was still smirking at his prank. She was in awe of his fearlessness, perched so high above them.

Aracely pulled Talia towards a long table laden with several stacks of plates. Aracely took one off a pile and showed Talia. Talia sucked in her breath. Incredibly, each dish of creamy white china had a colour image of the Mena Creek waterfalls and the castle. Plate after plate had the exact same picture, flawlessly reproduced. Four hundred times.

"How do they do that?" marvelled Talia.

"Yes, it's —"

Aracely was interrupted by a sudden smash. A folding chair had crashed to the floor. This was followed by a loud wail. Roberto's face reddened and he burst into tears.

Señor Candela clapped his hands and shouted at the girls.

"Take the twins out before one of them breaks something!"

The tension of the pre-wedding preparations was affecting him too and he seemed to have little patience. Talia scooped up the crying Roberto and tried to soothe him. He was a sturdy little boy with chubby legs and arms. His crying stopped almost immediately as his wide brown eyes took in Talia, becoming captivated with her. He sank his little fingers in her hair and pulled out a lock, hanging on tightly. Talia smiled in spite of her pain.

She carried the little boy out with her as they exited onto the balcony. From there they had a wonderful view of the falls and the gardens below. They proceeded down a steep staircase to a patio bordered by a stone balustrade.

The patio overlooked a swimming area at the base of the falls. Water roared over the cliff, sending out a spray of water droplets that shimmered in the sunlight.

Laughter drifted towards them from a couple idling in a small paddleboat in the middle of the pool. The lovers seemed blissfully unaware of the seven pairs of staring eyes. They spun about in the lazy current, intent only on each other.

As the group left the patio and went on to the rest of the garden, Talia could feel the coolness of the damp earth and the shady canopy of the trees.

Just beyond the patio area was a garden house with a rooftop bandstand. At the lower level were tennis courts, and a refreshment counter offering ice cream and soft drinks. They passed a long fountain where water shot up from tall spouts.

Aracely led them to the Tunnel of Love, a narrow passageway carved into the rock. As they approached, Lucia shrieked. "Run or you'll get bitten by a bat!"

"Don't be silly. The bats are asleep!" said Ofelia.

Whether that was true or not, no one wanted to risk dawdling, so they all ran until they reached the other end. Breathless with laughter, they exited into the sunshine.

A few feet from the tunnel they came upon a small stream with a bridge. Towards their left was yet another waterfall, although this one was much smaller than the one near the castle. Etched on a small plaque was the inscription *Little Angels Falls*.

"Where Mama comes to remember her dead babies," remarked Maria Eugenia.

"Dead babies?" asked Talia, shivering a little — less from the cool shade than from the thought of ghostly beings floating around them.

"Before Aracely, there were three dead girls," explained Maria Eugenia in a matter-of-fact tone. "They died as babies. One of them was dead before she was even born."

"What were their names?" asked Talia.

"Arabella, Magdalena, and Graciela."

They were all quiet for a moment. Even Roberto and Gloria were respectful as they thought about these children who would never have the chance to play in this wonderful park. Carved in the rock was an alcove in which a small statue of an angel posed, her serenity undisturbed by the rushing water. Before they came away, Aracely made the sign of the cross and threw a few petals onto the water as a blessing.

They did not return via the tunnel but took a longer route and reached a point where the gravel pathway veered off in several different directions. They argued briefly about which way to go.

"Mama said she wanted us back to polish silver," reminded Lucia.

"But we have to show Talia the bamboo grove and the fernery," insisted Maria Eugenia.

And so the tour continued, first through a long alley of tall Kauri pines, straight and majestic. At the end of that was a fernery, shrouded in damp shade. Delicate maidenhair fronds and staghorns were easy enough for Talia to recognise, but for the other more unusual varieties she needed to study the labels.

Aracely pressed the group to continue until they reached the wall of bamboo, marking the end of the property. They turned back and followed another pathway. Upon their return they stopped by the creek.

"Here, Robbie loves to feed the turtles."

Maria Eugenia dipped into her pocket and gave her little brother a few crumbs of bread. The little boy threw them down immediately, missing the edge of the water by far. He was given another handful and was guided closer towards the shore. This time some bits of food landed on the water's surface and the children were rewarded with the appearance of several small turtles. Little black eyes locked on the crumbs and narrow pink snouts darted out for a nibble.

Roberto clapped his hands together in delight. But when the breadcrumbs were all gone, his face clouded over. The turtles hung around for a little while longer but when they caught on that the food was all gone, they too made themselves scarce.

From somewhere above came the ringing of a bell.

"It's Mama. We'd better go," urged Lucia.

To the relief of the sisters, Talia offered to watch the toddlers rather than polish silverware. Aracely noticed that Talia had a knack for keeping the wee ones quietly content.

"Roberto has really taken to you." She remarked to Talia. "He doesn't cry as much with you around."

Talia smiled and led the children to play behind the Candela house in a fenced playground. It contained a grassy area with a seesaw and swings. Next to it was a paddock where a few horses and a couple of goats grazed.

As Talia leaned against the fence and fed the goats some grass, the worry and strain of the last few months seemed to seep out of her. Here they would not want for anything. Here she would not feel hungry or lonely. Even the goats seemed friendly.

She glanced back towards the castle and gave a shake of her head. It was all so incredible. Only yesterday she had been living in squalor and today she was settling in near a palace, where her long-lost friends lived a life of luxury with hot showers, piano lessons, and electricity.

Sometime later, as Talia pushed the toddlers on the swing, enjoying a peaceful moment of contemplation, she heard a strange noise. An odd bird call — one that was unfamiliar to her. The children immediately became alert, sitting up watchfully. Talia noticed their faces fill with excitement. Just then Alwyn appeared, pulling a miniature billy cart. It was decorated on the side with an image of the castle and the words *Castillo Candela*.

Roberto and Gloria tumbled off the swings and bounded towards Alwyn, as fast as their little legs could carry them.

"Clovis! Garnett!" Alwyn shouted as he entered the paddock. He wrestled the two recalcitrant goats into harnesses and led them out, hitching them to the cart.

Alwyn laughed as he plopped Gloria and Roberto side by side on the front seat. They giggled and squealed with delight as Alwyn led the goat cart away. Talia skipped along with them, wondering where this outing would lead them.

Alwyn brought the cart in front of the castle and around to the car park. As visitors left the castle grounds, they were intrigued by the charming sight. When they approached to have a closer look, Alwyn offered them souvenirs. Talia watched as more than a few dug into their pockets for a postcard or small bauble. The combination of the adorable twins, the mischievous goats, and Alwyn's beguiling manner seemed to persuade them to open their purses once again.

A man in a straw hat took out a camera and photographed the two children in the cart. He gave Alwyn tuppence for his trouble.

At last the billy cart was returned to the shed, and the goats and children were freed from their duties as miniature tourism ambassadors.

"Goodnight, Princess." Alwyn gave Talia a mock bow before he led the goats away.

Talia smiled to herself as she hustled the children into the Candela house. If only he knew just how far she was from being a princess. But it did not really matter, she thought, as just being at the gates of the castle was quite enough.

Chapter Fifteen
Not Another Princess
Mena Creek, North Queensland – September 1933

Talia, excited over the busy day, had trouble falling asleep right away and was still awake an hour later. She could not help but overhear fragments of her parents' conversation. Their words filled her with dread and her heart thumped in her chest.

"Are you not happy, Carmen?"

Her mother was sniffling.

"Yes, very happy."

"Then why are you crying?"

"I am not crying," Carmen replied.

This was not particularly convincing, as it was followed by more sniffles and a rather loud, barely-stifled sob.

Andre sighed. For a while, neither spoke.

"Is it because of her? — Beatrice is a difficult woman, I'll admit, but she is goodhearted. She wants everything just so."

"And I will try my best to oblige her," Carmen answered finally. "I am grateful to her for being able to stay here and I hope we can be here for a long time."

Talia exhaled in relief. She too hoped to be there for a long time, and that, whatever her mother's disagreement with Señora Candela was, it would sort itself out. She would hate to have to leave already. Castillo Candela was so unbelievably wonderful and magical. She couldn't wait for morning so she could explore some more. The tour that day had been rushed.

She was also eager to enjoy the company of the Candela girls and little Roberto. Alwyn too seemed like an intriguing, if somewhat odd, person.

At last nervous exhaustion got the better of Talia and she fell asleep.

In the morning, she felt more rested than she had in a long

while. The roar of the waterfalls drowned out the usual night cacophony — the manic bug sounds, the batting of insect wings against the mosquito net, and the raucous frogs. But here, the steady sound of water flowing over the rocks lulled Talia into a peaceful state and kept her there until the first rays of sunlight warmed her face.

Morning came with a hurried bustle. The grand wedding was approaching and all hands were required to bring the huge endeavour to success.

Talia was saddled with a large pail of potatoes to peel, all while watching the youngest of the Candela children in the play area. In the kitchen, her mother removed the skins of red peppers and diced onions in preparation for making paella.

"How's number six princess today?"

Talia looked up to see Alwyn, his eyes twinkling.

Talia retorted, "Since when does a princess peel potatoes?"

"When she's got a sharp knife."

Playfully, Alwyn picked up a long potato peel and wrapped it around his wrist. He took another peel and held it around his neck, creating a necklace.

"Number six princess has some pretty flash jewellery too."

Talia laughed, only half-annoyed at Alwyn's distractions. "Go on. Señora Candela will have my head if I don't get these done quicker."

He grabbed the potato peels and headed towards the goats. They spied him approaching and hurried to the gate. They leapt up, their hooves clambering against the cross boards, pushing each other in an effort to get closest to Alwyn.

He leaned forward and let Clovis gnaw the peel entwined around his arm. Talia couldn't help laughing. The children crowded at the fence, giggling. Talia thought that Alwyn was a little strange but the goats certainly didn't seem to mind.

When the last of the peels were gone, the goats' enthusiasm for Alwyn waned. They sniffed him for a while then turned their attention to Roberto and Gloria whose tiny faces and fingers protruded into the pen. Talia was at the ready and quickly pulled the children's hands back, safe from the goats' ever-hungry chops.

Talia led the children back to the seesaw and resumed the tedious job of peeling potatoes. She found herself making sure the peels were extra long, imagining that they would eventually be wrapped around Alwyn.

She looked up and saw him in the garden among the rows of staked plants, looking puzzled. He pinched off a few strands and brought them to his nose and inhaled. He frowned, uncertain. Talia got up and made her way over to him. He saw her and flushed slightly.

"Is this basil?" he asked, with a trace of embarrassment.

"No, those are chives. There — there's the basil." Talia pointed to a leafy bush, marked with a small tin label.

It was strange, Talia thought. Surely Alwyn had seen the names on the markers but then maybe not. He seemed a little flustered but quickly recovered.

"Thank you, — your majesty." He twirled the bundle of herbs in his hand as he made a curtsy, exiting as he backed away from her. Gloria and Roberto giggled at his theatrics.

"Isn't he silly?" Talia remarked to the children.

They giggled some more in agreement.

Talia marvelled at Alwyn's good-humoured attitude, which he maintained all the while keeping up a steady pace of work. On the day before the wedding, Talia and Aracely bumped into Alwyn as he was carrying an armful of freshly pressed linens.

"Where you going with that?" asked Aracely.

"This here's for the bride. She gonna wear this tomorrow," Alwyn replied.

"What?" Aracely was confused.

"This is her wedding dress. Such a big sheila."

Talia giggled. "Alwyn, you're rotten. What if she heard you?"

"She here already?" He made a point of looking around as

though really expecting to see her. "Mebbe she help peel potatoes, take a load off number six princess."

"I'm done with the potatoes, thank heav —"

Señora Candela's voice cut Talia off. "Alwyn, take those linens to the grand hall before they get soiled."

Talia and Alwyn snapped to attention and hustled to continue their work. Señora Candela's tone made it clear there was no time for joking around.

As soon as the damask cloths were laid out, the older girls, under the supervision of Señora Candela, began to set the tables with the new china. With almost mathematical precision, they laid out small salt and pepper shakers at every eighth chair. In between those, bowls of sugar with small spoons were set out, as well as ashtrays.

On the morning of the wedding Talia and Aracely went through the garden to cut fresh blooms, and following Señora Candela's specific instructions, plucked only blossoms that were fully open and free of any blemish. They were to gather orange and yellow blossoms for the guest tables, as well as white and purple for the head table.

Alwyn was raking the paths when Talia and Aracely came along. It was a daily chore of his to sweep away the fallen leaves and palm fronds, as well as cut back the prickly 'wait-a-while' vine that sent out shoots overnight.

When the girls had gathered up several baskets of flowers, they heaped them on a table and then sorted through the colourful sprays, trimming the stems to size. Lovely fragrances drifted up as they shook off insects and excess dew. Taking care to choose only the fullest blooms, they arranged the cuttings in small jade-green vases. When all the vases were full, Aracely interrupted her mother to ask if their work was alright, but Señora Candela was not quite satisfied and called out to Alwyn, asking him to bring up some strands of ivy and palm leaves.

He was back shortly with bits of greenery. Once these were

added to the pots, Señora Candela was finally satisfied and the posies were placed on the tables. The result was quite lovely with brilliant colour and trailing green contrasting with the ivory linens.

Alwyn helped bring in several large milk cans, delivered that morning from the nearby Malanda Creamery. He tipped the heavy cans and skimmed off the layers of cream into several smaller bowls.

Busy hands soon whipped the cream to a rich snowy thickness, folding in almond liqueur and piping it into flaky pastry tubes that lay ready. They were dusted with icing sugar and stored with the many other tarts and dessert squares prepared over the previous week.

Talia's eyes boggled at the array of sweets. There were Neenish tarts, Lamingtons, and Pink Pyramids, vanilla slices, pastel-tinted coconut macaroons and squares of chocolate fudge. But most astounding of all was the beautiful wedding cake. It was an elaborate multi-tiered confection, above which stood a miniature bridal couple in porcelain underneath a delicate archway dotted with tiny sugar rosebuds.

But there was little time to stop and admire the artistic handiwork, as there was much work to be done in the few hours remaining until the party.

It seemed no time at all before a gleaming carriage pulled up with horses in flower-festooned bridles. Other vehicles followed, carrying friends and relatives of the bride and groom.

The guests trickled through the castle grounds, mingling on the terrace, taking in the tantalizing aromas of the dinner they would soon enjoy. A photographer began to pose the bride and groom, snapping photos of them against the cascading falls, in front of gracefully arching bougainvillea and wattle bushes, and leaning along the balustrade with their extended families. Small children too were corralled into smiling and standing still while the perfect moment was captured forever.

Chapter Sixteen
A Kind Cut
Mena Creek, North Queensland – May, 1934

Under the dome of a large gum tree, Roberto lay sleeping as dappled sun danced across his face. Underneath the thin filmy skin of his eyelids, his eyeballs moved restlessly, as though absorbed in the adventures of some fantastic dream. Talia swished a fly away as she studied him. Sweet little Roberto. Six years old, yet still such a baby.

She had him to herself this afternoon. Although he had nearly recovered after a week-long fever, Señora Candela had still not let him accompany the rest of the family on an outing to Innisfail. He made a fuss about being excluded and his protests were made worse by the fact that he was still not quite well. He pouted and whined. His frustration, mixed with his lingering fever, only added to his flushed complexion.

Talia had tried to soothe him with cold compresses, which he pushed away after a few seconds. She also offered him bits of watermelon and tapioca pudding, but he refused those too. At last, he had fallen asleep out of exhaustion.

Now that he was quiet, Talia could turn her attention to her sketchbook. Intent on creating a watercolour of the castle, Talia studied the building where it sat among the thick layers of vegetation. She noticed how the sun fell around it, leaving pockets in dark shadow while reflecting its brilliance elsewhere. She tried to absorb the shapes and the colours using her eye rather than her mind to recreate what was before her.

Her charcoal pencil moved quickly as she made her first rough outline. She worked steadily except for occasional glances at Roberto who stirred from time to time without wakening.

At one point Talia got up to feel his forehead, lightly brushing aside his damp hair. He was warm but no warmer than anyone else

on this hot day. She smiled at him. He had taken to calling her
Auntie Talia, which endeared her to him even more. He was the
one person in the Candela family to whom she felt closest.

In spite of his having started school just a couple of months
earlier, he still seemed very young and vulnerable. Perhaps it was
due in part to his delicate nature — he was the first to catch every
illness. But it could also be attributed to his being mollycoddled by
his five adoring sisters, and being the only son, sheltered by his
doting parents.

Talia returned to her paper and resumed sketching the
contours of the castle. She particularly liked this viewpoint. It was
a perspective not often captured by the tourist photographers
because they did not have access to this side of the property.

Not long after, she heard Alwyn whistling and smiled to
herself. Then it became quiet save for the steady flow of water
from the falls and the occasional rustle of wind through the trees.

When Talia was satisfied with her outline of the castle, she
began to go through her basket of makeshift containers: salvaged
tobacco tins and chemist jars where she kept her homemade paints.
Alwyn had taught her how to make them from powders and plant
extracts found in the surrounding area. As she unscrewed the lid of
a small jar of sap from the bloodwood tree, a pungent smell rose
up. The other extracts too reminded her of the deepest parts of the
scrub, the nutty smell of damp rainforest, the sweet decay of
rotting leaves and bark, mixed with faint hints of pollen and
nectar.

She glanced at Roberto again and noticed him sleeping
peacefully, his hand draped over the edge of the cot.

She returned to her painting, looking up frequently to study
her subject, her eyes concentrating on certain details, the colours
and shadows at that moment in the afternoon. She became
completely lost in her work and did not notice the passage of time.

All of a sudden, Talia was startled as something flashed by,
followed by a thud. Then seconds later, she saw Alwyn run up. His

body was quivering, his eyes intent on the ground near the foot of Roberto's cot.

Talia caught a rustling movement in the grass. She gasped now that she saw what Alwyn had been staring at. There, inches from where Roberto lay, was the twisting body of a snake, decapitated by Alwyn's machete. The snake thrashed about until it was finally still. Through it all, Roberto did not stir, remaining blissfully asleep.

Even though the danger was past, Talia grabbed Roberto and raced back to the house with him. He was drowsy and unaware of the threat, but soon enough became infected by Talia's panic. He burst into tears and hugged her tightly. Both she and Roberto were still trembling and crying from the shock when Alwyn reappeared. He handed Talia the paper and paints she had left in the garden.

"It's really good."

"What?"

"The painting."

"Oh, that. I don't want it," she said, shaking her head in embarrassment. "It will just remind me of how I wasn't taking care of Roberto."

"Naaah. Don't be daft. You're a bonza nursemaid as far as I can tell. Those King Browns just sneak up like that."

"Is that what it was? A King Brown?" Talia blanched and slumped into a chair. Her chest was pounding.

"Don't tell his mother. I'll be in so much trouble."

"Don't tell me what?" And there was Señora Candela in the doorway of Roberto's room. Talia burst into tears. Roberto bounded up on the bed and looked up brightly.

"Mama, you'll never guess! King Brown was going to bite me!"

Señora Candela gasped.

"It's all right, Missus. He didn't get nowhere close before I stopped him," Alwyn reassured her.

"Yeah," said Roberto. "Stopped him by cutting off his head."

Roberto beamed. He sliced the air with his arms, as though he had not slept through the entire drama, but had witnessed it all. Señora Candela flew to her son and gripped him tight.

"*¿Mi hijito, que te pasó?*"

"I'm alright," he insisted.

She clutched his arms, examining his body for possible wounds. She was not convinced until she had thoroughly checked him over.

After Señora Candela had calmed down a little, she ordered her husband and Alwyn to go to the garden and ensure that the creature was indeed dead. The Candela sisters were required to wait inside until they were given the all clear.

Señor Candela returned a short time later. "*La culebra esta muerta*," he said, shaking his head as if to underscore how dangerous the situation had been.

One by one, the family tiptoed into the garden to have a look at the dead snake, now clotted with buzzing flies.

"Heavens," shivered Aracely. "It's huge!"

Señor Candela took out a measuring tape and stretched it across the length of the snake. He whistled. "Seven feet."

Talia recounted how the machete whizzed by and with precision got the snake as it was preparing to attack.

"*Es un milagro*," murmured Señora Candela.

"It's not really a miracle, Mama. Alwyn's a good shot," praised Lucia.

"Yes but it is a miracle that Alwyn was there," added Señor Candela.

"Alwyn is Robbie's guardian angel," said Aracely. Señora Candela nodded in agreement. There followed much discussion about what could have happened. Señora Candela stood staring at the snake with her hands to her cheeks in horror.

When Señor Candela was on the telephone later, he bragged about Alwyn's achievement. The switchboard operator must have heard and said something to her friends because the news soon got around. Not much later it reached a local reporter, Cam McElgunn, from the *South Johnstone Star*. Eager for a scoop, he motored out from his nearby office to interview Alwyn and photograph the dead snake. The snake was so long that Talia's father and Señor Candela had to help hold it up, so they were included in the photo as well.

Cam asked Alwyn a few questions, first starting out in Pidgin English and then switching to Standard English after he heard Alwyn's first answer. Alwyn demonstrated how he had thrown the machete from across the garden. The reporter retraced the path of the knife, counting his footsteps as he strode across the lawn.

"From here, you say?"

"Yes."

"That's incredible!" Cam shook his head in wonder. He saw Robbie hanging about and turned to him.

"And you, lil' fella, did you notice the snake come up?"

Roberto shook his head shyly. "No. I was sleeping."

Cam laughed and tousled Robbie's hair. "Good job you were."

When the story came out, Señor Candela purchased several copies of the newspaper.

YARD BOY KILLS GIANT SNAKE
Saves Six-Year-Old

Six-year-old Robbie Candela of Mena Creek was napping outside his parents' home at Castillo Candela when a seven-foot Eastern Brown snake crept towards him and prepared to attack. A sharp-eyed yard boy, Alwyn Cloncurry, spotted the snake and threw his machete at the reptile, severing its head in one go.

Robbie's parents, Mr. and Mrs. Ramon Candela, are convinced that their only son would have been killed by the snake had it not been for Alwyn's quick action.

Local snake expert Sam N. Lucas said that there are plenty of snakes out now with the warm weather and this particular one was probably attracted to the bowl of pudding next to the sleeping boy.

One copy of the clipping was pasted into a family scrapbook, one was given to Alwyn as a memento, and another was intended for the castle museum. The record of Alwyn's feat would join several other accounts and photographs of local events and famous visitors on the Castillo's wall of fame. Alwyn's image would hang alongside that of world-renowned cyclist Hubert Opperman who had been in the area en route to the Top End ten years before, a group of unnamed pioneers who had conquered a mammoth crocodile in the late 1800s, and Seymour Fontaine, an acrobat from Wirth's circus who had scaled the castle parapet in 1928.

Señor Candela had the photographs and clipping placed in a frame, and when it was ready, the family gathered in the museum to celebrate Alwyn and have a look at the addition to the display.

Señor Candela made a short speech praising Alwyn and pinned a blue ribbon to his chest, pronouncing him a hero. They all clapped and Alwyn turned pink, bending his head in embarrassment at all the attention.

Alwyn was all decked out for the occasion. His unruly hair had been cut short and smoothed down with a generous amount of Brylcreem. He was dressed in a new shirt and pants given to him by the Señora as a reward for saving her son. Talia thought he looked quite handsome and told him so.

"You'll have to stay out of the trees with your new clothes."

Robbie asked Talia for a closer look at the photo. Alwyn lifted him up and Talia read the clipping out loud.

Alwyn listened carefully and pointed to his name in the news article. "There Robbie, that's me."

Robbie nodded.

Señora Candela brought up a tray of coconut cookies and Talia's mother served them all lemonade.

The castle museum was only open on rare occasions for special guests to the park. Talia had rarely come up to this room, so she took the opportunity to wander around, looking over everything with fresh eyes.

One wall of the museum was dedicated to aboriginal artefacts — finely woven bags, bark paintings, and a message stick. Behind a glass case, there was an assortment of old guns, muskets and ammunition. And on a table near the entrance were miscellaneous items, a stuffed wombat, sharks teeth, seedpods, shells, and some barnacle-encrusted iron — all that was left of a ship that met its end on the nearby reefs.

While Señor Candela was proud of his collection, he had ambitions to expand it, in particular to include more material on the mining history of the area. He had mementos from the Cloncurry mines where he had invested money and reaped a small fortune in copper.

The name Cloncurry prompted Talia to ask Alwyn if he was related to the owner of the mine. But he shook his head, saying that he had gotten the name Cloncurry simply because that was where he was born. His father was an itinerant miner from Ireland who left before Alwyn came into the world.

"Never even met the bloke," Alwyn shrugged.

Aracely had told Talia at one time that Alwyn's mother was an aboriginal woman who contracted leprosy and was banished to a leper colony. Alwyn meanwhile had been living with other orphans on Palm Island when Señor Candela hired him at the age of nine.

Talia felt a pang of sadness to think that Alwyn's parents no longer had knowledge of their son, nor he of them. They did not know of his heroism, or his intelligence, nor that he had grown up into someone hard-working and resourceful. Would his father have been so eager to abandon him had he been able to see into the future and know who Alwyn would become?

There was one more stop on the museum tour. Señor Candela asked for everyone's attention, directing them to an object on the wall hidden under a piece of cloth. When he pulled off the cover, Talia let out a little cry. There, in an elegant frame, was her watercolour painting of the castle.

"*¡Qué precioso!* Where did you get that?" Señora Candela asked.

Señor Candela pointed to Talia and she blushed.

"Who? Talia?" Señora Candela glanced at Talia in surprise.

"Beatrice, this girl can do more than peel potatoes."

Señora Candela squinted at the picture and then turned around to face Talia, giving her an appraising look. Talia worried that the Señora might be angry with her for painting while she should have been watching Roberto, but there was no hint of this.

"Well, well. Nicely done," she remarked to Talia.

Talia caught Alwyn watching her. He raised his eyebrows and smiled. He did not seem to mind that she was stealing some of the limelight away from him.

Chapter Seventeen
Art and War
Mena Creek, North Queensland – 1936

Although Talia's world revolved around school, friends, and her work at the castle, she was thrust into the politics of her home country when news reached Mena Creek that civil war had broken out in Spain.

Rebel forces under fascist leader General Francisco Franco led brutal attacks on innocent civilians. Using military might supplied by Germany's Nazi dictator Adolf Hitler and Italy's fascist leader Benito Mussolini, whole cities were bombed, and women and children were machine-gunned in the street as they tried to flee.

The stories of the massacres of innocent people angered the Spanish immigrants of the Innisfail district. No other nation stepped in to help Spain, but individuals from all over the world volunteered to fight against the fascists. While most local residents were unable to participate directly in supporting their countrymen, they quickly organized to raise funds for the war relief effort.

Señor and Señora Candela offered to do their part to help the Spanish Relief Committee by hosting a costume ball, as well as sponsoring the prize for the pageant queen, Miss Spanish Innisfail.

On the afternoon of the fundraiser, there was a parade in Innisfail with floats representing the provinces of Spain. Flags from Andalusia, Valencia, and Catalonia, and other provinces were flown together, reflecting the way in which the smaller divisions that used to plague Spaniards fell away in face of the greater threat of fascism.

Gaëlla Monteréal, a classmate of Aracely's, was chosen as the winner of the pageant and rode on one of the open-topped cars, waving to the local Spaniards and other supporters lined up along the street. She had her photo taken with Señor and Señora

Candela, and the president of the Spanish Civil War Relief Committee. The procession of cars and buggies meandered through the countryside and ended at Castillo Candela, where the festivities were to continue.

There were several speeches preceding the party. Ignacio Funez, a local man who happened to be in Spain when the fighting erupted, told of his narrow escapes, describing in detail his wounds and the bayonet attack on others near him. When Ignacio peeled away a bandage to show the extent of his injuries, one of the guests, a middle-aged woman, fainted and was led outside to get some fresh air.

But soon the evening moved to lighter things — singing and music. A pig was raffled, as well as a crocheted tablecloth.

As the guests swarmed the dance floor, Talia came upon a line-up of people crowding a dark corner of the hall. She squeezed through to see what the queue was for and came face-to-face with the one-eyed woman, dressed as a gypsy. Talia's heart leapt into her throat. She felt the old terror return and hit her with the same force as it had nearly a decade earlier. Just at that moment 'La Encantadora' looked up and stared her directly in the eyes. The old woman's mouth curled into a smile, as though she recognised Talia right away from the four-year-old girl she had met so long ago.

While other partygoers had no hesitation in letting the one-eyed woman read their palms and hear her advice about the future, as the proceeds were for a good cause, Talia stayed clear of 'La Encantadora' for the rest of the evening.

"She's very good, you know."

"Yes," agreed a woman standing nearby. "She told me that I would meet my future husband at church, and there he was."

"And he's been on his knees ever since — praying for mercy, poor fellow," whispered someone behind the woman's back.

A titter of laughter followed, but the ridiculed woman pretended not to hear.

Talia came to understand much later that La Encantadora was no witch, but simply a kindly widow, Señora Cecilia Kenavo, who was an immigrant like the rest of them. She had arrived in Australia not long after Talia and her mother, following her sons to a strange new land. Cecilia had said good-bye to Sant Feliu and packed up her things, bringing along a wedding photo, her late husband's pocket watch, some old lace pieces, silver candlesticks, and her psychic 'gift' which had taken up no room at all in her bags but was most certainly the most valuable of all her possessions.

Cecilia suffered from arthritis in her hands and her English was so poor that she could not find regular work, but she lived simply and frugally, and the extra money from her readings supplemented the modest and intermittent monetary gifts that came from her sons.

The party continued with a mournful song performed by a soloist, a man browned by the sun with hands gnarled from manual labour, but whose voice was tender and full of feeling. The ballad undulated with deeply felt emotion, moving the audience with each swell and dip. When at last the song was done, the crowd of listeners erupted in thunderous applause.

"*¡Viva La República! ¡Viva la República!*" shouted several guests.

Talia found her arms shooting up along with the others. Her eyes welled with tears. At that moment, it seemed as though everyone in the hall felt the same pain and fear for those suffering in the civil war.

A surge of renewed energy for the struggle rippled through the gathering. Spirits were high. Voices spoke loudly defending the cause, and coins and bills were tossed and unfurled, loosened from the grasp of those who had earlier harboured uncertainty.

Excitement pulsated through the castle hall. As drinking and dancing increased, voices grew more fervent.

"*¡No pasarán!*"

Talia joined in a long sardana, linking her arms with others, feet tramping through the sawdust sprinkled over the polished boards. She felt connected to the community in a warm thread of humanity, feeling a bond of love and fellowship.

She saw Alwyn out of the corner of her eye. He paused to watch, his eyes full of wonder and envy. Talia lost her step for a second, and her connection with the other dancers was broken. But then someone grabbed her arm, and she was once more pulled along in the shaking throng.

When she turned to look back, Alwyn had disappeared.

Except for that brief moment when he had stood watching Talia, he had been working steadily all evening, collecting drink glasses and small plates, bringing these to the open kitchen where a water kettle boiled. He soaped them and rinsed them off, placing them on a rack to dry.

He was returning to the hall with a tray of clean glasses when he passed a group of men smoking cigars and sipping on liqueur. Their gravelly voices vacillated between excitement and anger.

Alwyn recognised Andre among them. Tipsy, his eyes enflamed, Talia's father raised his fist in an emphatic gesture. Then he brought it down to his chest and pounded fervently, directing his words to the wounded hero Funez.

"*¡Yo tambien! ¡Me voy a España!* — I cannot sit by and let my countrymen be slaughtered."

He continued, words spilling out. "*No puedo permitir que ese bárbaro mate a mi pueblo. ¡Lo haré por la comunidad!*"

"Are you sure?"

"*¿Estás seguro?*"

"You doubt me! — Of course, I am serious!"

The men thumped Andre on the back and shook his hand in congratulations. They wished him luck and asked him to forward messages for relatives back home.

Alwyn scurried past. He wanted to find Talia and warn her. When he located her at last, he was panting and sweating. She was taken aback by his distressed state.

"What's the matter?"

"I'm not sure, Talia," he paused, trying to catch his breath. "Your Dad was going on about Spain. The war and all."

"Isn't everybody tonight?"

"No, no. He was talking like he might just up and leave on the next boat."

Talia stared at Alwyn, trying to tell if he might be joking but there was no trace of humour in his eyes. This was one of those rare moments when he was serious.

"What makes you think that?" she asked slowly.

"I could be wrong but I heard him say he was going to Spain to fight the brute."

Talia's eyes widened. "Maybe you misunderstood."

Alwyn shrugged. "Maybe." He repeated as many of her father's words as he could remember.

It left Talia with an uneasy feeling. She tried to dismiss Alwyn's suspicions but throughout the rest of the evening, she caught snatches of conversation with her father's name whispered. She felt eyes staring at her.

Talia considered passing on what Alwyn had said to her mother, but decided to wait until after the party.

As the festivities began to wind down, someone shouted for silence. Talia watched with a sinking feeling as her father climbed up on the dais with Ignacio. The returned soldier put his arm over Andre's shoulder and that is when Talia's father announced he was going to Spain to fight.

As cheers and shouts of congratulations erupted, Talia turned to see her mother blanch and stiffen. In spite of Alwyn's warning, Talia was still deeply shocked. She regretted not going to her mother earlier with the rumour when she had first heard it. Had Carmen known, maybe she could have stopped Andre.

Suddenly well-wishers came towards them with congratulations, thanking them for Andre's gift to the cause.

Carmen was caught between the community's supportive reaction and her own disappointment and shock. She gave their friends and well-wishers a brave smile. They could not know that inwardly she seethed. Later when she was alone with Andre, she pleaded with him to change his mind, but it was no use.

"Why, Andre, why does it have to be you? We were going to start our own farm, and now you want to go away."

"I'm not going to let the bloody fascists run roughshod over my country."

"*This* is your country now. It has been for fifteen years."

"I'm doing it for everyone else who can't go back."

"What about your family? Don't we matter at all?"

Apparently not, Talia realised after her father had left, barely a week later.

The mood was sombre around the castle. Señor Candela had apparently tried to dissuade Andre, even threatening to put out his wife and daughter, but in the end he did follow through on that threat. He felt compassion for the Queixens women knowing they were now lost without Andre. He could not burden them with further worries. Besides, Carmen and Talia continued to work as hard as ever at Castillo Candela.

As Talia turned fourteen later that year, she decided not to continue with school and began to work full-time at the Castillo. The family was short its main breadwinner and she felt obliged to step in. Talia turned all her earnings over to her mother, only keeping a small portion for herself.

They were uncertain when and if Andre would return. The first letter they received came months after his departure and was already weeks old by the time it reached them. It had been routed through France by a fellow fighter.

Andre wrote of his exploits and his bravery, hiding in the Pyrenees with a band of fighters, enduring cold nights, trekking along icy mountain trails and sleeping in shepherd huts. The letter ended with his vowing to fight until the bitter end.

After the news had been duly shared with the Candela family, Carmen took the letter back and threw it into the wood stove, watching as the flames devoured the paper.

Chapter Eighteen
Friends at Work
Mena Creek, North Queensland – 1937

Apart from a few hours set aside to paint, Talia spent long days working at the Castillo, doing laundry, cleaning and helping with the park visitors. She collected empty glasses and dishes from the patio. She served lemonade and soda water to picnickers at the water's edge, frequently earning small tips. These she offered to her mother, knowing that money was scarce with her father away.

On summer afternoons the refreshment stand near the tennis courts served home-made ice cream. From week to week the flavours varied, but popular mainstays were coconut, mango, rum and raisin, and passion fruit. Talia took pleasure in cranking the ice cream paddle while crystals formed and the dessert thickened.

Children looked on longingly as Talia scooped plum-sized balls and plopped them in the wafer cones. More than likely they hoped for a more generous portion for their three pence. But Talia was firm and fair, knowing that the line-up for ice cream was always long, and she could not bear to see anyone disappointed.

As she and her mother waited for news of Andre on the battlefront, they gleaned bits of information from letters, news stories and clippings passed through the Spanish immigrant community.

Talia was always happiest when she could forget her worries and become totally enraptured by a new film. At Castillo Candela, they were fortunate that the great hall was used as a cinema four nights a week.

One of Talia's many tasks was to unfold the chairs and arrange them in rows on movie nights. She also helped Alwyn collect tickets and usher the guests to their seats. Once the guests were settled, Talia went up and down the aisles hawking small bags of popcorn, salted peanuts, humbugs or liquorice. Then, as the movie was about to begin, she would turn out the hall lights and hurry to join Alwyn in the projection booth. There they would spend the next two hours whispering and giggling over Alwyn's portrayals of characters from the movies they were watching.

His ability to perfectly mime the great screen actors, both in gesture and accent, was often more entertaining than the movie itself and frequently threw Talia into fits of hysteria.

"I got to get me a deep Florida tan if it takes me all afternoon!" he said, one evening, quoting Cary Grant in *Holiday*.

"I'm too white, Talia. Nobody will believe me that I've been in Florida for two weeks."

Talia was still laughing so hard at intermission, that she wheezed as she ran down the stairs. She wiped away tears of laughter, and tried hard to suppress her giggles as she passed out bags of popcorn and candy.

Most every movie night was like this, and only the occasional question from a stranger about her father would jolt her out of her buoyant mood.

As the same movie was repeated night after night, Alwyn's performances became more polished and more outrageous. Moreover, he could recall lines from films months afterwards in the most incongruous of situations.

Talia once ran into him as he was fixing the flooded toilets near the refreshment stand. At the time rain was coming down heavily and the stench from the broken toilets was awful. It was a miserable situation, but Alwyn, ever the joker, shrugged his shoulders, and said with a perfect Oklahoma accent "New York's alright but I wouldn't want to live there."

To judge Alwyn just by looking at him, with his brown-skin, gangly physique, unkempt hair and threadbare clothes, one would expect only half-sentences in broken English, but he was eloquent, and a quick study of mannerisms and speech.

Talia looked forward to the many hours spent in his company. He was a salve to all the hardships, worries and disappointments of the day. With him, she could forget the petty dramas and jealousies she sometimes experienced among the Candela sisters, as well as the minefield of her mother's difficult moods.

*   *   *

When her father first left, Talia worried that she and her mother might be asked to leave Castillo Candela, expecting that the little house behind the castle would go to a new groundsman, leaving Talia and her mother to find other living arrangements.

Andre had served as a buffer between Carmen and Señora Candela, and now that he was away, the relationship between the two women grew even more strained. Señora Candela would often hint to Carmen that they needed the cottage that Carmen and Talia occupied.

Finally, Carmen asked Señor Candela directly if they might be sent away. He seemed quite surprised by her question, and quickly reassured her that he would do no such thing, especially not to the family of a hero of the cause. At last Carmen was able to relax a little, and the Señora's veiled threats no longer had the same effect. She and Talia settled into a peaceful routine, that is, until an incident later that year.

Excitement bubbled up when it was learned the Castillo would host a tennis tournament involving the English tennis player, Theo Parkman.

As the tournament began, the castle was overrun with foreign guests and newspapermen who came daily to watch. Their cars jammed the parking lot and many came early to get the best seats on the patio adjacent to the tennis courts.

Talia was run off her feet fetching cigarettes and coffee, and in the afternoons, cold drinks and sandwiches. As well as pocketing many tips, she scooped up the Capstan cigarette cards that were carelessly tossed away. When she presented Roberto with a large bundle of these, he gave her a wonderful hug, thrilled that he could now complete his collection of the 'Flags of the Empire' series.

Every morning, the crushed brick courts were swept and the white chalk lines reapplied. Cigarette butts and other bits of litter were retrieved, patio tables dried to remove the dew from the night before, and awnings and shades unfurled.

Talia hurried up and down the stairs with trays laden with refreshments until her feet were worn out and her arms ached. And still more coins were added to her pockets from appreciative customers.

Talia got used to listening for the distinctive 'pling' of the ball as it hit the taut rackets, the near-quiet breathing of the attentive spectators, interspersed with polite clapping and exclamations. She was sad to think the event would soon be over.

One day a sudden cloudburst sent the players scampering from the court to take shelter in the snack bar under the terrace. The crush of people in the small space seemed to break down the divide between those who served and those who were served. A mood of jovial camaraderie emerged.

It was after the rainstorm that Talia noticed a change in her mother. The following morning, as Talia was waking up, she was struck by how much care her mother was taking with her appearance — putting on red lipstick, and brushing out her hair into a smoothly shaped bob. Carmen caught Talia staring at her.

Talia had long wanted to cut off her long hair. In this hot climate, it felt like a steamy woollen hat. How wonderful it would be to be rid of the braid that clung to her neck, trapping the sweat.

"Mama, can I cut my hair too?"

"Don't be silly, you're still a girl. It's not proper."

"But even Lucia and Ophelia have short hair, why can't I?"

"I don't want to hear you ask that again!"

"I'm the only one!"

Talia would have continued, but her mother cut her off with a sharp glare.

Talia could not understand why her mother was so intransigent on this matter of her hair. The long braid placed her back in an age of propriety that now seemed so out-dated. She saw most other girls her age free of this burden. Talia dreamed about what it would be like to swing her head in the breeze and feel currents of air around her neck.

She realised years later that it was her mother's misguided thinking that somehow she was protecting her daughter, shielding her from temptation and worldly ways by keeping her hair long, that it would preserve her innocence in a time when things were changing too fast.

The unfairness rankled Talia, but she dared not cross her mother. She let it go for the time being and once again was swept up in the preparation for the final day of the tournament.

After the last match was done, Theo and the other visitors hung around, laughing and relaxing. Theo and his entourage had a couple of days to spare before their return journey. He had been watching Carmen and she smiled whenever their eyes met.

He decided to make his move as she approached to replace the ashtray at his table.

"So, what's interesting around here? — That is, besides the pretty barmaids?"

She smiled, "There are many interesting sights."

"For instance?"

"Well, the Strangler Fig Tree."

"Ooooh — that sounds awfully dangerous. Does it reach out and grab you if you get too close?"

He lunged at her playfully, eliciting a peal of laughter from her.

"Now, how about something more welcoming? What other wonders are hidden in these parts?"

"The Malanda Jungle Show — many people go to this."

"Jungle show — how do you mean, with pygmies and such? A giant vat of water, boil one human during the matinee show and another for the sunset crowd?"

"No, no." She giggled. "There's dancing…"

"Tell you what," he said, leaning forward, touching her arm gently, "if you're not working tomorrow, how about you come with me on my tour and make sure I don't get strangled by a tree or turned into cannibal soup, hmm? How does that sound?"

She hesitated. Her eyes flitted to the side, as though checking to see if anyone was watching. At last she replied, "Yes, I would like this."

He smiled, flashing a set of brilliant white teeth. "Splendid. I'll pick you up out front at half-past nine."

In the morning, Carmen dressed in a cotton print dress and pulled a hat out of a box and pinned it to her hair. She told Talia that, in case anyone asked, she would be out for several hours.

"Where are you going, Mama?"

"Visiting, with friends."

Carmen had hoped to slip out quietly, but just as she was exiting, the Señora suddenly appeared as though out of nowhere. Carmen stopped, like a child caught with her hand in the cookie jar.

"You have plans for today?" the Señora asked, even though she already knew.

Talia's mother's cheeks reddened, her eyes flashed angrily.

"I don't think I need to answer to you."

"Your husband is putting his life on the line for Spain, and you go chasing a tennis player — it's disgraceful."

Carmen was caught off guard. She wondered how the Señora could have learned of her date with Theo.

While the two women were exchanging words, Theo pulled up to the main entrance in his elegant Hudson Roadster. He tapped lightly on the horn. When no one appeared, he exited the car, and approached the Candelas' cottage. He knocked on the door but there was no answer.

Theo paced impatiently, finishing one cigarette and then

lighting another. At last Alwyn approached him and delivered the message that Carmen would not be able to come out to meet him, that she was ill. Theo received the news with a shrug and squashed the cigarette underfoot, as though with that same gesture he had dispensed with his disappointment.

Carmen watched through the curtain as the Hudson Roadster backed up and spun out of the parking lot.

She pulled off her bracelet and earrings and threw them down on the dresser. She removed her dress and let it drop on the floor. Without bothering to wipe off her lipstick, she lay down on the bed. Facing away, she tucked her head under her arm and sank into a deep lassitude.

Out of defiance perhaps, Carmen did not appear for her regular duties the next day or the day after. She lay in bed, barely moving.

Finally Señora Candela showed up at the small house. In a stern voice, she asked Talia to leave the room. Even before her daughter was gone, Carmen lashed out at Señora Candela.

"You got that black boy to send him away!"

"I saved you from a far worse fate."

Talia could not help but overhear. She cringed at the harsh exchange, hoping that Alwyn had no idea of her mother's attitude towards him. It was unfortunate that he had been the messenger — a role that tainted him further in Carmen's blighted eyes.

Talia felt sad that more often than not it was Alwyn who was burdened with the despicable chores: cleaning the dunny, hauling away garbage, burying dead animals, and sending away unwanted suitors. He deserved far better.

When she had her first opportunity, Carmen cornered Alwyn and asked him what Theo had said. Alwyn answered diplomatically, saying Theo was sorry. It was a lie, of course. Theo hadn't spoken a word, and Carmen probably knew that deep in her heart.

In a bitter postscript, a letter from Andre arrived. Oddly, it was not addressed to Carmen but to Señor Candela. It was read aloud in the sitting room, where the two families politely assembled.

Andre wrote about hearing church bells clanging to warn of an air raid and running to hide in an underground *refugio*. He was impressed with the calm of the children in the face of the daily bomb attacks.

"When is he coming back?" Talia asked.

"He doesn't say," Señor Candela replied. "Once he has been away a year, perhaps others will step forward to take his place."

Carmen inwardly fumed that Andre had not bothered to write to her directly. She found it humiliating to hear his letter read to her by Señor Candela, all the more so after the recent embarrassing episode.

Chapter Nineteen
A Paralysing Sickness
Mena Creek, North Queensland – 1937

As spring crept towards summer, there was no hint of the panic and terror that would soon overtake the community.

It was October when the first stories began to filter through of an illness that was striking down children in towns north of Innisfail. The poliomyelitis virus that had plagued the area in 1911 was making a devastating return.

Near Cairns, schools were closed down and public events like dances and church services were abruptly cancelled. Beaches and parks emptied for fear of encountering the insidious illness. Señor Candela deliberated over whether to close down the Castillo, but he hesitated as the busy summer period was set to begin.

They did not have to deliberate for long, because one night the household awoke to terrifying screams. Señora Candela burst into Roberto's room to find him writhing in pain. His knee was drawn up close to his neck and his other leg was pulled sideways.

Señora Candela called for her husband, who came running, rubbing his eyes at the sight of his son in spasms of agony. One by one, the Candela girls were torn from their sleep, and they spilled out of their beds to see what the commotion was about.

Señora Candela, frantic with worry that her other children might catch Roberto's illness, sent them away and forbade them to go anywhere near Roberto's room.

Señor Candela telephoned for the doctor from Innisfail. Dr. Heaslip was delayed with several other cases and did not come until the following morning. He looked over Roberto and immediately diagnosed him with polio. His prognosis was grim and the old doctor recommended Roberto be taken to the hospital right away.

The Candelas rushed Roberto to the Innisfail hospital, but

once there his condition began to deteriorate. There was no cure available, and one could only hope and pray that the disease would not spread further in his body. The doctors even talked about the possibility that the polio could reach Roberto's lungs. If that should happen, they explained, he would have to be hooked up to an iron lung to help him breathe.

In the meantime, the physicians recommended cutting off Roberto's tendons from below the knee to keep the polio from spreading. This was a shocking proposal, but the Candelas were desperate to save Roberto, and after much handwringing decided to follow this medical advice, however awful it seemed.

Señora Candela looked at the bleak polio ward with row upon row of children constrained by metal braces and breathing contraptions that looked like personal prisons. She could not bear to think of Robbie encased in one of these.

She collapsed in tears and Señor Candela led her outside, where Alwyn was waiting anxiously. When Alwyn heard of the decision to sever Roberto's tendons, he became very upset. Sensing the Señora was already regretting the decision, he pressed her to change her mind.

"Ma'am, it's best not to cut anything. Once you cut it, it can't grow back. It's like a tree trunk."

Señora Candela appeared to be wavering.

"You cut, Robbie will never improve. But if you leave the limbs, maybe he'll walk again."

"Ramon, suppose what he is saying is true."

Señor Candela glared at Alwyn. "Stop confusing the situation. Besides, this is not your affair!"

Alwyn shook his head. "Don't cut the legs."

Señor Candela sighed. He spoke to his wife in Spanish, thinking Alwyn could not understand. "These are trained doctors, Beatrice. They know what they are doing."

In spite of a dressing down by Señor Candela, Alwyn persisted. He pleaded with Señora Candela, rightly assuming she would be easier to convince. "Don't let them do it just now. Best to wait. What's the harm in waiting?"

Señora Candela knew in her heart that what he said made sense. She grabbed Alwyn's arm and pulled him with her into the hospital. Ramon followed, protesting half-heartedly. They hurried to the ward, past nurses and orderlies until they found Roberto. Alwyn scooped him up and carried him out over Señor Candela's protests. Even though he did not agree, Señor Candela did not return Roberto to the ward.

But even after he came home, Roberto was still in great pain. And Alwyn knew the Candelas were at risk of taking Roberto back to the Innisfail hospital once again. Alwyn stayed by Robbie's side, trying to soothe the spasms by kneading the muscles.

It was only by chance that the Candelas heard on the radio of an alternative treatment by Sister Kenny, a nurse who had received some attention for her work with polio victims. She had a small clinic in Townsville to which the Candelas sped Robbie the instant they found the address.

Because Kenny's clinic was filled to bursting with patients, Roberto could not be admitted but Sister Kenny tutored Alwyn and the Candelas on how to care for Roberto. She had them take woollen strips soaked in boiling water and apply these to Roberto's limbs. Slowly this relaxed the tense muscles and helped straighten them.

For the first time in weeks, Roberto was no longer in unbearable pain. He no longer moaned or cried out when he was moved or his legs were straightened. It seemed the worst of the illness was over and he had turned a corner. Still there was much work to be done to strengthen his muscles and regain use of his limbs.

When the Candelas returned with Roberto, Sister Kenny instructed them on the next phase of treatment. In the days that followed, Alwyn was directed to help Roberto bend his knees and ankles. He massaged the limbs and tapped the muscles, as though gently awakening them. By the end of the summer Roberto had made good progress and was able to stand while leaning on Alwyn's arm.

When he returned to see Dr. Heaslip in Innisfail, the old doctor was impressed with Roberto's progress, although he half-wondered if the boy had not had polio at all, or had been afflicted with a less virulent form of it. When told of the treatment Roberto received in Townsville, Heaslip scoffed, refusing to give any credit to Sister Kenny's method or Alwyn's dedicated application of her therapies.

To help stabilize his gait, Roberto was fitted with a metal brace that he hated to wear. He often left the heavy contraption off so he could romp freely with Alwyn. The older boy would place Roberto on his back for a run through the Castillo grounds or for a swim beneath the falls.

One day, Señor Candela stood watching with his wife as Alwyn cavorted with Roberto in the garden below. A whistle pierced the air and Alwyn looked up to see the Señor gesture to him, beckoning him up to the terrace. Alwyn raced up the stone steps, wondering what was the matter. Had he been too rough with Roberto just then because he let him fall into a shrub?

By the time Alwyn reached the top of the staircase he was out of breath, not so much from the climb but from a strong feeling of apprehension.

The Candelas both wore serious expressions.

"Is everything alright?" Alwyn asked meekly.

"Yes," reassured Señor Candela, a smile on his face.

Señora Candela stepped forward and pressed her hands on Alwyn's cheeks. "Once again you saved Roberto. — How can we ever thank you?"

Señor Candela chuckled. "This time it has to be more than a new shirt."

The Candelas had discussed the matter a few days earlier, and the Señora had been surprised that her husband wanted to give

Alwyn a car.

"Are you sure?"

"It's the old Studebaker that's been sitting under a tree for years."

"Does it even run?"

"No, it doesn't run. It doesn't even crawl, but it can be fixed up."

"Where will he get the money for petrol?"

"From us, of course. And in an emergency, we will have someone else who can drive."

"I suppose," murmured the Señora. She was confident her husband knew what was best, but still she felt nervous for Alwyn's sake. Alwyn was taken aback that he should be offered a gift for helping Roberto, when all that had been on his mind was to keep him out of danger and keep the little fellow from suffering more.

Alwyn was so overwhelmed with gratitude to receive a car, of all things, that he did not seem to notice that the old rattletrap's canvas roof was concave from having carried bales of hay at one time, or that the upholstery was inhabited by mice.

For Alwyn, a car meant a certain freedom and status that he had not thought possible before. But getting a licence would be another thing.

Señor Candela sorted out the problem of missing paperwork by registering Alwyn under the name of a worker who had gone back to Spain and whom he knew would not be returning. For the purposes of getting a driver's licence, Alwyn became Pablo Del Rio. Alwyn promised not to say anything of this to Señora Candela or any of the others.

With great enthusiasm and only the most rudimentary understanding of mechanics, Alwyn set about fixing up the ancient automobile, patching up the holes with putty, replacing the gear shaft and tinkering with the engine until the rickety old clunker coughed to life.

Talia and Robbie joined Alwyn on the car's first excursion

down the road to Silkwood. They laughed each time the vehicle made rumbling noises or went ominously silent, threatening to stall. Talia squinted as dust filtered up from a hole in the floor and breezes from the broken side window blew against her face.

They clapped and cheered as the car creaked into the little town, puttering to a stop right next to the creamery. They bought ice cream and leaned against the Studebaker, relishing their successful journey. How odd they must have looked — a cripple, a girl with a dirt-smudged face and tangled hair, and a half-caste — giggling and licking dripping cones at the side of a patched-up old rust bucket.

They did not seem to notice or care that pedestrians crossed the road to avoid possible contamination from whatever had afflicted Robbie. Nor did the trio put any thought or worry into how they would get back to the castle if the car didn't start. For that instant, they were blissfully happy, feeling that all was well with the world.

The first few months of 1938 were like that — generous days of discovery, deepening friendship, and exploration. Alwyn taught Robbie how to hunt with a pellet gun and to fish so that frustration over his lame leg did not dominate his thoughts. He came to feel a sense of accomplishment under Alwyn's tutelage.

Alwyn taught Talia and Roberto how to survive in the bush, pointing out which foods were safe to eat and the medicines readily available in the plants and shrubs.

There were other escapades and outings in the old car. A boxing match in Tully where Rampagin' Ronnie was pitted against Lord Steel. The betting was fast and furious for the aboriginal pugilist, Ronnie, who easily won the bout. Afterwards they hung around and chatted with the boxer. Alwyn politely enquired about the fighter's career, as though perhaps seeing some hope for his own future in that man's path.

They made a day trip to Mission Beach and watched as Chinese kites, crackling paper dragons and tigers, swept above them in zany dips and swoops. They ate steamed dumplings, stir-fried noodles, and lychees from a food cart and drove away later drowsy from the sun and sticky treats.

It was on their trip home from that beach excursion that they had a dangerous accident.

Moving off the main road, they took a route that meandered through denser vegetation. Out of the corner of his eye Alwyn saw the animal leap out of the brush. And then, there was an awful thud against the front grille, and a further shock, as a fully-grown wallaby slid over the hood and bounced off the windshield.

Alwyn pulled over and jumped out of the car, attending to the animal, which was clearly in the throes of death.

Talia gasped as Alwyn removed a knife from his pocket, and without much thought or deliberation, slit the throat of the wounded animal on the spot.

"Heavens! Why did you do that?" cried Talia.

"Can't you see, it was suffering," explained Robbie.

"We could have saved it," Talia wept.

"No, Talia, its neck was broken."

Alwyn guided Talia's hand to the animal's neck so she could feel it for herself. She gasped. While leaning over the animal she noticed movement in the dead wallaby's pouch. Roberto had seen it too and lifted the opening. Out popped a small foot. It belonged to a baby wallaby.

Talia lunged towards it, covering it up to shield it from Alwyn.

"Let me see," he asked.

"No! You'll kill it!"

"I won't. I promise. Now, come on, let's have a look."

Talia finally let him approach the pouch, where he retrieved the young wallaby. Other than being a little startled, the animal appeared unharmed. His mother's body had shielded him in the accident.

They named the little fellow Macadam for the simple fact that it was alongside the bitumen that he was found. Little Mack was bottle-fed until he was weaned. He became part of the Castillo tourist attraction, along with the cart-pulling goats and the ever-hungry turtles. Mack adopted Alwyn as his master and leader. He followed Alwyn about the park like a loyal puppy dog, unaware that Alwyn had been responsible for his mother's death.

* * *

While 1938 began with the promise of expansion and enrichment, enjoyment of friends and new horizons, it ended on a far different note, as the situation deteriorated in Spain.

In early 1939, reports from the battlefront there brought little encouragement for the Republicans. And, finally, a telegram came from the International Brigade with the news that Andre had died in the fall of Barcelona in January 1939. His body was lost in the rubble from the bomb blasts.

A memorial service was held for him and the community mourned not just his death but also the loss of the Republican side in the civil war. However unjust it seemed, Franco was recognised as the new leader of Spain.

Talia had mixed feelings over the news of her father's death. He had been absent for such long periods of time, and she could not help wondering if each time he left her and her mother, he had been somewhat eager to do so. Still, she felt the loss of another human being to whom she had been connected. As an orphan of sorts, she knew she would miss the family life they had shared. It was a family that had rarely been intact, but now would never be so again.

Chapter Twenty
The Quiet Beginning
Mena Creek, North Queensland – 1939

Thousands of miles away, events were leading Europe towards war. At Mena Creek, they listened to reports on the wireless of Hitler's invasion of Poland, but beneath the palm breezes in North Queensland, the blitzkrieg in Poland was only a distant news story. The outbreak of the Second World War barely touched them at first.

Other than being an interesting subject of discussion for those with connections to Europe, the war had no immediate impact on Queenslanders and life went on as normal. Perhaps even better than normal, as there was a small improvement in the standard of living — wool sales and coal exports surged, and the lives of Australians finally became easier after years of depression.

Efforts to support the war effort were made in earnest, but not with a great sense of urgency. In the evening, the Candela girls and Talia would gather round the crystal set to listen to the radio serials, *When a Girl Marries*, *Martin's Corner*, *First Light Fraser* and *Hagen's Circus*, while doing their best to knit wool socks, gloves and caps.

Gloria, the youngest, was a disaster at knitting but would never admit it. Rather than pulling out her stitches, she continued confident with her result. The other girls laughed until tears ran down their cheeks as they imagined the look of surprise when some poor soldier received a glove with only four fingers or a pair of misshapen socks.

But these moments of comic relief became rarer as the war drew on. The local folk reacted with disbelief as the first casualties were posted in the *Innisfail Times* daily. It was unbelievable that the son of the local postmaster and the two eldest boys of their neighbours, the Farleys, were gone. When the young men had left home to join up, they had seemed so invincible, viewing their stint overseas more as an adventure than a dangerous war.

The mood became more sombre still as the lists of casualties — killed in action, died of wounds, and missing or wounded — were posted every few days.

Talia thought about these men as she pulled the strands of yarn from the ball of wool, dipping her needle in and out, creating row after row. With each stitch, she wished the soldiers well, and with each purl and hook, she sent a mute prayer. *Keep well. Come home safe. Keep well.*

She thought of her father from time to time, and wondered if he had suffered. Or was his death a sudden event, rounding a corner in a dark street in the middle of the night and falling to the cobblestones before he knew what had happened?

The reasons for war were unclear to her. She only knew that it left large gaps in their lives.

In December 1941, a dramatic event would turn their existence upside down and bring the war much closer to their doorstep. On the 7th of that month, the devastating bombing of Pearl Harbor in an unexpected attack by the Japanese changed the course of the war in the Pacific. Australians were caught off guard, feeling exposed given their proximity to Japan, and even more so as many Australian soldiers were away in North Africa.

But nothing could compare to the panic that set in when news came several months later that the Japanese had bombed Darwin on their northern coast. That tragedy left several hundred citizens dead. While Darwin was hundreds of miles away, it was far too close for comfort. Living so near the coast, the Innisfail area residents felt very vulnerable. They realised that the Japanese could be at their doorsteps at any moment. Nerves were on edge, and the slightest rumbling from a truck passing on the road or the faraway drone of an airplane brought about near panic until they were reassured that there was no immediate danger.

Those who could afford it placed their children in boarding

schools in Brisbane or Sydney. Others debated about whether to send their children to the safety of communities inland from the Northern coast, although some worried that the rail lines would also be targeted for bombing.

The older Candela girls had long finished high school, but the war delayed plans for their further education. The Candelas, like many of their neighbours, immediately began construction of a bomb shelter on their property. While that was underway, Señora Candela also had her husband create a secret safe beneath the rock garden in view of their window. There she stashed her silverware, gold coins, and antique family jewelry.

These small measures provided some sense of security but it was nothing in comparison to the arrival of 40,000 American troops in Queensland. The presence of a force of this magnitude greatly boosted the spirits of the locals. They could breathe a sigh of relief, knowing that they were not alone to withstand a possible Japanese invasion.

For Castillo Candela, the arrival of the soldiers not only gave a sense of security but also delivered a huge boost to the castle's income. Thousands of servicemen, when not on duty, required a place for 'rest and relaxation'. Endowed with generous pay, the Yanks could easily afford food, drinks and entertainment to get away from the stress and rigours of war. At Castillo Candela they were welcome customers.

Word got around that there was no lovelier, more magical place than Castillo Candela, with its cascading waters, peaceful garden, clear natural swimming pool, delicious Spanish food, and pretty dark-eyed girls.

Except for the youngest, Gloria, the Candela girls and Talia were in their late teens or early twenties. Aracely was very attractive and outgoing, while Ofelia, Lucia, and Maria-Eugenia were more reserved, but nonetheless very beautiful as well. Despite their generally good nature and friendly manners, Señor Candela kept careful watch on the visiting soldiers as they hovered near his daughters. Beer and Bundaberg rum could change behaviour dramatically. It was not served at the Castillo during the day, but sometimes soldiers arrived with their own supplies.

The same umbrella of protectiveness extended to Talia as well. She was now seventeen and had blossomed into a stunning beauty. Her good looks drew many flirtatious remarks and whistles from the soldiers. Carmen, however, strictly forbade her daughter from accepting any invitations from the American servicemen.

"Here today, gone tomorrow. Leave you in trouble," she warned.

"Maybe I'd like to go away to America," Talia replied.

But that was really just an empty threat. While Talia did daydream of the glamorous life led by the film stars in California, she had no desire to move there. She loved living and working at Castillo Candela. Even though she was really just a housekeeper, she was at home there, and felt part of the Candela family, albeit a lesser member. Most of all, she knew she would miss Alwyn if she were to go away.

A quiet romance had developed between them, growing almost imperceptibly, but each day becoming stronger. In the way in which a single raindrop trickles down through the thick jungle canopy to the smallest plants below, Talia relished every little contact with Alwyn. Like the low growing fern, she demanded very little and conserved the exhilaration of every moment they spent together.

Talia admired Alwyn, the way he tolerated with infinite patience the commonplace rudeness that his skin colour seemed to generate. She was not sure when she first realised that she loved him or when she knew she could not live without him. They had been in close proximity for so long, seeing each other daily, working side by side.

He could understand her simply with a glance. It was reassuring to know there was someone else on earth who knew her so well. Her moods. Her thoughts.

But hanging over them was the unacknowledged realisation that theirs was an impossible love. The inevitable conclusion loomed ahead somewhere. They lingered at the fork in the road, knowing that choosing one route or the other might precipitate the end of their time together. But events conspired to push them forward sooner than they might have otherwise wanted.

Early one quiet morning, Talia gathered up her paints and paper and strode down a path deep into the garden. She unfolded a small camp stool and set out her materials. She decided to paint a cluster of grey-green staghorn ferns nestled in the crook of a tree and was fully absorbed in recreating it on paper when she felt a disturbance in the air around her. Her hairs stood on end and goose bumps formed on her skin.

A man appeared before her, flashing a smile, his look leering and slightly menacing. His eyes were veined and glassy, his skin reddened from too much sun and alcohol.

"You're the ice cream girl, aren't ya?"

Talia remembered the soldier from the day before.

She felt cold in the pit of her stomach. Her mind scrambled. Was she within hearing range of the castle, she wondered. Probably not. Moreover, it was still early and she had left while the others were not yet awake.

She guessed the soldier had spent the night somewhere on the grounds. Perhaps he had broken into the shed and had fallen asleep there. His uniform was stained and dishevelled.

"What's that?" he asked, as he came closer, feigning interest in her painting, leaning over her. He reeked of beer and sweat.

She froze as his hand brushed against her leg. The folding chair wobbled and then collapsed from underneath her. She teetered backwards, landing hard on the ground. He pounced on her and as he pressed down on her she felt the hard edges of tree roots jab her back.

Blind panic seized her. Bewildered and angry at having been caught unawares, she clawed and flailed at him but he was like an enemy tank, simply rolling over her, crushing her.

And then suddenly it stopped. She could feel the weight lift off her.

Through her coursing tears and matted hair, she saw Alwyn. He had a look she had never seen before, his eyes hard and glinting. In his hand he brandished a wide tarnished machete which he pressed against the soldier's neck. The man staggered up carefully, wary of Alwyn. Alwyn thrust him to the side and in a terse voice ordered him to go. The man crawled up and fled.

Talia threw herself against Alwyn, grasping him in relief. She blubbered, letting the fear flow out of her in gulping tears. He comforted her, holding her until she was spent. And still he held onto her, and she was lulled, finding not just safety but love. In being thrown together, they learned by accident the true extent of their attraction for each other. Once in each other's arms they discovered how hard it was to let go.

Chapter Twenty-One
Forbidden
Mena Creek, North Queensland – 1941

It was as though they had inadvertently found their way inside a curling seashell, travelling first to one chamber and then to the next, finding each one more delicious and warm than the previous one, until they were in the smallest and last hollow, a tiny corner where they could escape from the outside world.

There they wanted to remain, but the best they could do was to try to return whenever they had the chance.

Talia stole away to help Alwyn in the projection room and they held hands in the dark. She let him kiss her hair, not minding when the plait came undone. As the celluloid reflections danced off their skin, they pressed their faces together, and finally their lips found each other.

And it became even harder to be apart.

They found ways to meet again and again. In a sudden rainstorm, he sheltered her under a giant banana palm. While the rain battered the wide ribboned leaves, they leaned close together, laughing at getting drenched. By the fence while feeding the goats, they let their fingers interlace while clasping the same bundle of hay; or by the change rooms, they dipped into the shadowy alcove for the briefest of kisses. He led her to the alley of Kauri pines and she found a tree where he had carved their initials.

It was a wonderful but very brief idyll. Their happiness must have made them stand out, for increasingly they drew sharp looks and suspicious stares.

But they continued exaltedly, like a dry leaf tossed in the wind, unstoppable, feeling a false sense of freedom, until the wind suddenly stopped, releasing them. The rake caught the leaf in its prongs. And so it was with them.

Señor Candela called Talia in for a meeting with her mother

and Señora Candela.

"Stay away from him," he ordered.

"But I love him and I want to marry him."

"That's nonsense."

"Why?"

"*¡No digas tonterías, Talia!*"

"Don't you all love him? Didn't he save Roberto's life? Twice!"

Their objections came out all at once.

"He's black."

"He's uneducated. He has no future."

"You can never have a life with him."

"I can't have a life without him."

"Has he asked you to marry him?"

"No, but I know he would."

"He cannot. It's not allowed."

"Besides, how would you live? Where would you live?"

Talia was blindsided. Shocked by their cold-heartedness.

"Couldn't we live here?"

"No, Talia. *No es posible.*"

Señor Candela drew himself up. He spoke sharply and with finality.

"Do not bring shame on this family, or your mother, a poor widow. And don't make me send him away. You would be responsible for making him homeless if you forced me to take that step."

He turned abruptly and left the room. No one else spoke after that.

Later on, when Talia was alone with her mother, the probing started up again, taking an ugly turn.

"Has he taken liberties with you?"

When she did not answer, Carmen persisted.

"Talia, tell me."

Talia must have given away something by her look, for

Carmen grabbed Talia by her hair and wrenched it. "It would be the most disgusting thing, his baby."

Talia's eyes welled with tears. Not from the pain of having her hair pulled but at the way her beautiful world had been sullied. The people she once looked up to and held in high esteem became distorted and ugly. How they could see any child as disgusting, least of all Alwyn's — Talia could not understand.

Talia and Alwyn were ordered to stay apart, and Alwyn was abiding by the warning.

It was a terrible blow. The loneliness was crushing. Unsure of how much the Candela sisters knew, or suspected, Talia revealed nothing to them, and was more guarded in their presence. The Castillo had become a miserable, barren place, almost overnight.

Talia was told to remain on the upper level of the castle grounds. She had access to the laundry shed, the vegetable garden and the back half of the Candela home, but that was all. At first she dared not wander outside her permitted area. Besides, she felt that she could not trust herself, worrying that if she saw Alwyn she would just throw herself into his arms.

Convinced that he could be sent away, she was careful over the next few days not to seek him out for fear of endangering his status or threatening his place on the staff by being careless. She had heard of grown men and women being removed by their employers to return to missions that were just like prisons. It would be far worse for both of them if he were sent back to Palm Island.

Yet she missed him terribly.

Many times she sensed he was nearby and stopped what she was doing. She found herself studying the foliage, on the off-chance he might be watching, hoping to catch a glimpse of him.

One day, while running wet laundry through the mangle, Talia thought she heard his signature bird call. She stopped and listened. Was Alwyn trying to communicate with her in his own language, secretly greeting her?

On another occasion, as she was scrubbing the tiles on the patio, she heard a rustle and she looked up suddenly towards the grille. She thought she could see him in the shadow of the tangled vegetation, but she was not sure. She hurried to the wrought-iron screen and pressed herself against it, but she could not see him. It was as though he had vanished or her mind was playing tricks.

She wondered what he was thinking about at that moment. Did he regret falling in love with her? Did he miss her as much as she missed him? Or maybe he was ready to let her go, realizing it had all been a mistake.

She ached to know how he felt.

Roberto had taken over Talia's responsibilities as helper during the nightly movie screenings, as she was no longer allowed near the projection room.

But she did not have the luxury of crying herself to sleep or moping for hours on end. They were all kept busy running the Castillo or doing war-relief work of various kinds.

One evening, she and Maria Eugenia were bundling up care packages for soldiers and writing cheery letters to servicemen who had no family. Writing to the lonely soldiers, Talia was overcome with sadness and felt she was on the verge of breaking down. She could not bear it any longer, and rather than write to her soldier pen pal, she decided to write to Alwyn instead. She pleaded with him to make a decision, to take a chance or let her go. It was a risk, but she felt compelled to push forward.

She became upset as she wrote the letter and it must have shown. Maria Eugenia looked curiously at Talia and asked "Who are you writing? You're not falling for a pen pal, are you?"

Rather than fall apart in front of Maria Eugenia, Talia got up suddenly and went to the window on the pretext of looking at the sky.

"Did you hear that?" Talia asked, feigning alarm.

Maria Eugenia cocked her head and listened.

"It's probably just thunder."

Talia composed herself before returning to the desk to finish the secret letter. With great apprehension Talia slipped the letter to Roberto and asked him to hand it to Alwyn, begging his discretion.

Roberto just shook his head. "He keeps asking me what you're up to."

"He does?" Talia's heart leapt.

"He's a mess."

"Really?" It was selfish but it made her a little happy to know that her absence could affect Alwyn this way.

"Last night during the screening, he forgot to put on the second reel."

Talia felt a twinge of guilt. "Oh, that's terrible."

Roberto sighed. "Alright, I'll give him the letter. But it's going to come to no good for either of you." He was solemn as he tucked the blue envelope in his pocket.

"Thank you all the same. If you were my brother — well, you are like a brother to me."

"A brother would steer you clear of this trouble, Talia."

That night, Talia lay awake listening to the wind shake the dry palm leaves and scatter loose objects. But the strong currents of air did little to relieve the oppressive humidity.

In her letter, Talia had asked Alwyn to meet her by the waterfall at midnight. By then, the moviegoers would be long gone and the park grounds would be quiet.

She listened to her mother's snoring, and reassured by the regular pattern of it, knew that Carmen was fast asleep. Talia slid out of bed and tiptoed out of the room.

Outside, the ground was moist with dew, and Talia's feet slipped as she hurried along. When she arrived at the balustrade, moonlight was trickling through the leafy canopy. She held her breath searching the empty patio, and listening to the night sounds, waiting to hear his signal.

And then it came. Clear and full. It was her beacon as she crept towards the water and let herself drop off the edge into the pool. Darkness shrouded her as she slipped towards the rocky outcropping under the falls.

No matter the season, the time of day, the water coursed steadily over the cliff and made its way down, heedless of the events and turmoil in the world around it. And so it was tonight.

Talia thought she could see someone through the curtain of water. She pressed on, clambering over the rocks. The basalt outcroppings scraped her palms and legs, but no matter. She climbed up hurriedly, gasping a little as a hand shot out through the cascade, gripping her and helping her up. Alwyn smiled as he pulled her towards him.

He held her close and they stayed that way for some time.

"It seems like forever since I last saw you."

"I try to get my eyes on you all the time."

"How?"

He laughed.

A crack of thunder reverberated. Lightning snaked across the sky, breaking into pieces across the columns of water. Talia snuggled closer to Alwyn.

"What are we going to do?" she asked.

He stroked her face, and looked into her eyes.

"I'm going to join up, Talia".

"What! Alwyn, no!"

"It's the only way we can get married."

"Please, Alwyn, not for me."

"I've thought about it. It's what I'm gonna do."

"I'd rather have just a little time with you than none at all."

"I'm not gonna let 'em have a crack at me."

The cascading water was nothing compared to the tears Talia shed as she begged Alwyn to change his mind.

"You're just like my father."

"Not so, Talia — I'm gonna come back."

He refused to let go of the notion that military service would be the only route to his becoming more acceptable to the community and ultimately worthy as Talia's future husband.

When Talia crept out of the water it was pouring hard. She crawled into bed shivering. She felt a stone-cold fear for Alwyn. It tormented her that it was for her sake that he was going off to war, a war that was growing bloodier as the weeks wore on.

In the morning, Talia felt weak and feverish. She could not get out of bed. Later, when her mother told her that Alwyn had gone missing, Talia's heart sank. He had gone ahead with his plan!

Her only hope was that he might be rejected by the army, but when Alwyn had not returned by the next day, it became clear that they must have accepted him.

Señor Candela sought Talia out, asking her what she knew of Alwyn's disappearance.

"I don't know," she lied.

Señor Candela sighed. "I think you do."

Talia remained silent.

"I could call the police. We're in a state of siege, Talia. The enemy is at our door. They won't take chances with anyone."

"He's gone to enlist."

Señor Candela nodded, a grim look on his face.

"What are you going to do?" she asked.

"I will have him brought back."

"Oh, thank God!"

Although she felt like a traitor, she was relieved by the hope that Señor Candela could possibly save Alwyn from the risk of death on the battlefront.

Chapter Twenty-Two
A Soldier Like No Other
Mena Creek, North Queensland – 1942

But Señor Candela could get nowhere with the staff at the Innisfail Recruitment Office. They had no record of anyone named Alwyn Cloncurry signing on. Nor did the officer recognise Alwyn from any of the photos Candela showed him.

Candela had long forgotten that he himself had given Alwyn an alternate identity — that of Pablo Del Rio. With this in hand, Alwyn made his way out of the district and headed south to sign on. He impressed the enlistment officer in Ingham with his knowledge of Spanish. So, in spite of *Pablo's* skimpy documentation — Alwyn claimed that all he had was a driver's licence because the rest had been lost in a flood — he was able to convince the officer that he was the son of wealthy cigar makers and badly wanted to fight against the Japs for what they had done to his family's estate in Manila. And yes, he was related to the film star Dolores Del Rio. In fact, the enlistment officer said he could see the family resemblance. The gift of a fine cigar did not hurt either. Warrant Officer Williams tucked it into his pocket and helped Pablo with his registration.

And so, within a matter of days, 'Pablo' was sent to Townsville for basic training.

What Williams did not know was that Pablo was not from a '*rio*' but a creek, and the closest he ever got to Spanish cigars was picking the butts out of ashtrays and reshaping them into handmade cigarillos. He had learned all of his Spanish listening to his employers, and with his gift of mimicry had mastered the accent very well.

But it didn't really matter that much, since fresh blood was badly needed as the war effort intensified. So the missing documentation was overlooked because a strapping young man like Pablo would be a welcome addition to the Blueys and the Curleys.

Basic training was a pleasant surprise for Alwyn. He found his fellow soldiers a friendly bunch, eager to 'do their bit'. They were focussed on strengthening their combat skills and getting to know their comrades in arms. This was all fine and well for Alwyn as he was happy to widen his horizons and make new friends.

There was a cloud however on this wonderful new horizon and that was Joshua Winter, son of an Atherton dairy farmer, who had been puzzling over where he had run into Alwyn before.

His scrutinizing gazes and frequently-repeated: "swear-to-God-I-know-you-from-somewhere," filled Alwyn with dread. Every time Joshua crossed paths with Alwyn, he made a guess as to where they might have met. One day he volleyed yet another theory at Alwyn.

"The Gordonvale Show?" suggested Joshua hopefully. "I'm thinking it's something to do with cows."

Alwyn suppressed a rising panic. He shook his head as calmly as he could. "Cows?"

It did indeed have to do with cows. Alwyn had helped Joshua unload milk cans many a time at Castillo Candela and they had chitchatted about the weather and other mundane things.

"Maybe we met at Willow Vale," Alwyn proposed, trying to throw Joshua off the scent. Though he had never set foot there himself, Alwyn knew Willow Vale was such a tiny fly speck on the map that it was highly unlikely that anyone at all was from there.

"Never even heard of the place," replied Joshua.

"It's south of Brisbane," offered Alwyn with forced casualness. His mouth was dry and his heart was beating fast.

Joshua frowned. "Nah, that can't be it."

Alwyn shrugged and mumbled, "Must have a double out there somewhere."

As Alwyn began to walk away, Joshua called out.

"It'll come to me," he said. "I never forget a face."

A chill ran through Alwyn. He felt as though he were already dodging bullets even before he had entered the battlefield, so persistent was Joshua's desire to solve the mystery of how he knew Alwyn. Should Joshua or anyone else find out his fraudulent identity, Alwyn feared he could be court-martialled and imprisoned, and worst of all — separated from Talia forever.

But perhaps he was losing her already through his neglect. During all the weeks of basic training, Alwyn had not yet written to her once. Meanwhile his fellow soldiers wrote to their loved ones frequently — from the back of a truck, or leaning against a sack of flour, or with one elbow propped up to their chins at the table in the mess hall — they had no problem filling reams of pages with words. Oh, how Alwyn envied them.

The night before they were to ship out, Alwyn settled down on his cot and finally determined to write his sweetheart a letter. He wanted to share his success in the first stage of being a soldier, his pride at wearing the khaki uniform and the 'digger' hat. He also wanted to reassure Talia that all was going as planned, but more importantly he wanted to put down on paper his commitment to her and his hope that they would marry once the war was over.

A fresh piece of paper stared up at him. He uncapped his fountain pen and attempted to scratch out a few words. *Alwyn loves Talia.* But then it occurred to him that using his real name would betray the fact that he was impersonating someone else so he scratched it out. Then, if he signed off as Del Rio, would Talia wonder who this strange fellow was. This worry, in combination with the necessity of maintaining his secret identity, and his poor writing skills, overwhelmed him. He dawdled over the letter, making no progress.

"Something for the mail bag, mate?"

Alwyn looked up to see a redheaded soldier at the foot of his bed, smirking. Craig 'Rusty' Doran was a lanky fellow, with a swashbuckling attitude. He was confident that he could tame the

Japs like he did the unruly horses on his family's sheep station. He had it in his head he would be home in time for the next shearing.

"Nah, not finished yet," Alwyn murmured.

To Alwyn's chagrin, Rusty lingered, as though prepared to wait until Alwyn had actually written his letter.

"Better send your girl something short and sweet. We're shipping out tomorrow."

"Problem is I just got too much to write."

"You do what I do. I write the same thing to all three: Stay true. You're the only one for me."

Rusty snickered at his own joke. Alwyn forced a smile, playing along. Alwyn was tempted to confide in this fellow and ask for his help but thought better of it. At last Rusty shrugged and moved on.

Alwyn pressed the flat of his hand across the paper as though by smoothing it he could make words somehow appear. He began to write 'Stay true' but hesitated at the word 'true'. It did not look right. Even if he were sure of how to spell it, it still seemed a trite thing to say to Talia. She would be true to him, this he knew in his heart, though he acknowledged he might not deserve it.

He tried again with 'you're the only one for me' but he became frustrated and crumpled up the paper, stuffing it into his jacket. He cursed himself for never having learned to write properly and vowed to master the skill as soon as he got back.

He had gone to school, but it was only for a brief couple of years, and in a classroom crowded with more than sixty rowdy youngsters. Various teachers came and went, each overwhelmed with the unruliness of the children and the heavy workload.

In spite of his lack of education, Alwyn had always managed by memorizing patterns and signs, and just plain figuring things out, but expressing his feelings for Talia and making amends for his hasty departure required something far beyond his present letter-writing abilities.

Nevertheless he promised himself he would try taking up the

pen at the next opportunity, but time and again he postponed the task until it was too late. Later he realized with painful regret that had he sent anything at all — a drawing, a short note, a pressed flower — it would have been better than nothing.

Even before they had shipped out to the Netherlands East Indies, their mission in the Pacific seemed to face incredible odds against the might of the Japanese. While Pearl Harbor was being attacked, the Japanese were also landing on the Malay Peninsula and at Luzon, in the Philippines. A week later, the Japanese attacked Hong Kong and by month's end, it was theirs too. Kuching in Borneo also fell to Japanese control. Most worrisome were the Japanese troops established on the Island of New Guinea and in the Solomon Islands, so close to Australia's northern coast.

The treacherousness of the air and waters plagued the convoy of ships that moved towards the battlefront in the Pacific. The Japanese ships and aircraft carriers prowled the same waters, and sent bombers that too often found their mark, throwing hundreds of soldiers and civilian evacuees to their deaths by drowning.

It was tense as the troop ship carrying Alwyn and his fellow soldiers channelled through the Sunda Strait in view of the low-lying shoreline of Java from where enemies could easily shoot at them, and so they were greatly relieved when they finally disembarked at Batavia.

The locals gave the troops an enthusiastic welcome, shouting greetings the men could not understand, although the exuberance and warmth was perfectly clear.

After settling in, Alwyn and his platoon were detailed to maintain landing strips for the Allied air forces as they made sorties against the Japanese. The hangars and airfields were prime targets for the enemy so the men worked on high alert at all times, taking cover at the droning sound of incoming aircraft or the peal of air raid warnings.

There was one particularly enjoyable interlude spent in the construction of a series of decoy aircraft in clearings a few miles from camp. Using paper and bamboo they created facsimiles of planes with the hope that they resembled Spitfires and Hurricanes enough to entice the enemy bombers to waste their payload on the wrong targets.

After their first pay parade, the men took off to explore nearby Batavia. It was a vibrant town with many Chinese and Indian-owned businesses. Men carried heavy baskets of food on poles balanced over their shoulders. Rickshaw taxis clopped through the streets busy with pedestrians. Here and there was evidence of Dutch colonial rule with its European style administrative buildings, while the influence of Chinese architecture was clear in many temples and elegant homes.

Alwyn, Rusty and Joshua stopped to buy chicken satay, banana fritters, and *nasi goreng* from a street vendor. The soldiers brought their meal to the riverbank and settled down for a picnic. Nearby, a group of women in colourful sarongs beat laundry against the rocks along the water's edge.

In between bites, the men teased Joshua whom they had just nicknamed 'Sloshy'. Joshua was clumsy by nature, but a recent gift of gin from some departing Dutch evacuees had augmented his reputation for awkwardness.

Rusty pointed to a splash of red sauce spilled on Sloshy's khaki shirt. "Crikey, have ya been shot?"

Alwyn laughed. "Are you alright, Sloshy? Should we call a medic?"

"Aaagh, bloody hell," grumbled Sloshy, trying to scrape away the stain.

"Give those ladies your shirt, mate, and they'll have it clean before roll call," said Rusty, gesturing to the women by the stream.

"Bugger off. Nobody's getting the shirt off my back," Sloshy grumbled, stretching out his long legs and leaning back for a nap.

As he rubbed his face, he complained under his breath about the noisy slapping of wet clothes on the flat rocks and the laughter of the women. To Alwyn, however, the sounds were soothing. It was a touch of simple domesticity that made it hard to believe that war was raging all around them.

A woman crossed to join the other ladies by the bank and Alwyn suddenly turned to stare at her. He felt his heart leap into his throat — the way the woman moved, the familiar shape of her head, her long black hair drawn into a braid. — It was not possible, he thought, yet he bounded up and ran towards her.

"Where's he heading?" Rusty asked.

Sloshy opened his eyes into narrow slits, peering with curiosity at Alwyn. Alwyn was upon the woman almost instantly and clamped a hand on her shoulder, not in an aggressive way, but rather with a desperate urgency.

"Talia," he whispered hoarsely.

The woman wheeled about and screamed. She retreated a few steps and nearly tripped. Alwyn's devastated expression must have frightened her even more for she backed away quickly, all the while hissing words at him. Alwyn dropped his head and sank to his knees. His army mates were baffled.

"What did she say to him?" Sloshy asked.

"I dunno," Rusty answered. "Shove off or something less polite, I figure."

"Come on, Pablo." Rusty said, pulling his friend up.

The mates were embarrassed by Alwyn's sudden strange behaviour, but they were more concerned that the fiercely chattering and scolding washerwomen would bring about some native style retribution, so the soldiers quickly decamped. Their riverside picnic was over.

There was no further opportunity to explore Batavia as recreational leave and excursions ended abruptly when the fighting intensified. The screaming of fighter planes, and the yammering of machine gun fire became regular sounds at the air base and in the surrounding area.

Receiving supplies, replenishing munitions, and keeping the fighter planes airborne grew increasingly difficult until finally there were no parts available to repair the few planes left, nor fuel to keep vehicles of any type running. The capture of Borneo had cut off sources of essential materials like rubber and oil, and Japanese attacks on sea and air transports had created a chokehold on Java.

More discouraging was the report that Singapore had also fallen to the Japanese. Military minds had wrongly determined that because Singapore was shielded to the north by impenetrable jungle and mountains that they merely needed to point their weapons to the sea to keep the city safe from attack, only to find the enemy was able to breach the northern barriers using bicycles and primitive all-terrain vehicles. And now, rumours flew that the Japanese were infiltrating Java using these same forms of transport.

Most of the Dutch civilians had already fled in earlier evacuations, but now as planes risked being grounded, air force personnel began to evacuate as well, flying out on the last few functioning aircraft.

The Allied soldiers left behind were disheartened. Even if there had been enough troop-carrying aircraft to convey them all out, the planes would more than likely be picked off by the Japanese Zero fighters. The men realised there was no way of safely getting off Java.

Word came a few days later that the Dutch had surrendered. The recommendation to the Australians from their major was to surrender as well, but before doing so, they were to destroy all military equipment to keep it from falling into the hands of the Japanese. Radars, guns, ammunition and vehicles were set ablaze or smashed.

Alwyn's platoon leader, Captain Jock Evers was reluctant to comply with the major's recommendation. He did not trust that once they were in the hands of their Japanese captors, they would be treated with fairness. He decided to take his chances and 'head for the hills', inviting anyone else on the platoon to join him too, but not before warning them of the risks in doing so. The men all knew that it was only a matter of time before the rest of them would be caught as well, but Rusty, Sloshy, and Alwyn were among those who decided to join Jock and continue their freedom for as long as they could.

Moreover, in a sentiment shared with several of his mates, Alwyn felt that they had only just arrived, and it was far too soon to give in. The four gathered up a supply of canned food, rifles, ammunition, tarpaulins and other gear and filled a truck.

One evening after the unit had completed a successful raid on a Japanese installation — setting two trucks and a storage shed on fire — they retreated in haste towards their hideout, ebullient from the success of their guerrilla mission.

In elevated whispers they applauded each other on the extent of the damage, and replayed the brilliance of their moves. It was at this time that something clicked in Sloshy's mind. He had found the answer to his puzzle over Alwyn's identity.

"Crikey, you're the sweeper boy from the castle!"

Alwyn flinched, waiting for the worst. But then Sloshy let out a roar of laughter.

Someone hissed, telling Sloshy to keep it down.

"You blunny lying sod," Sloshy chuckled.

Alwyn neither confirmed nor denied Sloshy's guess.

"Well, good on you for getting this far," Sloshy said quietly, clapping Alwyn on the shoulder.

"So is Pablo your real name?"

"It suits me — kind of like Sloshy suits you," Alwyn answered quietly.

"Piss off," Sloshy said with a smile.

Alwyn exhaled slowly. He allowed himself a measure of relief that this revelation did not have the expected disastrous outcome.

Sloshy understood Alwyn's hesitation to divulge any more of his story, but there was no reason to feel this way. Even if Sloshy had turned Alwyn in, at that point it would have received no reaction given the direness of their situation. All that mattered was that Alwyn was not the enemy, and who the enemy was would become all the more clear the following day.

Just before dawn, they were startled awake by the painful prodding of bayonet points and the glare of flashlights. A Japanese scout and some native guides must have followed their trail.

As daylight emerged, they got a better look at their captors, and were surprised by how harmless they seemed. They were mostly slender youths, some with small round spectacles that added to their boyishness, yet they brandished their rifles fiercely and screamed out orders.

The captive soldiers were taken to a former rubber plantation and crowded into some huts, each man allotted just enough room to stretch his legs. They met up with others from their unit, and it was a reunion of mixed emotions — disappointment that these fellows had been caught too, but relief that those they thought had been killed were still alive.

It had been a day and a half since the men had eaten and they were starving. When their first meal came, it was a single bucket of rice boiled in dirty water, but the men lined up with their Dixie cups, ready to receive their portion, which they quickly devoured.

Within a few days the order came to begin marching again. They were being moved to another camp, Tanjong Priok, a former dockworkers' quarters.

They traipsed through a jungle starting out at dawn, and arrived late that night, exhausted and hungry. Like many others, Sloshy was scratched and cut from the sharp bamboo stalks. Alwyn noted with concern several gashes on his friend's legs. He grabbed some leaves and crushed them, and urged Sloshy to apply the mashed pulp to the wounds. Without treatment, any skin sores easily became infected in the steamy moist heat and unsanitary conditions.

In the first weeks at Tanjong Priok many of the men fell ill to dysentery from the lack of clean drinking water or from fruit that was not properly peeled or washed. The frequent trips to the latrine and the paltry diet took their toll on the sick men and the prisoners quickly dropped in weight.

The heavy monsoonal rains pounded the camp and before long the grounds were a mess of mud and maggots. With the rains, there also came a surge in mosquitoes and other insects. The absence of 'mozzie' nets brought on many cases of malaria. Countless men suffered days of high fever and lethargy. Many of their fellow soldiers died in those first few weeks from disease and beatings from the Japanese guards.

The crushing hunger and weakness from their meagre rations finally convinced the prisoners to look upon many things that once seemed inedible as potential nourishment. Even the weevils found in the rice were seen as additional protein.

Alwyn cajoled his mates into considering snails and grubs. Morley MacTavish, or 'Taff' as he was called, eyed several glistening grubs that Alwyn was offering the fellows. The stocky Glaswegian teetered between revulsion and hunger.

"Ah cannae. Nooo."

"Give it a go, mate. No different from beche de mer."

"Don't know aboot no baich dai mair."

Alwyn demonstrated the delectability of the grubs by popping one in his mouth and chewing with gusto. Taff watched him warily.

"Mibbe, just give me a wee one, wit a bit o' rais, then."

Alwyn grinned, pleased to have a taker. He hid a few grubs in a dollop of rice and handed it to Taff. The Scotsman gulped it quickly, wincing as he chewed.

Taff made moves as though he would bring up the food but in the end kept it down, as though willing away the urge to vomit. The other men cheered and laughed at Taff. From then on there was further culinary experimentation. Several snakes and even a lizard or two became a meal for the famished prisoners.

Not long after they had been at Tanjong Priok, they were ordered once more to pack up as they were to be moved again. Several hundred men were rounded up and marched to the docks and then herded onto a decrepit freighter.

The prisoners slowly climbed down a single metal ladder, going as deep as five levels below the deck. The quarters were so cramped that there was no space between the sleeping hammocks that were arranged head to toe. Food was passed down in tubs to the men below. The men knew that should anything happen to the boat they would be doomed. The only reason to go up on deck was to use the 'toilets', which were nothing more than boxes fastened to the boat rails.

Their destination was Batu-Lintang, a camp near Kuching, Borneo.

Upon arrival at Batu-Lintang, any hopes the prisoners might have had that they would be housed in more decent and humane conditions were quickly dispelled. Two-thirds of the prisoners would never make it out alive by the time the camp was liberated on September 11, 1945. Before then thousands would succumb to the effects of severe beatings, over-work, disease, and starvation.

Alwyn realised, as did many others, that he needed to supplement the camp rations with protein and vitamins. During the forced labour trips outside the camp he plucked greens and harvested bark for infusions to stave off beri-beri, as well as mangosteen fruit to treat dysentery.

Within the prison compound however, there was fierce competition for fresh greens, and as soon as the smallest stalk emerged from the ground it was often picked before it could provide barely any nourishment. The level of desperation was such that there was no opportunity for plants to fully develop.

Conserving energy was another strategy for surviving on the starvation rations. But appearing to work without really exerting too much effort also carried the risk of a severe beating in the event that the Japanese guards became suspicious.

Alwyn watched helplessly as Sloshy began to lose strength and faltered during a forced work party north of the camp. They were hacking away at the jungle to make a clearing when Sloshy began to stumble. The other men did their best to cover for him by moving him to trees that were already partially severed. Unfortunately, the guard, a particularly nasty fellow whom they called the 'Crusher', caught on, and launched into a merciless attack on Sloshy.

The men feared for Sloshy's life, as he lay crumpled at the feet of the guard. Suddenly Alwyn began to shout, "Snake! Snake!" and danced around and hacked the ground with his machete, creating enough of a distraction that the brutal Nip ceased clubbing Sloshy.

In the days that followed, Sloshy, already weakened by beri-beri, and suffering from the aftermath of the beating, also came down with double pneumonia. He could no longer stand and stayed back from the daily work party.

Each day, his mates stopped by the infirmary — a fancy name for a series of simple huts — to look in on him. The former strapping lad, who had weighed fifteen stone at the beginning of the war, now weighed only seven stone.

One evening, Sloshy asked Alwyn to take out his photos from his belongings. He tilted them towards Alwyn, showing him those cherished images Alwyn had already seen many times before — Sloshy's sister Myrtle; Sloshy's parents standing at the rose arbour in their garden; and the Winter's farm, a sprawling homestead with a barn and a beautiful Queenslander house that sat midst gum trees and wattles.

Even as his friend lay dying, Alwyn could not help but feel a twinge of envy for Sloshy for all the comfort he had known in his life, and the love of a kind family.

"Promise me you won't use 'em for cigarette paper," Sloshy whispered, his breath raspy and low.

Alwyn smiled. At the camp, paper was scarce and even

precious letters and diaries were cut up and rolled around tea or papaya leaves to make what the natives called cheroots.

Alwyn watched as Sloshy held the photos in his hands, his fingers like sticks wrapped in thin parchment. His eyes sunken. From them Alwyn could see the glimmer of tears. When the photos dropped from his grasp, Alwyn knew his friend was dead.

Grief seized Alwyn. So many of their mates had died but losing Sloshy was terribly hard as he was like a brother to Alwyn, and his closest connection to 'home'. In fact, they had often joked that they had drunk milk from the same cow.

As the men prepared Sloshy for his burial, they were struck by how little he weighed. His remains were placed in the frequently re-used coffin with the false bottom, and lowered into a grave at the prison cemetery. A bamboo cross was fashioned and placed over the loose soil.

After Sloshy's death, an anger and resentment stirred in Alwyn that he could not shake off. Whatever the risks, he was determined to get his revenge on the Japanese guard who had abused Sloshy and hastened his untimely death.

Alwyn devised a plan, but before embarking on it, he warned Rusty, Taff and the others of his scheme, and told them to stay clear. Over the course of the next few days, Alwyn set out to carefully sever the limbs of several trees, leaving the branches precariously resting on one another so that with a small tug, they would collapse on anyone below. When the trap was complete, he began to whistle and sing, attracting the attention of the overly cruel Japanese guard.

"Hey, ya nasty scum. Australia number one. Nippon number one hundred. Nippon's losing the war!"

The Crusher looked at Alwyn with angry dismay.

"Come on over here, ya dirty mongrel," Alwyn jeered.

The brute did not hesitate. He bounded towards Alwyn, brandishing his bayonet and threatening the taunting POW. Alwyn nimbly stepped behind a palm, and forcefully tugged on a long vine that in turn sent the load of tree limbs crashing down, ending forever the bellowing of the hated guard.

Alwyn must have known he would be caught. When the Crusher was found mangled beneath the pile of chopped wood, the other guards wanted to punish all of the prisoners but Alwyn stepped up and claimed it was his fault. It was an accident he said, but they did not believe him.

Alwyn's mates watched in quiet shock as the guards whipped and slashed him over and over again until his chest was a series of ribboned wounds. Then the guards strung him up for the others to see, as a reminder of what would happen to anyone else attempting the same thing.

Alwyn's body slowly drained of blood. His empty eyes stared with the focus of a dead man on a row of ants labouring beneath his dangling legs.

When the prisoners returned to the site the following morning Alwyn was gone. They could only guess at what might have happened to him. They assumed that the Japs must have buried him, or worse, he had been dragged away by wild animals — a panther perhaps, but they never saw Alwyn again.

Chapter Twenty-Three
Hoping for News
Mena Creek, North Queensland – 1944

Talia felt sick to her stomach as she stood at the top of the steps. She swooned as an intense and sudden pain shot through her body. Her knees suddenly gave way and she fell forward, catapulting down the stairs and scattering the contents of the tray she had been carrying. The clatter of the dishes on the cement brought several park visitors running to her aid.

While there were no major cuts to her body, broken bones or other apparent injuries, Talia remained unconscious for several days. The priest from St. Patrick's in Innisfail was asked to come in to give Talia her last rites. The Candelas and Carmen kept vigil by her bed and candles were lit in the church for her.

The prayers seemed to work, for one night during a heavy rainstorm Talia sat bolt upright, her eyes wild and her mouth stretched wide, her teeth bared. It was hard to imagine she had been in a deep coma only seconds before. From the bottom of her throat came strange gurgling sounds and then she began to hiss and thrust her arms about.

Carmen, who had been watching over her daughter, had awoken quickly and felt her blood run cold at the sight of Talia so possessed. The girl's fiendish screams so frightened her mother that she could not move or call for help. Carmen wanted to believe it was just a bad dream and prayed for the nightmare to end. At last Talia seemed to calm a little. The screams dissipated and she slid back down. She closed her eyes and appeared to drop off to sleep.

It was not till morning, when the terror of the night before had begun to wear off a little, did it sink in that Talia had emerged from her coma. Carmen's relief that her daughter had begun to recover was tempered by a lingering fear of Talia's strange outburst.

Several weeks passed and only then did Talia finally manage to get out of bed. Even so, she was very weak and moved with great lethargy.

The Señora cajoled Talia into taking iron pills and made sure the girl had meat broths daily. The Candela sisters tried to enliven her mood with gossip and plans for the future once the war had ended. Yet Talia barely paid attention to these distractions, nor acknowledged the Candelas' kind gestures.

It was only when Aracely confided in her that she had fallen in love with an American soldier that Talia began to truly recover, showing an interest for the first time in outside events.

Aracely realised her parents were not likely to welcome the possibility of her marrying a foreigner, so she kept the relationship a secret.

"Promise not to tell," Aracely urged.

"Of course," Talia said. She sat up and reached for Aracely's hand, giving it a comforting squeeze.

"I don't know what I'm going to do. Papa will never allow me to marry an American," Aracely sighed.

"Probably not," agreed Talia. "But you mustn't let that stop you."

Talia looked at Aracely. "You'll find a way."

When she met Benny Vecchio for the first time, Talia immediately liked him and sensed he was a good person. Knowing the pain of her own thwarted romance, she acted as an intermediary between Aracely and him whenever the need arose.

She asked Benny one night if he could help her find Alwyn. Talia gave Benny an old photo of Alwyn and wrote his name on the back. When Benny asked details of where Alwyn had enlisted and where he was stationed, she was embarrassed to be ignorant of any of this information.

"Has he written to you at all?" Benny asked.

Talia shook her head, biting her lip to keep from crying.

"So maybe he's not even in the army?"

"I don't know. Only he said he was going to join up. So that's what I reckon he did."

"Well, I'll ask around," Benny offered.

Benny gave Talia an encouraging smile as he slid the photo into his uniform pocket. "I'm sure he'll turn up when this whole thing blows over."

Benny secretly confided to Aracely that he didn't think much of this Alwyn character not having written at all, but Aracely assured him the facts were likely to be more complicated than that.

No one ever could diagnose the illness that had afflicted Talia so severely. The recovery was as mysterious as the onset.

She told no one but she remembered clearly waking up from her coma and having the distinct impression she was there with Alwyn in the jungle protecting him and willing him to go on.

It was as if Talia's body knew something of Alwyn's pain, and it stooped and bent to absorb some of it for him. For a woman of only twenty-two, she looked much older and more careworn than her actual age. Her hair hung limp, and her complexion was dull. It did not help either that she made little effort to make herself attractive.

Even though there might have been indications of interest from visiting soldiers, a flirtatious remark or a smile, Talia rarely met their eyes. Her gaze was always fixed on a faraway point, unseeing, lost.

She read the newspapers and listened to the radio, getting upset at every report of ships sinking or soldiers shot in battle.

From time to time, as soldiers passed through the park, she would show them Alwyn's photo and ask them if they knew anything about him. Only once did she run into someone who thought he recognised Alwyn, recalling him as a Spaniard en route to Borneo. But that was all he could remember.

Talia was not convinced he had really met Alwyn. Yet she kept his words at the back of her mind — Borneo — a Spaniard.

And there the trail ended. Survivors of the Borneo mission were rare. Talia could only wait for the end of the war and hope Alwyn would return soon after.

While Talia's love life was in limbo, Aracely's flourished. Benny returned to Innisfail for a two-week furlough from Darwin. One evening, he arrived dressed to the nines, his hair shiny and his uniform carefully pressed. He asked to speak to Señor Candela.

An hour later he emerged from his meeting, beaming from cheek to cheek. He grabbed Aracely by the waist and pulled her close for a kiss. They had been given Señor Candela's blessing to marry.

Upon the heels of this piece of good news came other wonderful news. Victory was declared by the Allied forces. The war was over.

Carmen remarked later that she was surprised the Señor gave his permission for Aracely and Benny to get married.

Talia simply shrugged. She had her mind on other things. With the end of the war, she had great hopes Alwyn might be among the men returning home. With streams of soldiers heading back from the front, Talia began to pray for a miracle.

Soldiers first began to return from the South West Pacific on troop ships in September and October 1945 after being routed through a dispersal centre where they received medical care and identity papers. Talia approached the Ministry of War and the Office for Repatriation of Soldiers with the possibility of locating Alwyn, but his name was on none of their lists.

She scoured the newspapers for stories of returning men and pressed anyone in uniform for possible news of stragglers. Time after time she was disappointed. But she remained determined that she simply had not asked the right person or Alwyn had not yet been released.

It was at a surprise kitchen tea for Aracely that she overheard an unsettling conversation between two bridesmaids, Etta Patton and Mabel Swann. At first Talia thought they might be talking about her, but later realised they were speaking of someone else.

"Yeah, everyone else seems to be getting news, but she's not," Etta remarked.

"Poor thing. His name hasn't come up on any POW lists either, I take it."

"No, no. I told her he might be with the commandoes, still running around the jungle, no notion the war's over."

"That's always a possibility. But by now it's more than likely they just haven't found his body."

"I hope not. Poor Viola."

"This whole business of getting our boys home is taking an awful long time."

"It's quite unbearable for those still waiting."

Indeed, Talia thought. Quite unbearable.

Chapter Twenty-Four
The End and the Beginning
Mena Creek, North Queensland – 1946

The day of Aracely and Benny's wedding was fast approaching. It was to be a sumptuous event, or as lavish as it could be in the face of the ongoing rationing. They were not just celebrating the wedding of the Candelas' eldest daughter but also the end of the war, and the end of all the years of hardship and depression.

Ration coupons were pooled, and favours were exchanged with local fisherman to get lobster and prawns. Champagne and wine bottles from the Candelas' cellar were dusted off and brought up for the event. Señora Candela's antique jewellery and fine silverware were dug out of the rock garden and restored to a shiny finish. A big band ensemble from Rockhampton called 'Johnny and the Belle Tones' was booked for the night.

In the weeks leading up to the wedding, Talia worked long hours cleaning and polishing the castle hall, scrubbing the stone patio and railing. She touched up the murals of pastoral scenes and daydreamed about how different life would have been had she remained in Spain, in her small village.

One day shortly before the marriage, she scurried about the hall attending to the decorations and other last minute details when she heard a flutter above her. A sparrow had flown in and hopped from one rafter to another. It reminded her of the day she first met Alwyn as he perched in the rafters hanging streamers. She was overcome by a strong feeling of his presence, as though his spirit was there in the room with her.

Snippets of music drifted in from the radio. She heard Vera Lynn sing: *"We'll meet again, don't know where, don't know when."* Was this how she was meeting Alwyn again, through the presence of a small bird?

It was odd, but it gave Talia a sense of comfort that helped her through Aracely's wedding, something that she might have otherwise found very painful. Her own loss was magnified by the joy surrounding this wedding in Castillo Candela, and the knowledge that she might never marry her love in the castle, or anywhere for that matter.

Yet Talia had been very touched that Aracely had asked her to be maid of honour. Indeed it made her feel special. She only hoped it was not done out of pity.

The wedding was exquisite. It was as though the devastation of war and the ration constraints did not exist for the Candelas. Aracely floated on a cloud of happiness, looking resplendent in a gown Carmen had created and beaded with great care. She looked like the princess they had always known her to be.

Talia danced with Roberto and he apologised often for his lame leg, but Talia reassured him his limp was hardly noticeable. She felt another wave of melancholy sweep over her as she thought of how Alwyn had made it possible for Roberto to dance at all, and yet he was not here to share the celebration.

The party lasted until early the next morning when Mr. and Mrs. Benjamin Vecchio left for a honeymoon on Green Island. Only then did the Candelas have a chance to catch their breath.

In the first few hours of dawn following the grand party, birds pecked at the small kernels of rice scattered between the patio stones. Streamers hung limp, and tablecloths and dishes were piled high, waiting to be cleaned. But it would have to hold until later that day. For now, it was time to rest.

As they prepared to retire after the celebration, the elder Candelas could bask in the glow of the wonderful party and their family's good fortune. But their happy moment, as it turned out, would be very short-lived.

Chapter Twenty-Five
The Prince
Mena Creek, North Queensland – 1946

After the busy day and the hours of dancing, Señora Candela was more than happy to remove her shoes from her swollen feet. She surveyed the vast array of wedding gifts arranged on a table in the master bedroom. Their friends had been generous towards the bridal couple.

"Ramon, how should we send these?"

She said this more to herself than to her husband who was in the next room. Still she waited for him to reply. "All this glassware, it's so delicate."

Now louder, she added, "Do you think we should store it in case Aracely and Benny come back?"

Still there was no answer.

"Eh? Ramon? Ramon?"

She got up heavily from her chair and strode into the bathroom, stopping suddenly.

Her husband was sprawled on the floor, his face ashen and contorted. Señora Candela screamed and ran to his side.

His occasional stomach discomfort had not been the result of indigestion but the symptoms of pancreatic cancer. Now, as Señor Candela lay in the hospital, Señora Candela wondered how long he had been suffering without complaint. Amid her sorrow, she felt angry at his stubbornly stoic ways that would ultimately be his undoing.

The reason for Señor Candela's lack of reaction to Aracely's engagement now became clear to the family. He had been too ill to voice any disagreement.

It was a gloomy time as Señor Candela's condition deteriorated, and at the same time attendance at the park suddenly dropped with the evacuation of the soldiers.

Ramon came home from the hospital for the last few weeks of his illness, saying goodbye, one by one, to his children, and at last to Talia.

"*Perdoname, hija.*"

She could not hear him at first, because his voice was slurred from the morphine injections and the cancer that was taking hold in his upper body.

"*Perdoname.*"

Of course she knew the reason for the apology without his ever saying it. She wondered at what point he had begun to realise the mistake it had been to keep her away from Alwyn. She was sure he regretted not being able to say goodbye to Alwyn too.

Talia mused bitterly that at least the Señor and Alwyn could be reconciled in the next life. All would be forgiven between them, but for Talia, still in the here and now, it was too late.

Ramon Candela's death left a huge hole in the community, not just among Spanish-Australians but also among many other people from various communities and walks of life, from miles around. So many attended his funeral that the street near the church was jammed with cars. Mourners crowded outside the church entrance, too many to fit inside.

After the mass, the procession of women in black veils and men in dark suits wove through the cemetery like a line of crows, their heads bent in sorrow. The morning sun glowered on the town, making churchgoers uncomfortable in their funeral clothes. The crimson banana flowers hung like heavy teardrops.

Señora Candela clung to Roberto's arm as they walked with difficulty over the uneven ground. One was overcome with grief, and the other was just as sorrowful, but was also weighted down by his feeling of inadequacy and the terrifying realization that he would have to take over the business from his father. Roberto was not physically strong and was used to being sheltered. He had long lived in the shadow of his energetic, entrepreneurial father, and had never been encouraged to develop his own business acumen.

Following his father's death, Roberto struggled with his new responsibilities. He made many of his early decisions out of ignorance and in haste. He bought new projector equipment when attendance at screenings was down as moviegoers preferred to see films at the new theatre in town. Rather than pare down Castillo Candela, he sold other holdings to keep the castle property going.

There were also expenses related to sending Gloria to school in Melbourne and weddings for Maria Eugenia and Lucia.

Magnifying the problem was the fact that the thousands of soldiers once stationed in the area had all gone home and no longer frequented the castle and park. Moreover, a new highway had been built not far away and many travellers simply bypassed the Castillo, preferring to explore further afield in their new cars.

The castle property was bleeding cash.

One day not long after his father's death, as Roberto was looking over the books in despair, he asked Talia rather abruptly, "Would you still have me if I were a poor man?"

Talia was taken aback by the question. She said nothing at first.

"I don't know how my father did it."

Talia stared at the accounts, wide-eyed. She was surprised at the dismal earnings and even more so by the large expenses.

"So that's why I'm warning you, things could get a lot worse. But maybe if we were partners we could make it work."

Talia began to feel uneasy. "What do you mean, Roberto?"

"I'm asking you to marry me."

Talia placed one hand on the back of a chair and leaned against it. She felt her body go weak with shock.

"This could be yours. You could be queen of the castle. After years of mopping the floors, you deserve it."

She was speechless.

He stood up unsteadily and bent towards her. He brought his hands to her face, and lifting it, kissed her full on the mouth.

It was not a tender kiss, but one given out of desperation.

Talia felt sick with repulsion. She pried his hands off and pulled away.

He staggered back, looking as though he might fall. Talia caught his arm and steadied him.

He said with a touch of bitterness, "Is it because of my gammy leg?"

"No, Roberto. No. We grew up together — you're like a brother to me."

He scowled, "My thoughts about you of late have not been brotherly. Not at all, lovely Talia."

He reached his hand out to touch her hair but she shook her head and edged away from him.

Roberto's mouth pulled into a sneer. "You're not still thinking of that abo, are you?"

Talia froze.

"Don't speak of Alwyn like that."

From down the hall, Señora Candela's ears perked up at the sound of Talia and Roberto's agitated voices. She switched off the radio and cocked her head to listen. Concerned, she got up and hurried in the direction of the office.

As she swung the door of the office open, she caught Talia and Roberto in mid-argument. Her son was sweating and red-faced, his eyes wild, while Talia was pale and quiet.

"What's the matter?" the Señora asked, looking between the both of them.

Roberto wiped his brow and shrugged.

"Nothing. We were just talking bookkeeping."

"But I can help you with that, Roberto. I always helped your father," Señora Candela insisted.

Talia was inching her way out of the room while the Señora tried to calm her son. "No need to trouble Talia with that."

Just after Talia exited, Roberto looked up to see her gone. He brushed past his mother and hurried after Talia, his metal brace clanking as it met the hard tile floor.

"You just think about it. We can talk again in a few days," he said, calling after her.

Talia turned to look back at Roberto. She didn't want to hurt him. He looked so forlorn, but she felt angry on Alwyn's behalf. It was hard to reconcile the cherub-faced little boy she had always loved with this red-faced man with ugly words.

She replied firmly, "You already have my answer."

Roberto looked crushed. Anger flashed across his face.

Talia hurried away. In the background, Roberto's mother's voice asked, "What is it, son? Answer to what?"

"It's nothing!" he snapped.

But the Señora already had an inkling of what Talia and Roberto had been discussing. She decided it was time to speak honestly with her son. But not at Castillo Candela.

On the pretext of visiting her daughters in Melbourne, she lured Roberto away, promising him they would be back at the end of the rainy season.

Talia and her mother were left to keep watch over the Castillo. The park would be closed until February. In any event, few visitors came these days. Castillo Candela was now off the beaten track, requiring a detour. It now seemed quaint and outdated, a vestige from the pre-war years, especially in comparison to the more interesting attractions that could be found right on the new Bruce Highway stretching from Cairns to Brisbane.

It was a rainy day, barely two weeks after the Señora and Roberto had left, when a shiny car came crunching up the drive, swerving to a stop in front of the gates. A horn honked insistently.

Talia peered out and saw a man waving. It was Roberto. She was astonished to see him. She exited the house and approached his car.

"Come out for a drive," he invited, leaning from the open window.

"Where did you get this?" Talia asked.

Although Roberto had mastered the skill of driving in his

teenage years, he had never been encouraged to own a car himself and had always been chauffeured here and there.

On the way back from Melbourne, he got tired of waiting for his train connection and simply strolled into a dealership and purchased a car on a whim. He then drove up from Rockhampton at fifty miles an hour.

"Come on, you're getting soaked," he said.

He too was getting wet with the window rolled down. His hair and face glistened. His eyes were strangely bright.

Talia gave in, as much to get out of the rain as to find out what Roberto was up to. She slid into the passenger side and it was only then that she smelled the rum on his breath.

"What do you think? Pretty flash, eh?"

Roberto put the car in gear and backed out. He spun the brand new vehicle onto the road, over Talia's objections.

"Roberto, you shouldn't be driving. It's raining hard."

"Made it all the way from Macknade without taking a break. This thing flies over puddles like an aeroplane."

He was really pushing the car, zooming over the precarious gravel track, swerving to avoid the largest puddles and speeding up through others.

Talia screamed for Roberto to stop but he seemed bent on going still faster.

His leg brace made it difficult for him to brake quickly, and the alcohol made his judgement even worse.

"Roberto please — I'll marry you — is that what you want? I'll be your wife!"

But Talia's pleading did nothing to slow him down.

He laughed harshly and only pressed harder on the gas. Reckless and unstoppable.

"Robbie, please!"

Talia wept hysterically, pulling on his arm, but to no avail.

It was only when the road turned and a cow suddenly appeared a few yards ahead that Roberto found the brakes.

It was a beautiful brown jersey that had escaped when the water rose in its paddock. It looked askance at the oncoming car, but not really comprehending the danger. At the last second, however, it decided to move out of the way.

As Roberto's lame foot reached for the brakes, he tried to direct the car to safety, but it spun wildly, heedless of his intention. It rolled over the gravel as though on a wave of smooth ball bearings, careening haphazardly.

Talia caught a glimpse of the giant fig tree long before they made contact. She thought about the years and years the parasitical plant would have taken to wrap the host tree up and down, preparing for just this very moment when an out-of-control car would ram it hard.

As it did now.

The car met the multi-layered trunk. The front windshield shattered and the driver's side crumpled, caving in against Roberto.

Talia was still screaming as she slid against him.

The motor coughed and expelled a tuft of smoke, slowly wheezing and sputtering to a dead quiet. In the seconds that followed, only a small creaking could be heard from the accident scene.

And then the moans came, the frightful moans. Talia heard him and tried to pull away. He had cushioned her from the worst of the impact. With great difficulty, she turned to look at him.

He was bleeding where glass had cut his forehead. Between moans of pain, he sobbed, "I'm sorry, Talia."

Then, when he received no answer from her, he asked, "Are you alright?"

She supposed she was. But it was as though she was learning to move again, jogging her brain to direct her foot and arm to make larger movements. She shifted on the seat, facing him full on.

"Why, Roberto? What's got into you?"

He began to cry harder.

"Roberto, tell me."

"You're my sister, you know."

The words didn't register right away. Talia felt light-headed.

He continued, between sobs. "I'm not a Candela after all. Not by birth, anyway. Your mother is my mother." Saying these words seemed to exhaust him and he fell back against the door, eyes closed.

Talia's head throbbed, the pain making itself known to her brain. Her body exploded in a thousand points of agony. There was no more emotional and physical torture in the world than that felt by Talia at that moment.

Days later, outside the Innisfail hospital, Talia bought a copy of the *Northern Courier* from a newspaper boy, who stared at her yellow and purple bruises, almost forgetting to take the coin she offered him.

She brought the paper up to Roberto's ward. And as though it might matter to him, she read the weather report, the racing forum, and the cricket scores and was part way through a story about Prime Minister Chifley when Roberto interrupted her.

"I have a confession to make, Talia. — I must tell you." He paused, and then looked directly at her.

"I was trying to get us killed."

She set the paper down in her lap. She said nothing to him, but her upper body slumped as she bent over the news. Soon her shoulders began to shake and dark spots appeared on the headlines and columns.

When he came home from the hospital, they did not speak of it again.

The once-proud prince was hobbled by shame, which his physical injuries seemed to mirror. His arm was swathed in a cast, and he was riddled with scratches and bruises. While these eventually faded, there remained a veiled look in Roberto's eyes. Regret and self-loathing hovered over him like a vulture.

Except for some desultory activity, he ceased any pretence of trying to run Castillo Candela. He became overwhelmed by the bills that continued to pile up, and after a while, did not even bother to open them.

After a few weeks of almost daily rain, the radio warned of the approach of a tropical storm system.

In the morning, there was no rain but the humidity was oppressive. The sky was opaque, with the light of the sun diffused through a million expectant droplets. Talia and her mother held off on doing the laundry. They shuttered the windows and began to collect the small clay pots from the patio, bringing them inside.

By eleven in the morning, the wind had picked up considerably. The long sprays of bougainvillea broke free of the walls and began to nod and sway, pointing away as though urging them to flee. *Go now*, they seemed to warn. But where could they go?

And even if they had some place to hide out, they could not leave just yet, as there was much more tidying left to do. Had they known the futility of tying anything down, they would have dropped everything, and simply hurried away to safety. But hindsight is only that.

As soon as the first engorged droplet hit the ground, Carmen and Talia hurried more quickly to secure loose objects.

Talia remembered some small ferns she had set aside for planting and ran into the lower garden to gather them up. She would put them in the shed until the storm had passed.

The two women were not the only ones busy that morning preparing for the bad weather.

Eight miles upstream, a timber-getter named Hollis Rowley worked feverishly to haul in some Kauri pine logs that lay precariously close to the banks of Mena Creek. The swollen waterway lapped at the fringes of his property, taking over more and more land as rain fell. Thousands of gallons of water formed improvised rivulets and tributaries, and collected in the creek, attaining almost Amazonian breadth. A vast force, it surged towards the Coral Sea.

With a pulley and a pair of bullocks Hollis managed to bring the heavy logs to higher ground. But no sooner had he done so than the river claimed still more of his land. He watched in defeat as his full-grown logs, hewn over months, and valued at twenty pounds a board foot, were swept away in the turgid brown water as though they were nothing more than toothpicks.

Hollis dared not step into the fast-moving water to wrestle the logs back lest he meet the same fate. He knew he would not stand a chance against the powerful force.

He cursed as a small fortune in timber barrelled away and out of his reach, down the muddy channel. The wood sailed at top speed, passing Silkwood in the blink of an eye, pausing briefly to cluster around a bloodwood tree leaning into the creek, its limbs and roots still intact, until one by one the great Kauri pine logs shot between the branches of their land-bound relative, and continued on. The freed logs spun at a startling pace towards the railway bridge, not more than half a mile from the Castillo Candela. There the logs regrouped in military fashion, a three-ton formation of battering rams, readying to charge ahead.

Roberto, still wearing a cast on one arm, tugged awkwardly at the corners of the tarp that stretched over the broken windshield of his nearly new automobile. He climbed into the front seat and wound down the front passenger side window with his one good arm, then snatched the end of the tarp. He rolled the window up again, securing the tarp between the window and the frame.

As he exited the car, he was immediately struck by the eerie quiet. Puzzled, he walked to the cliff overlooking the falls and was astounded to see that the water flow had been reduced to a trickle. Such a thing had never occurred before and seemed especially baffling during a rainstorm.

Then he heard the creaking and the muffled thuds coming from the direction of the railway bridge.

Roberto stared at the horizon. His eyes widened and his face registered a cold fear, suddenly understanding why the water was not getting through.

He turned and ran back towards the castle, calling for Talia, whom he knew to be in the lower garden. He hurried towards the grand staircase, moving unusually fast for the cripple that he was.

Then he heard the sickening groan of metal. Followed by a resounding crack. Pummelled by the heavy logs, the railway bridge twisted and snapped. Rivets popped and flew off like bullets.

"Talia!"

Terrified for himself, but even more so for Talia, Roberto flew down the wet mossy stairs, arriving at the first landing, with its lookout over the falls and swimming area. He turned around and gulped. He had a prime view of the wall of water roaring towards him, a wall fortified by columns of logs.

Roberto was knocked off his feet by the charging water. He was caught up in the flow, but mercifully was slammed in the head by a log almost immediately, so he was not conscious during the terrible journey downstream.

Meanwhile, Talia, who had heard Roberto's cry and had seen the cascade cresting at the top of the castle, dropped the small pots of ferns and ran towards the tunnel. She took cover in the hollow without a second to spare. As soon as she was inside, a surge of water pulsed inwards, rising to her knees.

Fearing that the tunnel itself might collapse, she withdrew to the far end and took shelter at the edge, facing Little Angels Falls. She listened to the crashing sounds, the roar of the rushing water, but she had no real idea of the devastation being wrought.

At that moment, the logs were ramming the castle doors, forcing them open. Then they bashed through the walls to the other side, gutting the once lovely hall. Folding chairs and tables shot out of the makeshift openings, but not before being reduced to splinters. It took less than five minutes for Rowley's logs to barrel through and devastate years of the Candelas' work.

Talia saw the water subside from the tunnel entrance. But rather than risk being hit by a late surge of water or moving debris, she took a circuitous route to exit the valley, clambering up the south wall of the creek. She arrived at their little house, muddy and tear-streaked. She found her mother huddled inside, crying. Their shack had survived quite well while the castle itself was devastated.

"¿Y Roberto?" Carmen asked.

Talia shook her head. She considered telling her mother about Roberto calling to her from the upper terrace but thought it best not to say anything.

As soon as the storm cleared, they set about looking for him but the water in the creek remained high and they found nothing. When a search party failed to find his body after several days, Carmen took the unusual step of calling upon the one-eyed Encantadora to help locate him. By this time, the Candela women were en route from Melbourne. Otherwise, the Señora might have objected to using a most un-Catholic way of searching for Roberto.

The old clairvoyant would not come out to the Castillo because of the muddy roads but described exactly how and where Roberto would be found, pinpointing the site on a map of the shire. She even described the flotsam that would mark his watery grave — a jute bag hanging off the end of a branch.

And that is how they eventually found him — an old *Rose of Siam* rice bag, forming the canopy for his tomb. Roberto lay perfectly still, floating in the gold-brown water, like a fly trapped in amber.

His body was bloated, and with the extreme heat, a burial had to be arranged quickly. In the meantime, Señora Candela and the sisters had arrived by train from Melbourne. They were overcome with grief at Roberto's untimely death, and the shock of seeing their old home in ruins only added to their sadness.

Chapter Twenty-Six
The End of an Era
Mena Creek, North Queensland – 1947

There was no use trying to repair the damage, not that the Candelas had the heart for it any more. Restoration would have cost thousands of pounds, which they could no longer spare. The hardwood floors in the ballroom were warped from the water. The coloured glass panes of the entrance doors were shattered. Loads of silt and mud covered the floors.

Too much grief and destruction had washed over the old Castillo, and no amount of work or money could justify bringing it back to its former glorious state. Moreover, the Castillo had already begun to die even before the storm hit.

After Roberto's funeral, Señora Candela made quick work of going through their personal possessions, auctioning off the furniture in their English cottage, and those tools and bits of equipment that had not floated away.

Then she and her other daughters made plans to return to Melbourne — Aracely had not been able to attend the funeral. She had remained in America, pregnant with her first child.

With only a little encouragement from Gloria, Lucia, Ofelia, and Maria Eugenia, the Señora decided to move to Melbourne permanently. The Señora spent only enough time to gather a few mementos — the little that remained after the storm —and to oversee the closure of the park.

The abruptness of Señora Candela's decision hit Carmen and Talia hard, as they too were still in mourning. There was bitterness in the air as Carmen and Talia helped Señora Candela pack and prepare for her departure. It was as though she could not acknowledge that Carmen and Talia were also suffering. Talia felt the absence of Alwyn even more at that moment. How much easier it would have been had he been there to commiserate.

With their trunks packed, and the Castillo shuttered, the Candela women boarded the train heading south.

Talia was still deeply stricken by the death of Roberto, difficult as their relationship had been of late, but her mother was thrown into an even deeper melancholy. Her sadness was magnified by the fact that she had been forced to give up Roberto as a baby or face being shunned by Talia's birth father — a man who eventually left them anyway.

The closure of Castillo Candela and the permanent departure of the Candelas only deepened Talia and Carmen's grief. In one fell swoop they had lost a brother and a son, and had also been cut off from their home and their livelihood.

And then Talia worried that if Alwyn were to return he might not know where to find her.

Once more, Carmen and Talia were on their own and starting afresh. Before long they found rooms above Lok Fan's General Store in Innisfail. Carmen continued doing alterations and making wedding dresses. She had impressed a few locals with Aracely and Lucia's gowns, and more orders followed from that.

Adjusting to the city was quite difficult. At first Talia could not sleep because of the street noises: the rumble of traffic, the loud voices, and the honking horns. She rose in the morning more exhausted than when she had gone to bed.

She missed the lulling sound of the falls, the hum of the cicadas and the rustle of the wind in the palms. She missed the smells of the Castillo: the fragrant perfumes of frangipani and hibiscus; the aromas of Señora Candela's cooking and baking; and the fresh country air. The second-storey flat was also hot and confining. It lacked the cooling shade their old house had offered.

It was a struggle to adapt to these changes, and as though that were not enough, Talia had to find a job. But if the war had done anything, it had expanded the work opportunities for women. There were often openings at the fish cannery, and Talia went to make an enquiry there. She spoke to the foreman, who told her to come back in a couple of days. That same afternoon, when she returned to Fan's store, she noticed the old man scratching something on a piece of cardboard.

"You know, Mr. Fan, I can make a new set of signs for you." He took her up on her offer, and this was how Talia began her work as a sign painter.

Someone saw her sprucing up the banners in Lok Fan's store and from there she got an order to paint the sign for Deluxe Dry Cleaners. She painted a smiling businessman in a suit and hat.

Then she ran into Hilliard Dixon of Dixon's Bakery and found herself talking him into repainting his fleet of delivery trucks with a new logo and colour scheme of her own creation.

She never did return to the cannery to find out if a job had opened up. With Talia's mother doing alterations for a number of ready-to wear clothing stores, they had enough to get by and then some.

Talia bought an old 1928 Morris truck to help get around with her paints and ladder. She got herself some canvas overalls and sturdy boots at an army-surplus sale, and picked up a pair of old military binoculars and a canteen for her increasingly frequent treks into the scrub to paint. To escape the noises and smells of the town, she made a point of retreating often to the comparatively restful countryside.

After unpacking from their move, Talia was surprised and pleased to see how her artistic skills had improved. She debated keeping her old artwork, now mildewed and water-stained. In a burst of cleaning, she burned most of the pieces, except for the drawing of the staghorn fern, the one that marked the day when everything had suddenly changed for her and Alwyn.

It pleased Talia to stroll about Innisfail and see her handiwork posted here and there, and on vehicles passing by. Whenever and wherever she could, she volunteered her artistic services for shows, parties, and civic events. She became known for her talent and had no shortage of contracts.

But she still pursued her passion projects, making forays into the rain forest, to collect and paint the plants of North Queensland — plants she knew to be important to local aboriginals, thanks to Alwyn, but which were relatively unknown to many townsfolk.

At the Devon Cinema, she received a commission to paint a larger than life Bob Hope holding a camera and a baby's soother for the movie *My Favourite Brunette*. As she painted Bob Hope's face behind the camera, a smile formed on her lips, recalling Alwyn's impressions of the great comedian. With a pang, she thought about how much she would give to watch a movie with Alwyn again.

"Have you seen it?" a man's voice enquired.

Talia peered down from the ladder.

"Seen it? Oh, no. I'm just doing this artwork for the theatre. The picture won't be here till next week."

"That's quite something."

Below, a man looked up at her intently. He was a nice looking fellow and it was clear by his grinning face that he had found something amusing. She didn't really think he was laughing at her, although she was sure she must have looked quite ridiculous.

It was unfortunate that he had decided to approach her at this very moment, with her hair coming undone, and her wearing an old canvas shirt rolled up to her paint-spattered elbows. The hat too — how awful. It was another army-surplus find that had been boiled into a wobbly shape, but it did keep the sun off her face. Although not today, it seemed, as her cheeks felt warm and flushed.

She agreed to see the movie with him. Even though she could have gotten in for free, she did not tell him this. They went to several other picture shows too, and they strolled up and down the Esplanade in the evenings.

Dennis Inglemann was a 'solid' man, even by his own description. He was a 'brick off the old block' — a joking reference to the fact that his father was the founder of the

Inglemann Brick Factory in Tully. Many of the churches, schools, post offices, and city halls in the area had been constructed with Inglemann bricks and they were all still standing, many tropical storms and cyclones later. And Dennis, too, was dependable and reliable.

It was a new experience for Talia to be escorted to nice places in a brand new slate-green Holden. Dennis was always polite and came round to open the door for her. They sped up and down the coast in his car, visiting places that used to be days away by horse and cart.

Talia began to spend her hard-earned money on things she had never even thought of buying before — silk stockings, a bottle of *Evening in Paris* perfume, two new dresses and fashionable leather shoes with high heels.

She finally had her hair cut and styled into a shoulder length wave. She put rollers in it at night, not so much to curl her hair as to train it out of its wild tendencies.

Dennis seemed very pleased with any effort she made to embellish her appearance. Compliments and sweet endearments, like "heaven must be missing an angel" spilled easily from him.

When they watched a movie together, Talia would glance over at him, half-expecting some mocking imitation or mimicry. She was always surprised to see him simply watching the movie, enjoying it for what it was.

She thought about where they were going, and how fast and easily they travelled together, like the new highway, clear and smooth. When she reflected on it, she was surprised to realise it had only been a couple of months that she had been seeing him. She didn't think she was falling in love with Dennis, but she knew she cared for him. He was a very nice man.

Her twenty-sixth birthday was approaching, and she was still not married. It was not something she dwelled on, but her mother would not let her forget that Talia's status as an old maid would soon be firmly cemented.

Although Talia was not aware of this, Dennis seemed determined to do something about this problem. He knew her birthday coincided with Christmas so he made a date to pick her up just before dawn on December 25th. He wanted to treat her to a special breakfast picnic to catch the sunrise.

They drove for half an hour over a rugged road that climbed higher as the sun crept up. Finally Dennis turned off onto a smaller track and then pulled to a stop at a weedy piece of land that was dotted with a few survey stakes. Dennis took Talia's hand as though she were some delicate creature and led her to the edge of a plateau.

She gasped at the splendid vista. Pink strands of light were just making their way into the sky. The cane fields and dairy farms of the lush Atherton Tablelands came into view, bathed in a soft dawn glow.

"It's lovely."

"Yes, it's a great spot. I want to build a house here."

"It would be wonderful to paint up here."

"That's what I thought you'd say," he smiled broadly.

He went back to the car and hauled out a heavy picnic hamper and placed it on the ground, spreading out a tarpaulin.

Because it was her birthday, he had insisted that she not prepare any of the food. He proudly unwrapped bread and cheese, smoked ham and cookies with drops of apricot jam. He told her not to eat too much because they were expected at his family's house for Christmas dinner later.

"But there is so much food, Dennis. Who else is coming?" laughed Talia.

Dennis seemed especially nervous, which Talia thought was very sweet. He barely ate two bites himself. Finally, at a pause in their meal, he looked at her earnestly and asked, "What do you want to do with your life, Talia?"

She thought for a moment, looking across the verdant countryside.

"Well, it's probably too late —"

Dennis cocked his head, a trace of worry in his look.

"I want to be a botanist."

Dennis looked blank.

"And you?" she asked.

Dennis sputtered. "Well, I've got bricks in my bones."

He took a deep breath. "It's a good living, Talia."

It occurred to Talia that she might have offended him, and she blurted out quickly, "Yes, it certainly seems to be."

And then the real intent of his question started to dawn on her. It explained his nervousness and the elaborate production around the picnic.

Talia was caught off guard. This moment had arrived too quickly. How well did they really know each other? She was wondering what she would tell him as he unwrapped the bottle of champagne. She watched his hands unrolling the newspaper and setting the bottle of champagne near her. He was fumbling for something in his pocket when she saw the newspaper. A breeze picked it up and lazily rolled it off the tarpaulin, but not before she caught a glimpse of the headline.

To Dennis' surprise she jumped up and ran after the paper, barely catching it before it flew off the edge. He gasped as he saw her stop just short of the cliff.

He thought about how close he had been to losing her over the precarious rock face as she hurtled towards the wide-open sky, fingers uplifted towards the windborne newspaper.

But by then she was already gone to him anyway.

Dennis watched as Talia collapsed in a heap of sobs, clutching the newspaper. Her terrible crying poured out as she bent over the photographs of the missing men with their names listed below.

There was anguish in her crying, but also great hope. At last she understood why she hadn't been able to uncover a single trace of Alywn after all this time. But now — now knowing his enlisted name was Pablo Del Rio, it all made sense.

Talia never did get to see the engagement ring — not that it would have made any difference. Dennis quietly tucked it back into his pocket. Talia was so overcome with emotion that she forgot where she was and with whom.

The photo of Alwyn flung her back to the past in a fraction of a second. She was sure she could find him one day.

Pablo Del Rio!

Dennis and Talia hardly spoke on the ride back. Talia clung to the torn newspaper as though it were the most important thing in the world. For both of them, the return journey was tortuously slow. For him, it was a trip filled with humiliation and disappointment. For her, every second on the road was time not spent searching for Alwyn.

When Talia arrived home, she saw that Carmen was already dressed in a lovely summer dress, one she had just finished sewing. Her hair was styled and her lipstick fresh. Her face fell as she caught sight of Talia holding the newspaper.

"No! No!" she groaned.

"Had you seen this?" Talia held up the newspaper, giving her mother an accusing stare.

Carmen shrugged and raised her eyes.

"You hid this from me?" Talia could hardly believe her mother's deceit.

"Why would I show it to you? To what end? He is dead, Talia. Probably for several years now."

"We don't know that!"

"What good is going to come of all this, Talia? You and Dennis could have been married."

The scenario at the Inglemann home was just as devastating, although it played out more quietly. When Dennis finally arrived for Christmas dinner — without Talia, and smelling of liquor — he had finished the champagne by himself — his mother knew he had been rejected. She quickly removed the table settings meant for his girlfriend and her mother, and nothing more was ever said of Talia.

Talia needn't have worried for Dennis' sake. His pain, while acute, was, in the overall scheme of things, short-lived. Within three months, he was engaged to a new girlfriend, Bernice Westney.

Unlike Talia, Bernice immediately appreciated what a catch Dennis was. When he asked her what she wanted in life, she gave him the right answer — to be married and have children. She was rewarded with a three-quarter carat diamond ring, likely the same ring intended for Talia. But Bernice would never know this, nor did she have time to wonder as she launched headlong into preparations for their wedding.

Meanwhile Talia spent many hours calling the Office for the Return of Prisoners of War, the Office of Veteran's Affairs, both in Sydney and in Rockhampton, trying to glean some more information as to the whereabouts of Alwyn/a.k.a. Pablo Del Rio. But there was no new information to be had.

Some of the Veterans' Affairs staff put her on the spot regarding her connection to Pablo. The irregularities with Pablo's documentation did not help matters. The clerks were suspicious that Talia was unable to provide accurate next-of-kin information or any other details on Mr. Del Rio. She could not say he was her husband, nor even her fiancé, and this seemed a further hindrance to her enquiries.

Why hadn't Alwyn at least written her a letter? Just one letter that could have demonstrated a relationship with him. But she did not even have that.

"Can't you tell me if anyone was recovered from his unit?"

"I'm sorry, none that we know of."

"Would you notify me if anyone is rescued?"

"Fill out these forms, and we'll see what we can do."

Talia decided to track down the families of the men in the same battalion to see if she could learn something from them.

After some phone calls, she was put in touch with a former prisoner of war, Walter Hoven, who was staying in a returned soldiers' convalescent home in Townsville.

The home overlooked Ross Creek. When Talia arrived, she stood for a moment watching a small ferry cross the broad estuary from the south side.

A nurse greeted her and led her to Lt. Hoven, who had been sitting near the window and had probably seen Talia as she arrived only moments before. He did not stand when she entered and she noticed that his pants were neatly folded under the upper part of his legs.

"You can call me Wally," the former soldier said.

"It's lovely to meet you, Wally."

The parlour felt confining and Talia sensed the other veterans staring, so she asked Wally if they could move outside. She wheeled him out to the wide planked verandah and they sat for a while, looking out at the looming shape of Castle Hill.

Wally's sister had suggested that Wally might like some Capstan cigarettes, so Talia made sure to bring some along, as well as chocolates.

Wally grabbed the packet of smokes and fished one out with trembling fingers. He was a gaunt man with a deep cough, and blue eyes that held a sea full of bad memories.

At first, he spoke easily and fluidly of the early days of signing on — card games and practical jokes, slipping off the boat for the last few jaunts in Melbourne before they shipped out. But then his voice slowed and faltered. He paused often to draw on the cigarette. Finally he came to the part in his story about a march into the jungle on one of the Nips' many forced labour parties from Batu-Lintang prison.

"You'll think I'm mad as a hatter when I tell you this. I haven't told anyone here, so please don't go spreading the word. Don't want to be thrown in with the loonies."

He laughed — his laugh turning into a ragged cough.

"Out of nowhere, I heard a voice." He searched Talia's face to see if she might think he really was crazy. Then he went on.

"It was just after we finished the dig. Nobody was talking, and this voice was not one of my mates. It was very clear. He said *they're going to kill you all now.* — Just like that."

Talia nodded, listening solemnly.

"I felt like *he* was telling me how to do it, how to save myself." Walter pointed to the heavens. "*He* warned me."

"So when they pulled out the bayonets, I rolled into the pit and just played dead."

He paused to wipe his eyes.

"I felt bodies falling all around me. The ground was wet with blood. I just waited till they stopped. I don't know how long. A day and a night, and another day — then I crawled out. I didn't look back. It was no use."

Talia was shaking.

"Why me? Why save me and none of the others? I'll never know."

He continued after a moment. "Is there something special I am meant to do?"

Talia finally came to the point of her visit. She opened her purse and pulled out the newspaper clipping of the missing soldiers, including Alwyn.

"This fellow here, Pablo Del Rio. Did you ever meet him?"

Walter nodded gravely. He scrutinized Talia. "Yes, I remember him."

"Oh!"

"Yeah — Paulie."

"You know his real name is Alwyn. And he's not Spanish at all."

"You don't say? — Could have fooled me."

"Yes."

"He was your husband?"

"No, er — my fiancé."

Walter sighed, and then recounted with as much delicacy as possible the rough treatment of Alwyn and how they all believed he had been killed.

"I'm sorry — you're probably angry that I survived and not your Pablo."

Talia shook her head.

"You didn't see him die. He wasn't one of the ones in the pit."

"No, but — "

Talia felt like she wanted to run out of the hospital. That if she said goodbye properly, she would simply collapse in tears.

The longer she stayed, the worse Wally made her feel.

"Maybe that's why I'm here. To let you go. Get you to stop waiting. — You're very pretty you know. How old are you?"

Talia gave Walter another packet of cigarettes and thanked him for his time. He held onto her hand and wrung it with surprising strength considering his frail appearance.

"You'll come and see me again, I hope."

"I'd like to," she said, though it was the last thing she wanted to do.

As she left Townsville, the light was fading. The sun bled orange and red through wisps of cloud.

She wondered if this was his sunset — Alwyn's sunset. Would this be all she would ever know of his last day on earth?

Some forty miles north of the town, Talia's heart exploded. Her tears began to fall so fast, and she shook so hard, she could not drive anymore. She wrenched the steering wheel and turned off the main highway, finally bringing the truck to a stop at the side of the road. Without moving from the driver's seat, she wept until she was spent.

But after she was done, she did not have the energy to continue her journey. The thought of arriving home to tell her mother what she had learned would be too much to bear. Not tonight, not tomorrow night — maybe never.

She sank back in the seat and fell asleep. She awoke some time later, her body protesting the awkward position of her neck and the stifling heat inside the truck. She got out on wobbly feet, stretching out her stiffness. As she stood there, she caught the sound of excited voices.

Curious, she turned towards the sea, intrigued to see thin beams of light, filtered through the night and salt spray, darting like fireflies.

She followed the lights and voices across the dunes, her feet sinking as she clambered over the deep sand.

On the crest of the dune, she stopped to stare in awe. The full moon cast its glow on a wonderful miracle — a league of turtles slowly crawling away from a deposit of eggs in the sand, heading back to the water.

She drew closer and saw the rippled tread lines in the wet sand and the ancient beasts, calm and plodding, returning to the sea.

She was inspired by their amazing trust, to leave a part of their lives and the hope of their futures buried on the beach without a backward glance, knowing that their offspring would find their way to the water.

Talia shivered. Was this some sign, like the voice Walter had heard in his head? A sign for her to go on and simply trust that all would be well?

Chapter Twenty-Seven
Tea Leaves
Innisfail, North Queensland – 1949

After her break-up with Dennis, Talia's evenings no longer took place at the Starlight Ballroom or the Trocadero but at the kitchen table, where she sketched and wrote.

She let her hair grow long again and the bottle of *Evening in Paris* perfume was pushed to the back of the shelf. Her only perfumes now were the scent of real flowers, wooing her with fresh delight.

She abandoned her pumps and dresses, and was most often seen about in heavy canvas pants with large pockets, gumboots that went up to her knees, and a floppy hat. What an odd figure she must have cut, tramping through the swamps and the woods in her strange get-up.

She did not care that men might no longer see her as a pretty girl or consider her delicate. Women could stop worrying that she might steal the affections of their husbands or boyfriends, for Talia's main interest was out there in the scrub and along the creek banks.

Sometimes she worried she had missed out. She would cross paths with an old schoolmate and see her walking with her children. It was then Talia wondered at the madness of her choices.

She did wonder if she was going mad. She thought of him so often, she even felt his presence on occasion. Once she woke up in the dead of night, convinced she had heard him — his own unique bird call.

She raced out of bed and ran to the window, pulling it open and leaning out, searching up and down the street, only to find it empty. Afterwards she could not get back to sleep.

But mostly she tried to direct her thoughts to her painting

expeditions. The cherished days when she could carve out some free time to wander the hinterland, study and sketch plants, pull up their roots or take cuttings and seed pods and bring them home.

Once or twice, she had luck with articles she submitted to the *Northern Courier* or the *Sydney Morning Herald*. One was on the Candlenut, and the other on Wangal greens. Her articles focussed not just on the beauty of plants or trees but on their myriad uses as medicine and food.

Finally, in the spring of 1949, she bundled up her drawings and writings, and travelled to Sydney. She trekked across the bustling city by tram and on foot, going from one publishing house to another. She felt a little self-conscious in her out-dated clothes, so much at odds with the sophistication of Sydney.

The meetings were an exercise in humiliation and frustration. They would generally go as follows:

"So, you're not a trained botanist?"

"Well, I am self-trained."

"I see."

"But you do like the drawings?" Talia would ask hopefully.

"Oh, yes. They're very beautiful. Lots of nice detail."

That was because they felt sorry for her, but not enough to stop from adding: "However the cost to publish colour prints of these would be quite prohibitive."

"I suppose."

"And we're not sure who would want to buy your book. It's not suitable for tourists, or scientists really. I'm sorry, I don't think it's quite right for us."

They wished her the best of luck, giving her a look laden with pity at her delusions.

And so it went.

The last publishing house offered Talia the chance to submit drawings for a children's book. She smiled politely, agreeing to follow-up later with samples sketches of fairies under fern fronds and elves on toadstools, although she knew she never would.

She was so deeply disappointed, not just for herself but on Alwyn's behalf too, for it was he who had inspired her to take an interest in the plants of their country.

From there Talia travelled on to Melbourne, putting on a brave face as she visited the Candela sisters and the Señora. They must have been shocked to see Talia, so faded and unkempt.

Señora Candela, her hair now salt and pepper, but her bearing still regal, took Talia aside on the last evening of her stay and gave her an envelope.

Talia opened it, surprised to find it stuffed with bills.

"What's this?" she asked.

"Ramon set aside some money for each of his daughters so that when they married they would have a dowry, and he considered you as his daughter too. Even though you are not going to marry, I believe you should still have the money Ramon left for you. So here it is, *mi hija,* for whatever purpose you choose."

Talia knew right away what she would do with the money. She promptly ordered five hundred copies of *Medicinal and Nutritional Plants of North Queensland* from the printers.

In the end she could only afford ten colour plates, so the rest of her drawings were rendered in black and white. Because of this, she had to revise the text to describe the missing information about the colours. She dedicated the book to Alwyn, her teacher and inspiration. This was the wedding present she would never be able to give him.

In spite of the compromise on colour plates, there was a delicious feeling of elation when the books were delivered. The smell of the fresh ink and paper was intoxicating. Lok Fan agreed to make shelf space for her book next to the road maps and tourist guidebooks.

Talia gradually convinced a few other shopkeepers to carry her publication, but once there the copies sat on the shelf growing mouldy, dusty and flyspecked. Barely a few copies sold.

Then, one day, she received a note from the owner of a

bookshop in Ingham. He had sold all ten copies and wanted a few more. She promptly packaged ten more and sent them out to him. She was pleased yet baffled. Why Ingham, she wondered? Why ten copies all at once?

Talia continued with her work as a sign painter and muralist. For a few days in June she was contracted to create a pastoral scene on the wall of a restaurant in Innisfail. The owners, an Italian couple, Ricardo and Dina, plied her with delicious meals of creamy gnocchi, chicken cacciatore, and tiramisu.

One day, feeling very full after a heavy lunch, Talia decided to take a break and went for a short walk. Only blocks from the restaurant, she was more than surprised to stumble upon the one-eyed Encantadora, sitting on a stool under a shade tree.

Talia felt a shiver. It was like being surprised by a snake on a path. It didn't matter that the snake was not poisonous. It always made her feel uneasy. But in a way, she welcomed the chance meeting, as she had long wanted to know — if there was a way of knowing — was Alwyn still alive?

The Encantadora led her down the path to the back of the storefronts where she lived among the weeds, crates, and the rusting shell of an old Ford. She hobbled along in old torn canvas shoes and a shift dress.

Talia lost track of the time. While the one-eyed clairvoyant boiled coffee, Talia felt dizzy with anticipation — not that she really believed these things, but the old woman had been right often enough that she could not be completely ignored.

"*Vamos a ver. ¿Quieres saber si él aún vive?*"

Talia nodded, surprised that the Encantadora already knew that she wanted to know if Alwyn was still alive. She half-wondered if the old woman had even positioned herself on the street predicting that Talia would come along.

The Encantadora poured the coffee into the small chipped cup and bade Talia to drink it. The coffee scalded her lips, but she was too impatient to wait for it to cool down.

"*Tienes muchas preguntas, pero sólo una te ha estado preocupando durante todos esos años. ¿Que ha sido de él todo ese tiempo?*"

Yes, there was only one question in Talia's mind — the same question she had had for many years now as she waited for him.

The psychic grunted and clucked. She cradled her veined knobbly hands around the cup, turning it around and then flipping it over onto the saucer. The slurry of coffee grounds smeared the cup, making a pattern. "*Vamos a ver.*"

Talia looked to the Encantadora with anticipation. The old woman cackled with laughter, giving Talia a gummy smile.

"*Ah, si — en las hojas del té, encontrarás tu respuesta.* "

"What do you mean I'll have my answer in the *tea leaves*?"

"Tea leaves. Yes."

"Not coffee? But you're reading coffee grounds!"

Laughter spilled from the Encantadora. She rocked back and forth, unable to stop.

Talia was livid. "You think this is a joke!"

The Encantadora shook her head, still shaking with giggles. It made Talia furious that her very serious question was treated with such levity. She stomped out of the clairvoyant's home and fumed all the way back to the restaurant.

By the time she got back, she had barely calmed down. Perhaps she let the screen door slam a little too hard because Ricardo and Dina looked up sharply.

Talia felt her hand was shaking a little, either from her anger or from the effect of the strong coffee. "Tea leaves, indeed!"

Tea leaves would reveal the truth about whether Alwyn was alive, the psychic said. How ridiculous! It was more than likely the old lady was just trying to get her to come back for another reading using tea leaves instead of coffee grounds, but Talia would not fall for that trick. She wondered now why she had ever been afraid of that silly creature.

Chapter Twenty-Eight
Back to the Roots
Innisfail, North Queensland – 1949

Although her book never sold many copies, from time to time people who recognised Talia from the photograph on the dust jacket would stop her in the street. They would compliment her on the illustrations, and often wanted to discuss a rare plant they had discovered — more often than not a non-native species. Nevertheless, Talia was always polite and tried to be helpful. After all she was pleased to have any admirers at all.

So when she received a call to go to the Viewmount Tea Plantation to talk to Hank or a Mr. Hank about her book, she presumed it would be just another one of these kinds of conversations. The best she could hope for was to suggest that she be kept in mind for a sign painting job should the need arise. In any event, she relished the opportunity to get a glimpse of the unusual gardens she had heard about, with tea shrubs carefully transplanted from Ceylon.

An Indian man in a long pale tunic waved at her as her old Morris truck nosed its way into the entrance. He gestured for her to park under a shade tree but the vehicle died a few feet short of the target, as though resisting being ordered about.

Talia stepped out of the truck and gave the door a hefty shove. She thought it had closed, but just as she turned away, she heard a creak, and then felt a bump against her back. She made several other attempts to shut the obstinate door but to no avail. Finally, thoroughly flustered and embarrassed, she turned to face the man who was waiting patiently and she gave a dismissive wave.

"It's alright. I'll just leave it be."

"Do you mind if I try?"

Talia shrugged and let him pass in front of her. His long

fingers gripped the handle, then he twisted it, and lifted it. Then she heard a firm click. When the man stepped back the door was solidly in place. He turned to her with a bemused smile and offered his hand.

"Miss Queixens, I presume."

"Yes."

"Subhankar Dutta."

"Nice to meet you, Mr. Dutta."

"The pleasure is mine."

"Thank you for the help with the door."

"Not at all."

He smiled at her, his head bobbing. He was so tall he had to bend slightly to look at her. It made it seem as though he were bowing to her.

"The drive was alright?"

"Yes, thanks." Talia felt awkward. She wished she had a better idea of the purpose of the meeting.

"I'm here to see Hank."

"Well, that would be me." His eyes wrinkled in merriment at her reaction. "Hank is short for Sub-hank-ar."

Talia nodded and laughed. "Oh, I see."

"I don't suppose I look like a Hank to most people."

Subhankar gestured towards a bungalow. He led her across its spacious verandah, and through ornately carved door, then inside to a drawing room with large windows facing the garden. A palm fan whirred above them, stirring the air redolent with mysterious and fragrant smells. Talia inhaled deeply.

"What would you like to drink? — Don't feel you have to say tea," he chuckled.

"But I do like tea," said Talia.

"Wonderful. We have a few choices."

He presented her with several tins, and opened them releasing perfumes of bergamot, ginger and spices. Subhankar plucked a few leaves from each and dropped them in Talia's hands so she could crush and smell them.

In the end, she could not refuse his offers to try several varieties of tea. She cradled the delicate china bowls in her palm while she sipped and savoured the assorted flavours. All the while Subhankar explained to her the importance of good growing conditions, the timing of the harvest, and the drying and roasting process, and how these affected each type of tea differently.

When Talia thought she just might float away on a river of tea, Subhankar rose and suggested a tour of the grounds. They stood briefly on the back patio overlooking the rolling hills lined with neat rows of tea shrubs.

"They do best on land with a bit of elevation which of course also makes for a wonderful view."

Subhankar's pride in both his successes and failures was apparent as he spoke of the development of the plantation from the early days until the present. He pointed out his new plantings, some of which were thriving and others barely surviving.

Although Talia was fascinated, she still wondered exactly why Subhankar had called her out to the plantation. She noticed the faded panel van, but it had no sign. And all the tea packets already had beautiful artwork. It was puzzling. What could he want? Surely he had not brought her here to chat the entire afternoon. As pleasant as it was, Talia hoped that was not all.

"I most enjoyed your book. I must tell you I had no idea Innisfail was home to such an accomplished artist."

"Thank you."

"What are your plans for it?"

It was an odd question. Talia didn't really know how to answer. "I hope to sell a few more copies to cover the cost of printing," she stammered.

It was as though he did not really hear this dismal assessment of her work. He continued brightly. "Are you thinking of doing a series?"

Talia sputtered with laughter. "Good heavens, no!"

He looked puzzled by this response.

Talia tried to explain. "The truth is I had five hundred copies printed and most will either be eaten by silverfish or grow mildew before another one is sold. It was probably a mistake, although I don't really regret it. It was a wonderful project."

"Most certainly!"

"But perhaps I would have been better off setting the money aside for an icebox or a new clutch for my truck."

"Nonsense!"

Talia cupped her hands around her eyes to get a better look at him. His face was in shadow and it was hard to read his expression.

"What you really need is to capture a more comprehensive sampling," said Subhankar confidently.

"But I have no dowry left."

"I'm sorry. I don't follow."

"Mr. Dutta, I would love nothing better than to traipse through the scrub from Darwin to Charters Towers, collecting plants and seeds and painting lovely pictures of them, but I would have no time to work."

"And if it *were* your work?"

Talia was taken aback.

"Are there jobs like that to be had?"

"Well, yes! Right here."

Talia looked puzzled.

Subhankar leapt on. "I'm sorry, I thought that is why you came."

"I came because there was a message from you inviting me."

"Well, I invited you because you replied to my job posting, and included a copy of your book."

Talia shook her head. "No — uh. I did not."

"You *did* write this book?" Subhankar held up a copy of *Medicinal and Nutritional Plants of North Queensland.*

"Yes, I did, but …"

His voice took on a trace of annoyance. "Well, then I should like to offer you the job of botanical researcher and illustrator."

Talia's mouth opened wide, but she could not speak.

Subhankar continued, perhaps taking Talia's silence as a negotiating tactic, for he sweetened his offer as she remained mute.

"Very well, I'll give you six pounds a week, but that's as high as I can go. Plus the use of a new car, and an assistant on occasion if he can spare the time."

Talia felt her heart quicken and had trouble breathing.

"Do you need some time to think it over?"

"No," she said quietly.

Subhankar was taken aback. "No, you are refusing the job or, no, you don't need more time."

"Yes."

Subhankar frowned.

"That is, yes, to the job!" she laughed.

Once Talia had calmed down, she thanked Subhankar profusely and apologised for the misunderstanding. Before she left, they discussed arrangements for her to begin her employment.

As she got to her truck, she secretly prayed Subhankar would not watch while she tried to start the vehicle. To her chagrin he did not go away, but stood there smiling as she wrenched the crank handle over and over again.

She was pink with embarrassment by the time the engine of the old Morris finally turned over. Her cheeks coloured some more with the memory of the deep mortification she had felt at not knowing the reason for the meeting.

But as she pulled out of the drive, she let out a burst of laughter and waved enthusiastically to Subhankar. Humiliation notwithstanding, this had to be one of the most wonderful days of her life.

As she drove away from the tea plantation, she hummed with pleasure. Everything around her looked especially wonderful. The tumbledown fences and green paddocks, all of it was glorious, bathed in the afternoon light. She thought about this strange and stupendous turn of luck. She was so deeply engaged in contemplating the prospect of her new responsibilities that she did not pay attention to where she was driving and suddenly found herself approaching a familiar turn in the road. Then there she was — at the edge of Castillo Candela.

Instinctively she slowed down. An old 'No Trespassing' sign hung askew. Faded paint on a weathered board made it known that the property was up for sale. The second she moved to shift gears, she knew what would happen. The clutch rattled and choked, and the motor sputtered to a dead stop. Talia drew in a deep breath. She put the truck in neutral and let it roll towards the sagging gate.

There she sat for a minute, peering through the heavy vegetation at the outline of the castle ruins. Finally she got out of the truck and headed for the fence. She scaled it easily.

She was astounded by the tangle of vegetation, for she remembered the entrance as always being open and accessible. As if in return for years of being strictly tamed and manicured, nature had grown back with a vengeance. It smothered the old buildings and battered walls. Yet somehow Talia managed to get through. It was as though someone had recently hacked out the most narrow of paths, just wide enough for her.

While parts of the old Castillo were boarded up, the front door itself was ajar, hanging on rusted hinges. The planks were weathered and spotted with lichen. Termites had gnawed intricate patterns through the wood.

Talia squeezed between the door and frame, her eyes adjusting to the semi-darkness. The floorboards had lifted off the foundation, buckling and curling. The walls were speckled with mould. She gulped as something large slithered near her foot. She relaxed, recognizing a harmless carpet python.

The dreary deterioration of the once grand room saddened Talia, and she understood why she had not been back in the intervening years. She withdrew and made her way towards the grand staircase alongside the waterfall. The cement steps were slick with moss, so Talia held firmly to the decayed railing as she descended to the lower patio.

It was wonderful and sad at the same time. Nature continued to bestow its gifts of astounding beauty: clear vivid sounds of an infinite variety; riotous colours; and manifold fragrances. Generous and bounteous, it continued to provide in this small oasis — in contrast to the human inadequacy, failed dreams, and disappointments that had once been part of the place. And Mena Creek — on and on it went, the tiny course of water, spilling over the falls and flowing towards the sea as it had always done. A comforting constant. Timeless.

Talia continued into the heart of the old castle grounds, feeling full of love and gratitude for the place that had been the source of so much of what she had cherished in her life. The spirits of loved ones gone or dead were still there.

She pressed on deeper into the fold of nature, padding on a thick carpet of leaves, undisturbed since — *wait, what was that*? So strong were her memories that she imagined she was even hearing *him*.

She shook off the inexplicable impression and descended further into the valley, feeling the dampness like cold wet fingers stroking her arms. Shivering a little, thinking of the ghosts of those who had lived and died here, Talia hurried on.

She went on past the fernery, gasping in delight to see old plantings still thriving and an orchid in full bloom clinging to a stone wall. She continued to the avenue of giant Kauri palms. She tried to find the old carving — which tree was it? Yes, there it was. *A.C. loves T.Q.* How the bark had grown around the carving like a healing wound. A sticky sap oozed from the letters, as though the tree were weeping on behalf of the separated lovers.

Behind her there was a sharp cracking noise. Too large for the wind. An animal perhaps — a very large animal judging by the sound. Talia felt uneasy, and somewhat foolish as well for having wandered here alone into the depths of the abandoned grounds.

"Helloooo?" her voice quavered.

She gasped as a galah tore out of a jasmine bush and burst in front of her. Talia exhaled deeply, trying to calm herself. How had the gardens here become so eerie, so unwelcoming? Why was she so on edge?

She moved on. In spite of her nervousness she was not willing just yet to give up on her exploration. Beyond the pine trees, she found the clearing on the shores of the creek where she used to feed the turtles so long ago.

She reached into her pockets looking for something to lure them but found only a few packets of tea leaves. A gift from Subhankar. She opened one of the packets and grabbed the dry bits, sprinkling them on the water and faintly hoping the turtles would appear. She could not blame them if they did not bother to show for tea leaves — *tea leaves?* Something twigged in her brain. What was it about *tea leaves*?

At last rounded shadows appeared in the water and noses pushed up, nipping at the tea. Talia laughed. Had they been there all this time? The turtles should have been disappointed with the tea leaves, but they snapped up her offering without hesitation. Not wanting the little creatures to go just yet, Talia opened the second packet, and threw the remaining dried tea on the water. She caught a faint scent of Bergamot as the strands dispersed.

Just then it came to her — the Encantadora's words. *You will have your answer in the tea leaves,* the old lady had said. At the time, Talia had dismissed the clairvoyant's predictions, thinking the old woman had only wanted Talia to pay for another reading. Now as Talia stared at the green-brown water she wondered if the Encantadora's words held more meaning.

Talia shivered. She knew she must get help with her old truck before it got dark. She started to make her way back, pausing at the patio overlooking the water. A strange bird call erupted, breaking the silence. Her skin prickled. She spun around searching for the source. Was she hallucinating? Softly, she spoke his name, "Alwyn?"

There was a crashing sound and Talia tensed. "Alwyn?" she called again, more urgently and louder now, lest he not hear her.

And then she saw him — pushing his way through the folds of vegetation. Or was she seeing a ghost?

This could not be Alwyn. No. This man was too gaunt, his face too worn and tired. But the way he spoke to her *was* Alwyn.

"Hey, number six princess."

She screamed his name as she flew into his arms, thrilled to have him within her grasp but appalled at the same time by his rail-thin frame.

He pressed his face into her hair and clutched her. They did not move for a long time as though afraid they could be separated again. Their breathing found the same rhythm, their fingers interlaced, cheek pressed against forehead, until it was as though the membranes dividing them had fallen away.

He brushed a smear of pollen from her wet cheeks and looked deep into her eyes, a trace of humour in his voice.

"So did you get the job, Talia?"

"Oh, my God, Alwyn! It was you!"

He chuckled. She wanted to punch him but her fist became unfurled as it came in contact with him. Instead she squeezed his sinewy arms.

"Oh, Alwyn! — How long have you been back?"

He gave her a pained look. He hesitated before answering. "You were seeing some fellow — he had a fancy car — I reckoned you were happy."

She cried, "Oh, Alwyn, nooo — Don't tell me! You've been here all this time!"

He looked guilty. "I went off again, worked a bit up north, and then got back not too long ago. Started up with Hank. He's a good sort. You'll like him."

Talia shook her head, incredulous. "Alwyn, why didn't you tell me you were back? — You would have let me marry Dennis?"

He sighed deeply. "If that was what you wanted."

Talia squeezed his arm. "No, no." She moaned softly. "Oh, Alwyn — they had me convinced you were dead."

He gave a short laugh. "I was, just about. The Japs beat Mr. Del Rio pretty bad." Alwyn paused, adding quietly, "He died — but I got through."

Later when he removed his shirt, she saw the full extent of his wounds and for a moment she could not breathe as she stared at the horrific scars. It was as though a machine had raked his chest and back, leaving deep furrows and puckers in the skin. She pressed her hand into the deepest hollow, willing her love to heal him. Without speaking they moved towards the water and let themselves glide into it together. It held them up and cradled them, warm and smooth like a balm. Laughing and crying, they climbed the rocks, and the spray from the falls crashed over them like a thousand blessings, protective and restorative, long overdue.

"So Talia, do you think we can give it a go?"

"What, the truck?"

He laughed. "That old bomb! Not a chance."

Then Alwyn became more serious. He took her hands in his, brushing the skin and staring at them as though they might have the remedy to all the misgivings he still harboured. His voice was gravelly, catching in his throat.

"I meant, us — getting married."

Talia quivered. Her eyes filled.

Alwyn looked worried. He faltered, "But maybe I kept you waiting too long."

She shook her head. "I would have waited for you until Mena Creek ran dry and then some."

"So, is that a yes?"

Talia felt a pang as she gazed into his worried eyes. She gave him a look brimming with tenderness. "That's a *sí, Señor.*"

He broke into a wide smile and roared with delight. He scooped Talia up as though she were nothing more than a bundle of feathers and pulled her close and kissed her. She laughed as they tumbled again into Mena Creek. As they spun around, bodies entwined, the fading light cast a golden circle around them.